To all of those who suffer from PTSD,
Fight like hell.
I'm glad you're still here.

PLAYLIST

"Simple Man" by Lynyrd Skynyrd

"Hurt" by Johnny Cash

"Writer In The Dark" by Lorde

"Friends in Low Places" by Garth Brooks

"Four Out Of Five" by Arctic Monkeys

"Nothing's Gonna Hurt You Baby" by Cigarettes After Sex

"Apocalypse" by Cigarettes After Sex

"Hope in Hell" by Pistol Fire

"Come and Go" by Juiceworld

"Don't Take the Girl" by Tim McGraw

ROYAL BASTARDS CODE

PROTECT: The club and your brothers come before anything else, and must be protected at all costs. **CLUB** is **FAMILY**.

RESPECT: Earn it & Give it. Respect club law. Respect the patch. Respect your brothers. Disrespect a member and there will be hell to pay.

HONOR: Being patched in is an honor, not a right. Your colors are sacred, not to be left alone, and **NEVER** let them touch the ground.

OL' LADIES: Never disrespect a member's or brother's Ol'Lady. **PERIOD.**

CHURCH is **MANDATORY.**

LOYALTY: Takes precedence over all, including well-being.

HONESTY: Never **LIE, CHEAT,** or **STEAL** from another member or the club.

TERRITORY: You are to respect your brother's property and follow their Chapter's club rules.

TRUST: Years to earn it…seconds to lose it.

NEVER RIDE OFF: Brothers do not abandon their family.

Truly's BIKER

A note to the reader,

Truly's Biker is a dark romance.

Triggers include: violence, graphic and gory scenes, emotional trauma and subsequent PTSD, talk of sexual violence (but no acts of sexual violence), a taboo or forbidden relationship, and just general bad behavior.

There is no cheating or other woman/other man drama.

The Royal Bastards are bikers and this book is a dramatization of what I think a 1%er club might look like. Read it for the escapism and entertainment of a good girl falling for a bad man, not for relationship inspiration.

And don't let anyone make you feel bad for enjoying the books you like to read.

XOXO,
Misty

PROLOGUE

Roch

When I die, there'll be no white light to walk into. My road to hell is paved in fire for all the shit I've done. I shouldn't give a fuck about stupid shit like penance.

Yet here I am.

As I limp my way up the walkway to a single level ranch-style house, I shove my hand in my pocket and clutch the worn letter I'm delivering. The house looks exactly how Ricky explained. Older, but maintained, and next door to a veterinary clinic his wife, Aiyana, owns and runs.

Acid shoots up my throat, leaving a sour taste in my mouth. I reach the porch and pull out the piece of scrap paper that's blood-stained and barely fucking legible. It's all that's left of Ricky now.

I rap my knuckles on the door and wait. It cracks a sliver, but I don't see anyone.

"Who are you?" a child's voice asks, and I lower my eyes. One dark eyeball stares back at me from three feet down.

"Will," I say, but I hardly use my voice anymore, so it comes out hoarse. I clear my throat. "Frienda your dad's."

"My dad died. He was a hero." She opens the door a little more, and I get my first look at the kid. Long, dark hair frames an angelic face with chubby cheeks and almond-shaped, brown eyes that're too big for her face. She looks nothing like Ricky.

I nod in agreement. He was a hero. He should be standing here looking at his daughter. Not me.

I don't deserve shit.

"Mom home?"

"She's next door working on Mrs. Mitchell's chihuahua, Karen. Her teeth are rotten 'cause Mrs. Mitchell never brushed them." She steps onto the porch and grabs my hand like I'm not a scary motherfucker who hasn't had a shave or haircut in fuck knows how long.

My instinct is to jerk away. I don't let anyone touch me. Never again. But she's a kid. Ricky's kid. So I allow her to tug me across the grass to the clinic while she prattles on.

"Mrs. Mitchell died yesterday, and the shelter wants to find Karen a new home, but they can't because of the teeth." She smiles big and points to her mouth. "So Mama is yanking them all out. But it's okay. Karen can eat soft food and live a happy life. That's what Mama says anyway. I'd hate to live with no teeth. How would you eat taffy? Gum it, I guess."

"Oh."

"I wanted to keep Karen because she's so little and cute, but Mama said she'll find a forever home, and I already have a dog. But Ginger is big and smells and drools all over." She drags me around back, her tiny hand still in mine. "Anyway, so she left me home alone while she takes care of Karen."

My mind works to keep up with all her words. I spent two years only hearing Farsi. My ears aren't used to discerning things I can understand. Especially not from a child who doesn't even take a breath between words. My head throbs. I need to hand over this letter and get the fuck out of here.

"She's in here. Come on." The kid opens the back door, and I step inside a sterile hallway. She slips past me and takes my hand again. "She's probably done. It's been hours."

She opens another door, pokes her head in, and quickly shuts it. She moves to the next one, but this time she yanks me in after her. Inside, is a wall of kennels with some kind of critter in each of them. Standing in front of one, is a tall woman who looks a lot like the girl—golden brown skin, near-black hair, tall, and thin.

"Mama, this man's looking for you." She steps behind me and pushes me forward. It's fucking annoying to be manhandled by someone so small, but I swallow the irritation and remember she belongs to Ricky.

"Who are you?" The woman storms over, grabs the girl by the arm, and steps in front of her to block her from me.

"Will. Knew Ricky." I don't tell her if she wants to keep her kid safe, she should probably instruct her to not answer the door.

"Ricky?" she gasps. I watch as her face falls, her lips turn down in a frown, and her shoulders slump. The look of devastation. Been there. Seen it. Lived it.

"Here." I thrust the letter at her.

"You knew Ricky?" she asks, taking it from me, and I nod. She unfolds the paper and reads her husband's final words. Tears fall down her cheeks, and her hand covers her mouth.

I don't need to be here for this. I did what I said I'd do, and now I can move on. I turn around and walk out the same way I came in without a word. I head straight for my Harley and throw a leg over it. I've almost gotten away when I hear shouting over the loud rumble from the engine. Aiyana runs toward me, the girl close behind.

I look up at the cloudless sky and take a deep breath. Don't need this bullshit.

"Will, wait!" she calls out. I turn my bike off but don't dismount. "You were with him, weren't you? Over there? You were the one who tried to save him."

I don't know what to say. Yeah, I tried. But I failed, so it don't count for shit.

I nod.

"Thank you."

I nod again.

"Can you stay for dinner? I have questions."

I shouldn't. I don't want to be interrogated. The intrusiveness will unleash all the demons in my head. It's not pretty when that happens.

But it's my best friend's widow. I owe it to him.

"Okay." I step off the bike, and suddenly the little girl is at my side, reaching for my hand again. Aiyana looks at her nervously, but doesn't say anything.

"My name is Truly. I'm eight. How old are you?" She peers up at me while leading me inside the house. The first room we come to is a sitting room, decorated with pictures of wild horses.

"Twenty-two."

"That's old, but not as old as Mama. She's thirty."

"Truly," Aiyana scolds, gesturing for me to sit on a rattan sofa with olive green cushions. "Don't ask people their age. It's rude."

4

I shake my hand free and sit down. Truly nearly jumps onto my lap, but I nudge her to my side. What the hell is up with this kid? I'm a big man with stringy hair and a burly beard. I scare most grownups with my size and appearance; why don't I scare her?

"It's not rude since I told him my age. You said if I share first, it makes people comfortable to share themselves." She tucks a strand of hair behind her ear, revealing a small heart-shaped birthmark the color of a strawberry on the flap of cartilage where her cheek meets her ear.

Strange.

"Sorry about her. It's what I get for homeschooling. She has no social skills."

"I do too. Everyone at the clinic says I'm very polite and well-spoken for my age." Truly folds her scrawny arms in defiance.

"Why don't you go play in your room for a while, and I'll let you know when the pizza gets here?"

"Pizza? You never order pizza." She eyes her mom suspiciously.

"I'll change my mind if you don't listen," Aiyana warns.

"Fine, but I want pepperoni."

"Okay. Now scoot."

Truly jumps off the couch and runs down the hallway, chattering to herself the whole way there until I finally hear a door shut, leaving Aiyana and me in silence.

"She's precocious."

"Like Ricky," I observe, and it brings a smile to Aiyana's face.

"That she is. Thank you for coming in. How long have you been back?"

"Month." I rest my forearms on my thighs and stare at my hands.

"I only know what I heard on the news. The Army discharged you for abandoning your post to save Ricky. Is that right?"

I nod. She's being polite. It wasn't just a discharge, it was the dishonorable type. I abandoned my post against orders to save my best friend. Got myself taken prisoner in the process, and it was all for nothing because he was killed anyway.

"How long were you held?" She has the decency to at least sound hesitant to question me.

The Army had no problem drilling me over and over until I couldn't make sense of their questions. I know what they were doing. Trying to get me to confess I'd been turned. I barely convinced them otherwise, given the fact I don't talk much. Not anymore at least.

Words mean shit. They didn't help when I was begging for Ricky's life. They didn't help when I was begging to be released. They definitely didn't help when I sat in front of the command sergeant to explain why I ran into that compound after learning about Ricky's abduction, and what happened while I was a prisoner of war.

"Six months." I weave my fingers together and squeeze until I feel the pain of my knuckles grinding together.

"How long were you there before they…" She trails off, not wanting to say the words.

I know what she's asking. How long was I with Ricky before they killed him? Before they dragged him from the concrete cell we shared and decapitated him in front of a live stream with the commanding officers back at the Pentagon. Or wherever they are, sitting in their padded office chairs, making life and death decisions about what's going on thousands of miles away in the desert of Afghanistan.

Kill them. Kill them all. Do what they did to you. Make them pay.

I shake the voices from my head and remind myself I'm not there anymore. I'm in fucking Reno, Nevada. Still a desert, but not the kind that leaves sand between your teeth when you breathe and blistering sunburns regardless of the SPF you rub on your skin every day.

"Four months."

"He told me about you, you know." She adjusts herself to face me. "He said you were smart. Brave. Always had his back."

I nod, remembering how he and I became friends.

Ricky had no self-preservation. He'd run into a building without even scoping it out. He'd jump at the chance to be part of every operation, despite having a kid and wife at home.

I knew my time would be best served keeping him safe because he sure as shit wasn't going to do it himself. He was also nice to me when no one had been nice to me my whole life. Joined the Army at eighteen because I had nothing and no one. It was life on the streets or enlist.

Then suddenly, I had Ricky.

"Thank you for that." She reaches over and rests a hand on mine. It feels like a million bees stinging my skin. She must notice the pained look on my face because she jerks her hand away. "Sorry."

"S'okay."

"I should order that pizza. Pepperoni okay? If that's not what you like, Truly will get over it."

I nod.

"Okay, be right back." She disappears down the hall.

I stand up and walk over to the mantel. Pictures are crowded together across the wood slab. They show a younger-looking Ricky and Aiyana, baby pictures of the girl, and them as a family.

One, in particular, is of the three of them on a tarmac with Ricky in his uniform. If I were to guess, I'd say that was their last family picture.

"Okay, it'll be here in twenty minutes. I have to go check on a few animals. Want to come?"

I nod reluctantly, and she yells down the hall for Truly to come along. She comes scurrying out and immediately grips my hand. It doesn't sting.

Probably because she's just a kid, and she can't hurt me.

We walk out the front door and back over to the clinic. Aiyana opens each kennel and makes sure every animal is okay. When she gets to the last one, she lifts out a tiny brown and white, long-haired chihuahua. It fits in the palm of her hand. I've never seen anything so small and pathetic.

"This is Karen. She's only two years old, but her owner constantly shared ice cream and suckers with her and never brushed her teeth. The lady died yesterday, and Karen was left alone. We're getting her in top shape so she can be adopted. Want to hold her?" She holds out the small critter, and I take a step back.

"She won't bite, silly. She has no teeth," Truly says, and lifts my hand up to accept the dog.

She looks even smaller in my big palm. She's dead asleep, and her tongue is lolling out of her mouth, but she's warm and cuddly. I cradle her against my chest as she yawns, stretching her short legs in all directions.

She's cute. And so fragile. If she were placed with a family who wasn't careful, they could step on her or sit on her.

She needs protection.

"She likes you." Aiyana beams at me.

"Maybe you should keep her," Truly says, bouncing on her heels to get a better look. Swear this kid never holds still.

"She does need a home." Aiyana shoves her hands in her back pockets and rocks back on her heels.

Something stirs in my gut. I've got no business taking in a dog: I live in a motel, ride a motorcycle, don't have a job or a future, and I'm not right in the head. It's not smart for me to take on any kind of responsibility.

Despite all this, my mouth opens and says, "Okay."

"Really?" Truly shouts, and I wince.

"Hush, baby. You're loud," Aiyana scolds. I have to give her credit. She's observant and seems to understand me. "You can take her today, if you want. Tooth extraction isn't major surgery, and as long as you bring her back in a couple days for a check-up, she's all yours."

I nod.

"It's settled then." Aiyana closes the kennel. "Pizza should be here soon. Let's go back to the house."

I cup both hands around the dog as we walk back across the lawn. I've never held anything so breakable.

When we get back inside the house, Karen rouses and looks up at me with her black eyes. There's no fear there. Not like when most people look at me. She crawls up my chest, and I follow her with my hand, ready to catch her if she falls. She stumbles around the back of my neck and into the hood of my hoodie. I feel her walk circles, her long fur tickling my neck until she finds a comfortable spot and lays down.

I hear a sigh and look over to see Truly and Aiyana gaping at me. It makes me uncomfortable. I wonder if I did something wrong. Like maybe the dog shouldn't be back there.

This was a dumb fucking idea. I don't know how to take care of a dog. I reach back to remove her, already prepared to give Karen back, but Aiyana stops me.

"Leave her there. It probably feels nice and cozy. Like a nest. It's a perfect spot, actually."

I nod and lower my hands.

The pizza comes not too long after that. Truly talks the entire time, which is a good thing because it leaves no room for me to. The kid can hold an entire conversation on her own. Mouth full of food and everything.

Soon after, I stand up and walk to the door, ready to go back to my dark, dank motel where there are no little girls or curious women to ask me questions.

"Leaving already?" Aiyana asks.

I nod.

"Here's some dog food and a leash to get you started." She hands me a plastic bag. "And you'll come back in a couple days for me to check her out?"

I nod.

"Bye, Will. I'll miss you." Truly hugs me around my waist, squeezing tight. I don't know what to do, so I pat the top of her head twice. She jumps back and says, "Wait! I have something for you."

I look at Aiyana, confused, and she shrugs her shoulders. A minute later, Truly returns with something in her hand. She holds it up to me proudly, and I accept it.

I stare at it a minute, trying to figure out what it is. It's a charm made from red, yellow, and orange beads threaded over some wire. There's an infinity symbol in the middle with two long strips coming off either end. It looks like scissors that were pulled apart and stretched. I don't get it.

"Truly," Aiyana scolds, causing me to look over at them.

"What? I want him to have it."

"S'okay?" I ask, not wanting to cause a rift in case this thing is important.

The daughter and mother have a conversation with their eyes. Truly must win because Aiyana nods with a tight smile, and the girl wraps her arms around my leg again.

Aiyana urges her off of me and I walk over to my bike, tucking the charm in my pocket.

I don't know if it's safe to have a dog in my hood while I ride my bike, but I'm assuming one of the two girls waving at me from the porch would've told me it's a bad idea if it wasn't.

I tug on the strings to the hood so it's tight around my neck, ensuring she won't fall out. Then I start the engine and drive away.

What the fuck just happened?

Chapter
ONE

Roch
Eleven years later…

"**S**he's at the Golden Nugget. Room 519," Sly, the club treasurer and hacker, says through the earpiece in my helmet. He hangs up, not waiting for a response.

I flip a u-ey and backtrack to Fremont.

Sly's the only one who knows why I disappeared for a few days. Everyone else thinks I'm off on a long ride, needing a break after all the shit went down with the Corsettis. Dom Corsetti took Loki's old lady, Bridgette—raped and tortured her. But we got her back and sent Dom to Hades. Fucking glad too. Not many people in this world I can say I like, but Bridgette's one of them.

It's been a couple months, and everyone is still reeling. It's why I didn't tell them why I left. That, and because this isn't club business. It's personal. Aiyana and Truly are personal, and I keep that shit separate from my club life. They're family, and I don't need anyone knowing they mean something to me. It'd make them a target.

I hop on the freeway going north.

I'm in fucking Las Vegas, where the lights are too fucking bright and everything is too fucking loud, because Truly ran off with some asshole. Aiyana called me frantic a few days ago, begging me to find her.

I brought Sly in to help. He was able to track her location through her cell phone and then hack into the hotel guest registry to find out what room she's in.

I pull into the parking garage and hop off my bike. The hot desert air is thicker here than in Reno. Makes it hard to breathe.

The curious eyes of the gamblers follow me through the lobby. I don't exactly blend in with my leather cut, metal jewelry, and intimidating size.

I take the elevator up, feeling my blood pressure rise with each floor I ascend. I don't know what Truly was thinking.

The day she turned eighteen, a switch flipped in her head. She went from a sweet and innocent girl I couldn't get to shut up, to a mouthy brat who makes stupid-ass decisions.

The past year has been Aiyana asking me to find Truly or pick her up from some shady party or rescue her from any number of poor decisions she's made. She's an adult who has never been taught what happens in the real world.

She wears rose-colored glasses and doesn't understand the consequences of her actions.

Like running away with a loser who has multiple felonies for assault. Found that out through Sly too.

It's none of my business who Truly dates or spends time with until I find out she's going to get hurt. That's when I step in to save her. Most of the time kicking and screaming.

I storm down the hall to Room 519. Loud music blares, and the faint skunky stench of weed permeates around the door. Fucking great.

I don't bother knocking. Instead, I kick in the door and find Truly straddling some skinny asshole on a king-size bed. Her shirt's off, and his hands are on her tits. I see fucking red. She may be nineteen, but she's still a kid. She shouldn't be doing adult things like fucking some clown in a seedy hotel room in Vegas.

They don't hear my approach over the headache-inducing rap music playing. I reach for the guy, ripping him off the bed, and send him tumbling to the ground. Truly falls onto the mattress, her eyes bugging out.

"Will?" she shrieks.

I ignore her and lift the piece of shit off the ground by the fabric of his designer T-shirt. I slam my fist into his face three times in rapid succession. Blood sprays onto everything within a two-foot vicinity. He howls in pain, so I punch him in the throat to shut him up.

Kill him.

Kill him.

Kill him.

"Stop!" a shrill voice screams from behind me, snapping me back into the moment.

I drop the loser to the ground. He lands with a resounding *thud*. I wipe the warm, thick blood from my eyes and turn around to see a frightened Truly. She covers her face with her hands and sobs. I feel a vague tugging on my heart. I know I should say or do something to comfort her. That's what normal people do.

But I'm not normal, and I don't know how to be.

"S'okay," I mumble even though it's not okay. None of this is okay.

All to save this spoiled girl who's so naïve, she doesn't recognize danger in the form of some wannabe gangster who thinks he can be the next Snoop Dog or some shit when really, he's a peon with no future.

I step into the bathroom and use the threadbare washcloth to wipe the blood from my face. When I return, Truly's crouching on the ground next to her dip shit boyfriend, trying to rouse him.

"I'm staying here with Lizard."

"Tru" I warn.

"I hate you!" she shouts.

"Now."

"Go home, Will." She glares at me with mascara and tears streaming down her face.

Fuck. I've never been able to handle her crying, but I can't leave her here.

"Kickin' and screamin'," I threaten.

"You wouldn't." She narrows her eyes at me.

I nod and stalk toward her. I owe her mom this much. No matter how hard I fought to push Aiyana away over the last eleven years, she forced herself into my life. She looked after me and made me part of her family. Not sure I'd be alive if it weren't for her.

I grip Truly's arm and bring her to her feet.

I'm suddenly aware she still doesn't have a shirt on. Her tiny tits are barely covered by a black lacy bra I can see her nipples through. I quickly look away. She shakes her arm free and stomps over to the bed to pull on a top that hardly helps the situation. Her entire midriff is showing, and she's paired it with shorts that cover as much as a pair of underwear would.

"Go," I growl.

"I'm nineteen, Will. I don't have to go anywhere. I'm an adult."

"Roch," I correct.

"I'm not calling you by some stupid name your gang made up. You're Will. The same sad man who showed up at my door eleven years ago to tell me you couldn't save my dad."

Ouch.

Burning hot anger fills me. I fight to stop myself from throwing her over my knee and spanking her like a child. She sure as shit ain't acting like the grown-up she claims to be.

I'm done talking. I grab her backpack and her hand, dragging her from the room. The asshole on the ground stirs and makes a gurgling noise. Good, he's alive. I won't have to involve the club and have prospects come clean up my mess.

Luckily, Truly isn't interested in drawing attention to herself, and she wipes the black lines from her face on the elevator down to the lobby, glaring at me while I stare back. She thinks her dirty looks can hurt me.

Think again, little girl. Can't hurt a hollow heart.

I walk with a hand on her lower back all the way to the parking garage, in case she gets any ideas about ditching me. She doesn't. When we reach my bike, she stops short.

"You rode all the way here?"

I nod. Does she think my nonexistent sedan is in the shop?

I stuff her backpack in one of my leather saddlebags and hop on. She continues to stand there, gawking.

"On." I hook a thumb over my shoulder.

"It's like a six-hour ride home."

"On," I repeat through gritted teeth, handing her a helmet.

She throws her arms in the air, the motion exposing the lining of that way-too-grown-up bra. I wonder if her mom knows she wears stuff like that. In my eyes, she's still a mouthy, intrusive kid. Not this sexed-up kitten she's portraying.

Matter of fact, I still remember the first time Aiyana bought her a training bra. I stopped by with one of the dogs for Aiyana to look at and Truly was on the porch, pouting. I sat next to her and nudged her with my shoulder. She told me she didn't want boobs or a bra. I was shocked as shit she would say something like that to me, but that's how she always was. No filter, and no understanding of topics she should keep private.

Now look at her. Hiding things. Keeping secrets. Wearing next to nothing. I don't even recognize her anymore. I wish we could go back to the days she held my hand and yammered on nonsensically. She drove me crazy, but at least I knew who she was.

She caves, shoving the helmet on her head and hopping on the back of my bike like she's done a million times before. I start the engine, but don't go anywhere since she's not holding on to me. She knows the rules.

I wait her out. Minutes go by, but I stay parked.

She's stubborn, but I've got nothing if I don't have time.

Eventually, I feel her hands rest on my sides. *Not good enough.* I tug them around me until I feel her pressed against my back. She's stiff, and her anger is palpable, but I don't give a shit. She can stay pissed.

I'm not her friend.

At least not right now.

When I'm certain she won't pull away, I take off down Fremont. Thankfully, it's a Sunday afternoon and traffic's light.

We hit the highway and find open road. I twist the throttle, accelerating until we're going fast enough to release endorphins, but not so fast I'll kill us.

I know Truly likes speed too, so it's not a surprise when I feel one hand release me, and through the side-view mirror, I watch as she throws a fist in the air. She can't resist the open road, a fast bike, and a long ride.

Ever since Aiyana agreed to let me take Truly for her first ride when she was eleven, I've taken her to abandoned roads and shown her what it feels like to fly.

Back then, my Harley was old and only worked half the time I needed it to. I sold it for scraps not long after I joined the Royal Bastards and started making money. Real money. More money than I've ever had at one time. Now I have a custom, matte-gray Harley Sport Glide. She's the sexiest bitch I've ever ridden.

As the hours pass, I get lost in my head, thinking about how much things have changed since I left the Army. At first, I was lost. I couldn't get a job since a dishonorable discharge is treated the same as a felony. My savings account was dwindling, and if it weren't for Karen, I probably would've killed myself. I felt like I'd given everything I had to the Army, and they turned their backs on me when all I did was try to save one of our own.

I stopped at a bar one night, ready to drink myself into oblivion when a man in a leather cut approached me. It was Trucker, the prez of the Royal Bastards. He said I looked like someone who needed to belong. He told me about the club and what it meant to be a brother. Turned out he was right; the club was exactly what I was missing.

I became a prospect the next day. Being bullied and

bossed around by arrogant assholes for a year wasn't a big deal for me. I'd been through basic training, which was the same thing. Only instead of cleaning toilets, scrubbing floors, and making beds, I was serving beer, cleaning up puke, and dropping bodies out in the middle of the desert.

Trucker's not prez anymore, though. Now it's his son, Loki. I was all for the change in power. Trucker lost his mind when his wife was killed by the Corsetti family. His erratic behavior would've gotten us all killed if someone hadn't stopped him.

Loki's great at his job. He gave all the younger guys, me included, positions on the board. My experience with weapons from being in the Army made him nominate me to be the Sergeant-at-Arms. I accepted because the Royal Bastards were the best thing to happen to me, other than Aiyana and Truly, and I didn't want to disappoint them.

I feel Truly's cheek rest against my back. Maybe it's an apology. Maybe she's tired. Don't fucking know. Never have fully understood the girl. Not when she was handing me some beaded charm that I secretly sewed into the inside of my vest. Not when she was twelve and telling me about her boobs. And definitely not now that she's running away with a dumb ass who can't even get a swing in during a fight.

One thing I do know is I love her and her mom. They accepted me even though I'm menacing as hell and can't string a sentence together. They didn't blame me when I was the one who showed up at their door and not Ricky. They made me feel like I'd done something right by trying to save him. Next to my club, they're all I've got, and I'll be damned if I let Truly slip through the cracks.

It doesn't take us six hours to get home; it takes five and a half. The sky turned dark about a hundred miles back, but it didn't slow me down. We drove straight home, except for two gas station stops.

The second my bike is parked out front of her house, Truly hops off.

"I was slapping you fifty miles ago because I had to pee, asshole," she yells as she runs up the walkway, tossing the helmet onto the grass.

My lips twitch because I knew what she was asking of me. Just didn't care enough to break. I follow her inside, knowing Aiyana's going to have questions. There are a few things I'll keep secret for Truly's sake, but this isn't one of them.

"She was in Vegas?" Aiyana asks the second I walk through the threshold.

I nod.

"Sly called and told me. She was with that kid, wasn't she? That Eminem wannabe little shit, huh?" She paces back and forth with a hand covering her forehead.

I nod.

"I knew it. I knew he was trouble."

I take a seat on the old rattan sofa and cross an ankle over my knee. Might as well get comfortable. This is going to take a minute.

"I don't know what to do with her, Will. She's nineteen. I can't tell her what to do."

"Convent," I suggest.

"You think they'll take her?" Aiyana's hand drops, and she looks at me.

"Joke."

"Oh, right." She slumps onto the couch. "What do I do?"

I shrug. Never had a kid. Don't know how to control them.

"Thank you, Will."

"Roch."

"I'll never understand these nicknames you guys give each other."

"Road name."

"Whatever." She waves me off.

Aiyana was nervous for me when she found out I'd joined the club. We have a reputation around town, and while she doesn't know exactly how we make our money, she's heard rumors. Rumors I've denied over and over to protect her.

The Royal Bastards have had a few ways of making money since I joined up. Right now, we're hitmen. I'm a hitman. There's no pussyfooting around it. None of us are good people, and we've all got a place with Hades when we die.

"Late," I say and stand up. It's been a long-ass day, and I need to get back to my dogs. Bridgette promised to watch them, but she spoils them, and it takes days to get them acting right after she's been around.

"I'll see you later. Thanks again." She squeezes my shoulder as I walk out. I don't bother saying goodbye to Truly. She's likely plotting my death in her diary or some shit anyway.

Don't give a damn. She's safe and home with her mom. Right where she needs to be.

Chapter
TWO

Truly

I flop face-first onto my bed and cry into my pillow. I'm beyond mortified. Not only because I was dragged out of a hotel room like a petulant child by Roch, but I was also shirtless and straddling Lizard.

I didn't even want to be there. I don't know why I was. That's a lie. I know exactly why I skipped town with that loser. The same reason I do all the dumb shit I do. To get Will's... no, Roch's attention. The only time he's not with his brothers at that stupid club is when I'm getting into trouble, and Mom calls him to find me.

It's childish, I know. But he refuses to see me as anything but the eight-year-old I was when we met.

I think back to the first time we met. I watched as he got off his bike and sauntered up the path to the front door. Most kids would be frightened of his massive frame and the hardened set of his jaw. But not me. I thought he looked sad and like he needed a friend.

I decided I'd do anything to see his tightly pursed lips break into a smile. It's been eleven years, and I've yet to see him do anything but scowl.

I haven't given up, though.

Not that my behavior lately has given him any reason to be happy. He's tired of my antics. Mom is too. I must have a dark spirit living inside me because I can't seem to stop myself.

Then again, if he came around more often, for reasons other than to get check-ups for his dogs, I wouldn't feel the need to get his attention in other ways.

A knock on my bedroom door startles me from my thoughts, and I dry my eyes on my pillow before sitting up.

"What?" I yell out.

"Can I come in?"

"It's not locked."

The door opens, and Mom walks in, taking a seat next to me on the bed.

"Care to explain yourself?" Her wide, brown eyes study me carefully.

"I needed to get away."

"Get away from what?" she asks, not in a sarcastic way, but because she's genuinely curious. My heart aches with how much I love this woman. She's nothing but understanding and caring. She's confused by my recent tantrums and desperately wants to know what's going on with me.

It's infuriating.

"Everything," I huff out.

"Me?" She frowns.

"Everything," I repeat. "Life. School. The clinic."

"And me."

I don't confirm or deny. It's not her specifically, but in a way, yes. It's her too. I spent eighteen years never having a moment away from her. Dad joined the Army before she became pregnant, and I think to keep a piece of him close during the years he was deployed, she clung to me.

She didn't allow me to go to school with the other kids, and all playdates I had with the neighbors were at our house. She never even hired a babysitter for when she was working at the clinic. She just brought me along.

When Dad died, she went from a stage four clinger to a stage five. I wish he were still around. I don't have a lot of memories of him, but the ones I do have, are full of happiness and fun. He was light-hearted to Mom's serious. She'd be worrying about one thing or another, and he'd scoop her up and whisk her off to dance with him, all while he sang off-key in her ear. Mom would laugh and smile in a way she never did when he was away.

I never saw that side of her again after he died.

"I'm sorry, Mom. What else can I say? I needed a break. Lizard had studio time booked in Vegas, and I don't know... I guess it sounded like a fun opportunity."

"*Lizard* is a loser." She rests her hand on my thigh.

"Yeah, he is." I smile.

"What kind of name is that, anyway? He came out of the womb, and his mommy took one look at him and said, 'There he is. My darling baby boy, Lizard.' Is that it?" She's smiling now too.

"Probably. He *is* reptilian looking," I muse.

"It's the pointy nose and jaw."

"Don't forget the beady eyes."

"Right. Can't forget those." She wraps an arm around me, and I rest my head on her shoulder. "I was worried."

"I know. I'm sorry."

"You've had a lot of sorrowful moments lately."

"One or two."

"Is it your college courses? Are they too much for you? I know homeschooling put you at a disadvantage socially, but—"

"It's not that. I like my classes."

I started taking classes at the University of Nevada, Reno, at sixteen. I had my associate degree when I graduated my homeschool program, and I'm now working on my bachelor's. At this rate, I'll have my Doctor of Veterinarian degree by twenty-four.

"You have to help me understand then, kid. I can't keep relying on Will to drop everything and find you each time you decide to stay out all night or disappear with lizards."

"Why? Because drinking booze and sleeping with club whores is an important job?"

She gasps. "What do you know about any of that? You better not be hanging out at the club."

"I'm not, Mom." I stand up and walk over to my dresser. I pull open a few drawers and gather clean clothes so I can take a shower and wash the day off. "Besides, Will wouldn't let me even if I wanted to."

"He better not. I'd kill him."

"But I wish he would," I say under my breath. Mom doesn't know about the torch I'm holding for the surly biker. She'd lock me up in a heartbeat if she did. She hates the club and wishes Will wasn't part of it. I don't know why.

"What was that?"

"Nothing. I'm going to shower. I'm covered in dirt from the ride home."

"Okay." She walks to the door, but stops at the threshold. "Can you please promise no more disappearing acts?"

"Fine. I promise. Once word gets around a biker will show up to bash anyone's face in who messes with me, I'll be a social pariah anyway."

"I'm not even going to ask."

"Probably for the best."

"I love you, Tru-bear."

"Love you too, Mom."

She leaves me alone, and I walk across the hall to the bathroom. I strip and stare at my naked body in the mirror. Maybe if I had big boobs and curves, Will would see me differently. Instead, I'm willowy with plum-sized boobs and too big-eyes. I yank my hair free from its low ponytail. It's stick straight and deep chestnut brown. If I had blond hair with loose curls, I'd bet he'd give me a second look.

I flip my reflection off and step into the hot spray.

As I scrub every inch of my body clean, I think about what an epic failure today was. The only positive thing to come from this was riding home on the back of Will's bike. I've always loved being his passenger.

When I was a kid, it made me feel grown-up and cool. But now, it's a sensual experience. It's having free reign to hold Will tight, feeling the way his abdominal muscles clench tight under my palms. It's pressing my sensitive breasts into his sweaty back and knowing I'll smell like him for the rest of the day. Most of all, it's the vibration between my legs. It's the grinding into the seat, seeking friction, and being on the brink of orgasm with him right there, not knowing what I'm doing.

It's dirty and wrong.

And I love every second of it.

The next morning I wake up to a text message from Will. Well, there's not any actual text, only a thumbs-up emoji followed by a question mark.

Me: Yep. Thanks for saving my honor, white knight.

Will: Dark knight.

Me: Didn't mean to discredit your reputation.

Will: Be good.

Me: Are you saying my normal inclination is to be bad?

He responds with a shrugging emoji. Even in a text he doesn't use full sentences. 1 once asked him why he doesn't talk much. All he said was, "No need." Like that explains everything. Mom thinks he has PTSD or something from being a prisoner of war. I wish I'd known him before so I could know for sure.

Me: What's on your agenda today?

His answering emoji is a motorcycle. I debate giving him shit about being a badass biker who uses emojis to communicate, but I don't want to make him self-conscious. Ever since I got my first cell phone at sixteen, he's made it a point to occasionally check-in, and I don't want to lose that.

If I allowed myself, I'd text him every day. But I worry that would drive him away, so I let him take the lead. I respond when he initiates, and when he disappears mid-conversation, I let it go and wait for the next time he pops into my texts.

I'm a hopeless loser.

Me: Off to class. Talk later.

I'm not surprised when he doesn't reply.

I collect my laptop and various notebooks I need for

class, and shove them in my backpack. Then I grab an apple from the fruit basket on the dining table and walk out the door. I hop into my Mini Cooper and crank on nineties country. It's a guilty pleasure I'd never admit to listening to. But it's what Dad always listened to, and I feel close to him whenever I hear Garth Brooks or Travis Tritt.

Twenty minutes later, I walk into my biology class, and take a seat next to my lab partner, Max. He's cute in a tall and lanky kind of way, but his dimples are what sets him apart. Since we've been working together all year, we've become friendly. I get the impression he'd like for it to be more, but I only have eyes for a blond, bearded biker with California surfer good looks and the body of a god.

"Nice of you to show up for class," he jokes, nudging my shoulder with his own.

"Sorry about that. I was on vacation," I lie.

"Where'd you go?"

"Vegas."

"That's not a vacation. You can get crowded casinos and all you can eat buffets at the GSR." A few strands of his brown hair flops over his eyes and he pushes it back onto his head.

"True, but the strip clubs are so much better there," I say to get a rise out of him. I didn't go anywhere near a strip club. If we weren't at the ghetto studio where Lizard recorded his lame-ass vocals, then we were back at the hotel so he could work on convincing me to have sex with him. I was on the verge of giving in when Will showed up.

"Oh yeah? That's what you're into? Seeing silicone parts bounce around for a few dollars? I'd much rather see you up on a stage," he flirts.

"That will never happen, but you can keep hoping," I sass before I open my backpack and pull out my laptop. "So what did I miss?"

"There's a lab due in three days. Professor Stevens wanted to assign me to another partner since you hadn't been showing up, but I told him you were sick and would be back in a few days. Thanks for not making a liar out of me."

"You're welcome. I guess that means we should book the lab. When are you free?"

"Tomorrow evening? Say around seven? We could grab dinner after." One of his dark brows quirks up.

"Are you buying?" I ask.

"You drive a hard bargain, but sure. My treat."

"Then I'm in."

Chapter
THREE

Roch

I wake up to a cold, wet nose pressing into my closed eyelid. A puff of warm breath blows across my face, and I swat the dog away. I blink open my eyes to see Frankie, one of the eleven pit bulls Aiyana has talked me into adopting. Maybe it's survivor's guilt or some shit, since I lived and her husband died, but whether it's tracking down Truly or taking in another dog, I can't tell that woman no.

I've tried.

I sit up and stretch, scanning the bed to see who slept with me last night. Frankie, Molly, and Stan stare back at me, along with Karen, who sleeps on a small dog bed on the pillow next to mine. She sits up and stretches big before prancing over to me.

I scoop her up and take her to the sink. The casita I live in is on club property in the backyard and made up of one big room, sectioned off into separate zones.

Near the front door, there's a living room area with a

couple beat-up sofas the dogs like to nap on. Further inside, it transitions into a kitchen with a mini-fridge, a hot plate, and a couple cabinets for storage. In the back is where my bed is, along with a toilet and a sink in the corner. I never have company, so there's no need for privacy.

I stayed inside a room in the clubhouse for a while after I started prospecting, but it didn't take long for Trucker to offer me this place. No one likes having the boring, quiet one around all the time. I make them nervous, and they think I judge them for banging random chicks and drinking enough tequila and whiskey to kill an average man's liver every night since I don't indulge.

Truth is, I don't give a shit what they do. It's just not my thing. After I got home from the war, I was changed. Didn't feel the need to sleep around, and my mind is a crazy enough place without it being doused in booze or drugs.

I brush my teeth and wash my face, along with Karen's, while looking around my cramped space. I don't mind being banished out here by myself. I prefer the seclusion, and it allows me to be closer to my pack of dogs.

The guys grumbled when I started bringing home rescues until I showed them how protective they can be. They didn't mind after that. My dogs are the most intimidating alarm system money can buy.

I set Karen on the ground and dig out a clean pair of jeans and a fresh hoodie from my dresser. After getting dressed, I take the dogs outside to do their business. Karen runs around like a little mama, checking on all the bigger dogs before scratching at my leg to be lifted up so she can tuck herself away in my hood. She's thirteen years old and not very active anymore, preferring naps to playtime.

"Roch. 'Bout time you woke up," Goblin, our enforcer, calls out from the back door of the main building. "Church."

I nod and follow him inside.

The clubhouse stinks like pussy and booze. It's embedded in the paint on the walls and soaked into the wood flooring. It's the signature scent of the Royal Bastards. Most people would be grossed out, but I find it comforting. The same way my brothers are and this clubhouse is. These people, this clubhouse, gave me a place I belong—a family. We don't always see eye to eye, but what brothers do?

They'd kill for me.

Die for me.

That's what's important.

I stop at the bar and rap my knuckles on the wood to get the prospect's attention. Think his name is Miles or Mikey. Don't fucking remember. He took Jake's place after he made the ultimate sacrifice trying to save Bridgette. Jake might've only been a prospect, but he was days from patching in, and I'd already considered him one of my brothers.

Fucking miss that kid.

"S'up, Roch? Coffee?" Miles or Mikey asks, and I nod.

He fills a mug with the black sludge we brew and hands it over. I lift my chin at him and proceed into the Chapel. Everyone's already seated around the table with the Royal Bastards emblem carved into it.

Moto and Sly have their heads together, bullshitting about something, Goblin has his newspaper open in front of his face, Bullet looks star struck given he's newly patched in and hasn't been to church more than twice, and Loki and Khan are flipping through a folder that no doubt has our next job in it.

Even Trucker's here. He's been around a lot more than usual since the shit with Dom Corsetti. It's good to have him back. He'd been like a dad to me until the day his wife was murdered.

I take my place next to Goblin and have my first sip of coffee. Caffeine is the only drug I allow in my system, and I drink a lot of it.

"All right. Listen up," Loki calls out from the head of the table, banging the gavel. "Now that Dom's gone, it opens guns back up for us. Miguel reached out and asked if we wanted our gig back."

"You want to go back to guns?" Moto asks.

"It was a lot easier and safer. At least with arms, Miguel pays to keep the authorities in our pocket. Right now, we got no one if something happens during a kill. It was always supposed to be something to get us by until we found the next thing. Plus, we know the trade. We know who we're dealing with and how to do it. It's a better option than trying something new." Loki kicks his feet up on the table.

I like the idea. Going on long rides, transporting guns, wasn't difficult. It put me on my bike more, and it wasn't as messy. It fucking sucked when we had to lose our business to end the war with Dom, but back then, we were slowly getting picked off. There was no other choice.

"And you think Miguel is being straight with us? This isn't some kind of ploy with Anthony to take us down?" Goblin takes another drag of his cig.

"I don't think so. Miguel was pissed when he had to start dealing with that fuck wad, Dom. He's always been loyal to us," Khan chimes in.

"Let's take a vote." Loki sets his feet on the ground and leans over the table. "All in favor, say aye."

Each of my brothers votes to move back into guns, including me. It's the right choice. Not as lucrative, but we did well enough.

"Vote's unanimous. We're back in the gun business." Loki slams the gavel down, and my brothers whoop and holler. Even I slam a fist on the table. When everyone quiets, he continues, "I have our last job. His name is Eric McClean. He's a distributor for Leon King who thought he could skim off the top. He's racked up a hundred grand in product debt with no way to pay."

"Why doesn't Leon off the guy himself? You'd think the meth king of Northern Nevada could handle his own shit." Goblin lights a cig and blows out a puff of smoke. The scent hits my nose, and I wave it away from my face.

"He's being watched after one of his stash houses was raided, and he can't afford being tied to a murder," Loki shrugs. "It'll be an easy ten grand."

"McClean got any ties? Anyone who'll miss him?" Moto asks.

"That'll be Sly's job to figure out, but I doubt it." Loki passes a single sheet of paper to Sly because he can bust into any government database.

"On it."

"Let me know what you find." Loki rests his forearms on the table. "Anyone heard anything from the Corsettis? Anthony's been MIA since the warehouse explosion, and it's making me nervous."

"My friend who knows Anthony's cousin said they've all gone underground," Sly says.

"That's what I'm hearing too. I'm guessing they're regrouping. They've shut down all their businesses, legal and otherwise, but I doubt that'll last long," Moto says.

"We need to make sure we stay on top of this. I don't need their dad showing up seeking revenge. I'm not letting anything touch my club or Birdie. I don't want any surprises." Loki's eyes turn dark and deadly. I pity the asshole who decides to mess with his old lady again. "Anything else we need to discuss?"

We all shake our heads.

"Then let's get the fuck out of here." Loki slams the gavel down, and everyone stands to leave. "Roch, stick around."

I sit back down. Feels a little like being called into the principal's office, and I wonder what I did to get singled out.

"What's going on with you? You disappeared for almost a week. Had Birdie takin' care of the dogs. Where were you?"

"Vegas." My finger taps a tune on the wooden table.

"Why?"

"Ride," I answer, and watch as Loki's frustration grows.

It's none of his business what I was doing. If I needed help or it had to do with the club, I'd make sure he was clued in. I saw what happened to Bridgette for being associated with Loki. I'd never forgive myself if Aiyana or Truly were hurt because of me. They don't belong in this world.

The one and only time I allowed my brothers into the other half of my life was after the warehouse explosion. We all had injuries that could link us back to the incident, so we needed someone who could patch us up and keep our secret. Aiyana was pissed at me, and I don't blame her, but I didn't see another option.

No matter what, I'll never put them at risk again.

"Anything to do with that woman and little girl?" Loki smirks like we share a secret.

"No."

"Okay. You'll let me know if you need the club's help with anything?"

I nod.

"Birdie's coming by today," he says.

He doesn't like the friendship she and I have developed, but he tolerates it for her sake. If it were up to him, she'd never even look at another man. I get it because I feel protective of Aiyana and Truly, but for different reasons. Aiyana is a mother figure to me and Truly's like a little sister.

That doesn't feel right.

Maybe like a cousin?

I nod.

"I'll send her back when she gets here."

We leave the Chapel, and I make a beeline for the bar where Moto and Sly are sitting. Sly has his laptop out, and I'm assuming he's researching this McClean kid.

"Looks like he sells mostly to college kids," Sly says, scrolling down a Facebook page. He closes that tab and opens up a different page. "Let's see what else our boy is up to."

I watch in fascination as he flips through screens and programs I don't understand. Don't own a computer, and the extent of my electronics knowledge comes from Truly, who taught me to use my iPhone.

Within five minutes, he's hacked into McClean's Cloud files and is digging around.

"Our boy is naughty. Looks like on top of stealing meth from his employer, he also enjoys drugging girls and taking dirty pictures of them," Sly notes, scrolling through pictures of unconscious girls. "Let me hack his Messenger."

A few more clicks of the keyboard and a list of contacts fills the screen. He opens them one by one, laughing at how many times the guy blindly messages girls and gets rejected. The fifth contact down, there's a conversation about a party happening tonight.

"This might be our in. It's fast, but there's not much to plan out," Sly says and then spins around on his stool. "Hey, Prez. Come here."

Loki looks over Sly's shoulder and reads the message.

"I want you and Roch inside. Make nice with the kid and lead him out of the party. Khan and Goblin can be in the van waiting," Loki instructs.

"Me?" I ask, wondering why he's sending me in. I'm usually the one in the van, doing the dirty work.

"Have you seen your face? You look trustworthy." He reaches over and pinches one of my cheeks. I bat him away. "That gonna be a problem?"

I shake my head.

"What's a problem?" Bridgette asks, wrapping an arm around Loki's middle.

"Nothing, darlin'. You okay?" He turns her in his arms and kisses her while grabbing a handful of her ass. I back away and go behind the bar to pour myself more coffee.

I could've ended up a pussy chaser like my brothers, but after having every freedom stripped from me and watching my best friend be murdered, I realized how dark the world is. Now, the only thing I crave is blood and revenge.

When I take a life, it's the faces of the men who took Ricky from me that I see. I'll never be able to retaliate against the ones who deserve it most, but each kill tames the beast who wants to reign hell on earth to make them pay. Maybe if I let it all out, the burning fire within would be extinguished. Since that can't happen, the most I can hope for is to keep it under control.

I take my coffee outside and sit down on a plastic chair in the backyard. Karen climbs out of my hood, her tongue flopping out of the side of her mouth. She lies on my shoulder and stretches long. Scratching under her chin, I watch her eyes close, and a peaceful look wash over her.

"I thought I'd find you out here." Bridgette takes a seat next to me. Her blond hair is in loose curls over her shoulders, and she's wearing a baby pink sundress. "Did you have a nice vacation?"

I nod.

"You're not going to tell me what you were doing, are you?"

I shake my head.

"Does it have anything to do with Aiyana and Truly?"

I nod. I still won't talk to her about it, but I'll give her that much. Bridgette's the only one who knows Truly's name. While she was recovering from her injuries after we rescued her, I spent a lot of time at her side since Loki had to deal with club business. She asked a lot of questions. I didn't say much, never do, but I at least gave names.

"Are they okay?"

I nod.

"I was thinking about stopping by the clinic one of these days to thank them for helping me. I'd probably be dead without them, so it's the least I can do."

"No," I say through gritted teeth. No one can go near them. Not even Bridgette. She's too closely linked to the club.

"Fine. Will you at least tell her how thankful I am?"

I nod, but it's a lie. Aiyana and I have an unspoken agreement to never talk about that day again.

"I think that girl had a crush on you. She had 'the look.'"

I scoop Karen up and stand. Bridgette doesn't know what she's talking about, and I can tell this conversation is quickly heading into dangerous territory. I don't like getting angry when she's around. Loki doesn't like it either, so it's best if I walk away.

"Don't be like that. I was just teasing you." She gives me a wide and toothy smile.

"Don't joke," I say. I lost my sense of humor the first time I was placed in a foster home.

"Fine. Fine." She holds up her hands placatingly. "Want to take a walk with the dogs?"

Swear to God, each dog freezes in place at the "w" word.

I nod, and we head over to the back gate that leads out into the open desert. I release the dogs with a wave of my hand, and they take off through the sagebrush and dirt.

"I'm sorry about pushing you. It wasn't fair. You're keeping those women a secret and probably for a good reason, but you can't blame me for being curious."

"Killed the cat," I warn.

"Fine. I'll leave it alone. But know I'm always here for you if you ever need womanly advice or anything."

Girls are so fucking stupid. They've romanticized their lives to the point where they think the key to happiness is finding love. There's nothing in this world that could bring enjoyment to my life other than seeing Ricky alive and well. But I saw his lifeless head bounce on the ground, spurting blood before his body collapsed next to it.

He ain't coming back.

And neither is my happiness.

Chapter

FOUR

Truly

"How about you come with me to a party tonight?" Max asks with his mouth full of pizza.

We finished our lab and decided on an easy dinner in the dining hall on campus.

"I don't know if my mom will be okay with that. She's kind of pissed at me right now." I think back to the conversation we had last night.

"Uh-oh. What did you do?"

"I took off with a guy." I smirk.

"Boyfriend?" he asks.

All evening he's been standing too close to be considered friendly and has made every effort to touch me in some way, like bumping my shoulder or lightly slapping my arm when he made a joke. Even now, he's sitting next to me in the booth, instead of across from me like a normal person.

"No. Just a friend." I should say yes to deter his advances, but my pride is wounded after being treated like a child by Will, and the attention feels good.

"You're an adult. Your mom should back off and let you live your life."

"Yes, but I live at home." I rip my crust into chunks, tossing them back onto my plate.

"Come on, just for an hour. If you aren't having fun, we'll leave. No questions asked."

"All right. But just for an hour." I look down at my outfit. I'm wearing high-waisted black jeans with holes in the knees, a white crop top, and a lightweight camo print jacket.

It'll work.

"All right. Let's go." He stacks my plate on his and drops them over in the bin. When he returns, he grabs my hand and guides me out of the dining hall and to his car.

Ten minutes later, we pull up to a rundown house. There's trash in the front yard and random guys sitting in lawn chairs on the porch. They don't look like college students, they look like junkies with faraway gazes and hunched-over postures.

"Are you sure we're in the right place?" I ask with my hand on the door handle.

"Yeah, this is it." Max leans over me to look out the passenger window.

"How did you hear about this party?"

"Some guy from my business class. He said it was gonna be lit."

"Looks more like a bunch of losers who are getting lit." A pit forms in my stomach. I have a bad feeling about this. Will would shit a brick if he knew where I was.

"Don't pussy out. You said you'd give it an hour."

"Fine. But don't ditch me." I step out of the car and zip my coat closed. Covering up seems smart right about now.

41

"I'll stay next to you the whole time," Max says, walking around the car and taking my hand.

Inside is a little better. The worn furniture has been pushed to the edge of the living room, and loud electronic dance music blares from the speakers. It smells like alcohol and weed, and there are a ton of people milling about. I recognize a few kids from the college, but no one I associate with.

Not that I have a lot of friends, because I don't. I never have. Being homeschooled, I wasn't around many kids my age. It made me precocious and unrelatable to my peers.

Taking college courses at sixteen didn't help either, but by seventeen, the college guys finally gave me attention. At first, I thought it made me special. I was excited to fit in for once in my life, and I made a lot of bad choices. That's when I realized the worse my decisions were, the more Will would come around.

It was negative attention, but it was better than being ignored.

There was the time I went to a club with a douchebag who ditched me for the first blonde he could get his hands on. I texted Mom to come get me, but she sent Will. A few weeks later, he had to pick me up from a party after the guy I was with got loaded and wanted to drive me home. I can't even regret any of it, though, because each time, I was put on the back of Will's bike.

I pull my phone out of my purse and keep it in my hand, just in case. One call, and Will would come running to save me.

As we make our way through the house, Max stops to say hi and introduce me to a few people. At one point, I see him swap cash for a baggie of pills from some loser, but I ignore it. Drugs and booze are commonplace in college. I don't partake in the hard stuff, but I occasionally have a drink or two, sometimes three.

Whatever, I'm a college kid. That's what we do.

We find the kitchen, where Max pours us cups of beer from the keg. I take a sip, but spit it back before I can swallow. It tastes like lukewarm piss.

"Not a fan?" Max chuckles.

"No." I set the cup down on the counter.

"What about a mixed drink?" He opens the fridge like he owns the place and digs around until he finds a carton of orange juice. He dumps my beer and scoops some ice from the freezer into the cup, pours orange juice over it, and tops it with some vodka from the counter. He hands it to me. "Better?"

I take a sip and nod.

"Yep. Let's go back in the living room."

"Sure."

We approach a group standing in a circle talking. Max does the whole bro hug thing to one of the guys, who then introduces us to the rest of the crowd.

As they talk, my eyes wander. The one who gave Max pills earlier is making the rounds, most people choosing to purchase whatever he's selling.

He approaches two larger men who have their backs to me. The shaggy blond hair and thick build of one of them remind me a lot of Will. Even his posture is similar. Then he turns to the side, and I get a look at his profile.

Holy fuck.

It is Will. What is he doing here?

The dealer passes a baggy over to him, and he accepts it, clapping the guy on the back. He's doing drugs now? What the hell?

"Truly, where are you going?" Max reaches out to grab me, but I dodge him and storm over to Will.

"So you're a druggy now?" I huff from behind him and cross my arms over my chest.

He slowly turns around as though he's delaying reality. I wait patiently until he faces me, his brows furrowed and lips pursed.

"Now's not the time to be silent. What are you doing at a college party?" I snag the baggy from his hands. "And buying pills?"

"Ooh, someone's in trouble," the dealer squeals and laughs. "Your girl needs to lighten up."

Will glares at him, then takes me roughly by the elbow and leads me toward the front door.

"Truly? Who's this asshole?" Max asks with more confidence than he should feel. I have to give him credit, though. Even when Will transforms into Roch and gives him a death stare, he doesn't back down.

"I'll be right back." I drag a nail down Max's chest, causing Will's grip on my elbow to tighten painfully. It fills me with satisfaction.

We walk outside, and I jerk from his hold.

"What the hell?" I bite out.

He places his hands on his hips and looks to the sky in frustration. Partly directed at me, but I know the other part is because he can't say the words he wants to. I hate seeing him struggle like this, it has me regretting approaching him the way I did.

"Home," he demands. "Now."

"You go home. I don't need to go anywhere."

"Too young."

"I'm not too young to be at a college party, Will. In case you haven't noticed, I'm a college student. You're the one who shouldn't be here. You're thirty-three years old!"

"Hey, man. We gotta get back in there." The other guy who was with him taps him on the shoulder, looking uncomfortable. I recognize him from the day they all showed up at the clinic broken and bleeding. He reaches a hand out to me that I take. "Hi. We never actually met before. Name's Sly."

"Hi. I'm Truly." I give him a tight smile.

Will huffs loudly, kicking the ground, sending rocks and dirt flying into the air. Through all the times I've made him angry, I've never seen him this worked up. My annoyance slips away. He doesn't want me here. There must be a reason for it.

"Home," he repeats, pointing a finger at me.

"Fine. I'll go."

He nods and follows Sly inside, craning his neck to take one last glance at me. Max comes out of the house seconds later, looking annoyed.

"What was that about?"

"He's a family friend. He wants me to go home." I stare through the front window hoping to get a peek at what's going on.

"What's his name?"

"Will," I reply and give him my attention. "Why?"

"Just wondering. He looks familiar." He shrugs. "Anyway, ready to go?"

"Yeah, sure." An idea hits me. "Let me run to the bathroom first."

"Okay. I'll wait in the car." He pulls out his keys and walks toward the road where the car is parked.

I sneak back into the house and hide around a corner, spying on Will. He doesn't do drugs. I know it. There's something else going on, and I'm determined to figure out what it is.

Sly puts an arm around the dealer, chatting him up. The three of them walk into the kitchen, and I follow, making sure to put enough distance between us that I won't get caught. I assume they're getting a drink, but the kitchen is empty when I peek from around the corner. The only place they could've gone is the backyard.

I wait a few seconds before leaving out the back. They're not in the yard. There are only a few people huddled around a fire pit, laughing and drinking. I scan the area and see a gate.

"Did some guys just walk out that way?" I ask the group.

"I think so, but I wasn't paying attention," a dude-bro says and pats his lap. "If your friends left, you could come join me."

"Gross," I mutter, and I open the gate to see if I can spot them.

There's a van parked across the back alley. It's dark, but I can see three shadowed forms next to the side door. I inch closer, crossing the street, and ducking behind a dumpster. From this angle, the streetlight illuminates the faces of the three men. Sly's holding the drug dealer's arms behind him, shoving him into the back of the van.

"What the fuck, man?" the dealer cries out.

"You pissed off the wrong guy, bro," Sly says.

They scuffle, their feet scraping and dragging along the asphalt. Will rears a fist back and slams it into the dealer's face. I flinch. The crunch of bone on bone is sickening and sends chills down my spine. I've been on the receiving end of Will's anger—he's an asshole and even scary sometimes—but he's never aggressive with me. I squeeze my eyes shut as I listen to the sound of Will beating the shit out of the guy.

"Roch, that's enough. Let's take this somewhere more private," Sly whisper shouts, and then it's silent except for Will's panting breaths.

What the hell is going on? I want to pop out and demand answers, but I'm frozen. My teeth chatter together even though I'm sweating, and my thighs burn from squatting so long. I really need to get out of here, but I'm afraid they'll hear my steps.

Mom always warned me to stay away from Will's motorcycle club. She told me they were into dangerous stuff. I assumed she meant they scrapped cars and resold them. Or maybe laundered money.

It's much worse than that. So, so much worse.

They shove the guy into the van, the door slides shut, and the engine turns over. I tuck myself further behind the dumpster and feel my arm slide against god knows what. I become engulfed in the putrid scent of rotting food. I gag, but remain put until the van drives past me, and even then, I wait longer.

When I feel safe enough, I squeeze out of my hiding place. My hands are trembling, and I feel like I might throw up. I brush myself off and walk back into the house on shaky legs. I need to get ahold of myself before getting into Max's car. He'll surely know something happened by looking at me.

I push through the crowd in search of the bathroom and find it empty, well almost. The vanity is covered in dirt and hair, the toilet is almost overflowing with piss and toilet paper, and a girl is sleeping on the tiled floor. She's going to regret all her life decisions tomorrow. I turn on the water and splash my face, gazing into the mirror. I'm pale, and my eyes are wide, still trying to make sense of what I just saw.

I lift my shirt to dry my face and leave the disgusting room. Feeling slightly more steady, I return to Max's car and get in.

"What the hell happened to you? I've been waiting for a half-hour." He turns on the engine and takes off down the road.

"There was a line."

"You look spooked. You sure nothing happened in there?"

"Yeah. I think I'm tired. Can you take me to my car?"

"Sure." His eyes flip from the road to me and back again. "How do you know that guy again? Will, you said his name was?"

"Like I said, he's a family friend. He knew my dad."

"You should probably stay away from him." His fingers tap a tune on the steering wheel. "He seems like an asshole."

"He's not. He's… intense."

"How much do you know about him?"

Apparently, nothing after what I saw tonight.

"I've known him for eleven years." I shift in my seat. I don't want to talk about Will with him. I don't want to talk about him at all. I need to get home, go to bed, and hopefully wake up to find this was all a nightmare.

"What does he do for work?"

All these questions hurt my confused brain.

"Why?"

"I don't know. He seemed extra protective over you, and I thought it was weird."

"Are you jealous?" It suddenly clicks why he's so intrigued. He's protecting what he sees as his property. Which I'm not. We aren't even dating.

"No. Why would I be?" he huffs, but it's a little too defensive.

"I don't know." I smile softly. It's cute he has a crush on me. Would it be so bad for me to date someone attainable? Someone who doesn't beat the shit out of people in alleys and then toss their unconscious bodies in a van? Nope. That's the smart choice to make.

We pull into the school parking lot, and I direct him over to my car.

"*That's* what you drive?" he asks.

"What's wrong with a Mini Cooper?" I look over at my pepper white, hardtop, two-door car. Maybe it's on the older side, but I love it.

"It's so small."

"It only looks that way. It's much roomier on the inside." I open the door and step out. "Thanks for tonight."

"Can we do it again sometime? Maybe without the cafeteria food and the running into your "family friend" stuff?" He air quotes family friend.

"Maybe." I grin. "See you in class on Monday."

The second I'm behind the wheel of my car, and driving down the road, the uneasy feeling from the party returns. I can't help but wonder what they're doing to that guy right at this very minute. Are they beating the shit out of him even more? *Are they killing him?*

I can't think about it. In a small way, it would be my fault for not saying anything. Not calling the police. My skin crawls thinking Will would kill someone in cold blood.

No, that wasn't Will. The guy I saw back there was Roch. I see the difference now.

He'll never be Will to me again.

Chapter
FIVE

Roch

Tonight was a fucking disaster.

It's the second time my two worlds have collided, and it can't happen again. My mind didn't know how to handle it. I had a job to do, a mission, but it was interrupted by seeing *her* there. Part of me wanted to throw her over my shoulder and get her the fuck out of there like I've done so many times before. The other part felt obligated to see the shit with McClean through.

What was she doing there anyway? The only people there were junkies and miscreants. Like me. I belonged there. She didn't.

We pull up to the clubhouse, and I help the guys drag McClean to the basement. Regardless of the cyclone in my head, I still have a job to do. Once he's in the kill room, I suspend him by his hands from the ceiling like a puppet. Sly steps out of the room. He's got a weak stomach and prefers to be on the research end of shit.

I don't have a weak stomach, though. Not anymore.

McClean stirs, his head swaying side to side. I pull out my hand-carved obsidian knife. It's ten times sharper than a razor blade. When he sees the object in my hand, he wails so loud it pierces my skull and stabs into my brain.

Don't feel particularly hateful toward the asshole in front of me, so I make it quick. I slice through his carotid artery first. This rouses him, and he gasps, his eyes nearly bugging out of his head. I move to his leg, slicing through his jeans and femoral artery in one movement.

I could leave him like this, and it wouldn't take long to bleed out, but I'm tired and want to be done, so I turn him around and stab into his back, piercing his aorta.

The frightened look in his eyes drains, along with his blood. I turn the hose on to keep the flow moving down the waste pipe. We don't usually use the kill room for easy jobs, like this one. We save the basement for when we need information from someone. For everyone else, we drive them out to the middle of the Great Basin Desert and, after a quick death, the vultures and other opportunistic animals take care of the rest.

But things had already gone to shit with this one, and he needed to disappear quick. We'll throw him in a bath of Hydrofluoric acid, and McClean will disappear forever.

It's easier this way, but there's a higher risk of being caught. One drop of blood is all it would take. The cleanup alone is time-consuming and painstaking—neither of which I enjoy. But everything about tonight has been tormenting. Why not add clean-up to the mix?

"Hey, man. Heard shit got complicated." Khan ducks through the doorway and into the room. He's a fucking giant, in height and mass.

I nod. No point in denying it. Sly was there.

"The girl gonna be an issue?"

I clench my jaw and shake my head. This. This is why I keep Aiyana and Truly away from club life. Not that I think my brothers would go behind my back and tie up loose ends, but him even asking is enough to make me want to force them into hiding.

"Didn't think so, but Prez wanted me to ask." He rubs at the back of his neck. "You okay?"

I nod and continue to spray.

"Fucking hell. Get out of here. Let me finish up." He rips the hose from my hand.

My lips twitch. The guys tend to confuse my silence with emotion. Often times, it works out in my favor. Like now. I wash my hands and my blade before leaving Khan to finish my dirty work. I should feel guilty, but it's their own ignorance and failure to understand me, so I don't.

When I get to the top of the stairs, I see there's a party in full swing that wasn't happening when I went down to the basement. It's not as wild as it could be. Probably because Bridgette is here.

"Roch, sweetie. How the hell are you?" Tabitha sways her hips as she approaches me. I don't fucking understand why chicks do that. It looks awkward and obvious.

I give her a nod.

"Your babies have been fed, and Karen is tucked in for the night." She interlocks her elbow with mine. I should shake her off, but she tends to get pissy and not help with the dogs when I brush her off.

She stays latched to me until I get outside and am immediately swarmed by eighty-pound pits. All of these dogs were in fighting rings at some point in their lives. Aiyana has a soft spot for rescues and donates her veterinary care to them, but rarely will someone take on a dog who has a violent past.

She knows the dogs and I have that in common. It makes me a good choice for their rehab and retirement.

I lift a hand up and they all sit down, tails wagging while they wait patiently for attention. I take my time loving on them, making sure each one knows they're safe and cared for. I'm vaguely aware of Tabitha watching.

"You're gentle with them." She crouches alongside me and doles out some affection of her own. "Who's a good boy?"

"Girl."

"Oops. I have it in my head all dogs are boys and all cats are girls." She giggles when a wet tongue swipes up her face.

Tabitha ain't so bad. She's got dark in her heart too. Can't blame her after finding her in some politician's closet when she was eighteen. She'd been locked up in there for two years, only let out when the asshole who bought her wanted to use her like a doll.

"Dumb," I say, hoping she'll know I'm joking.

I'm rewarded with a slap to my arm. "Ha. You do have a sense of humor."

I feel my phone vibrate in my pocket. I stand up to pull it out and look. It's Truly calling me. She never calls. Always texts because she knows I won't answer. But after what happened tonight, I don't hesitate to lift the phone to my ear.

"I'll see you later, okay?" Tabitha waves and walks back to the party, hips moving side to side dramatically.

I click the green button and hold the phone to my ear.

"We need to talk. Not in a text or over the phone. Can I come over?" she blurts out.

"No." Not a chance I'm letting her anywhere near this clubhouse.

"That's what I thought you were going to say, but I came prepared with threats. I saw what happened in the back alley. I saw you beat that guy up. I don't want to go to the police, but I also don't want this on my conscience. So if you want to keep this between us, you will let me come over, and we can talk about it."

Fuck.

She has no idea what she's getting herself into. No clue the consequences of even threatening something like that.

I sigh loudly.

"Is that a yes?"

"Yes."

"I'm on my way. Text me the address." She hangs up.

I quickly type out directions and tell her to park in the street. I walk around the side of the clubhouse, hoping to avoid anyone seeing me. I cross the gravel parking lot out front and approach another of the new prospects. This one I remember the name of, Ford.

"Hey, Roch. Not joining the party?" He immediately perks up and stands straight when he sees me.

"No." This guy needs to leave. For at least five minutes.

"Need anything?"

"Beer," I mutter.

"You want me to go inside and get you beer?" he asks incredulously.

"Yes," I growl.

"Sure. Okay." He looks from the clubhouse to the gate he's supposed to be guarding. "Can you stay here and keep watch?"

I nod.

"Okay, be back in a minute." He jogs inside.

I hope it'll give Truly enough time to get here and through the gate. I pace from one end of the lot, to the other until I see headlights. The car slows to a stop, and a pair of long legs walk toward me. When did Truly get legs like that? I avert my gaze, pissed for even having a thought like that.

The lights above the compound hit her face, and my stomach sinks. She's upset. She might've even been crying, judging by the flush on her cheeks and her swollen eyes.

"Hi," she mumbles.

I slide the wrought iron gate open enough to let her pass, before closing and manually locking it back up. I usher her to the backyard quickly. The dogs rush over, and being her mom's daughter, she immediately lowers herself to the ground to say hello to all of them.

"Come," I say, pointing to the casita. My brothers can't see her here. This is such a dumb fucking idea. I kept her hidden from this life for eleven years, and now I can't keep her away.

"Fine." She gets to her feet and snaps her fingers, inviting the dogs to follow. No one loves these mutts as much as I do, but she's a close second.

After we're inside, I lock the door and close the curtains. It's typical of me to hide out during parties anyway.

"So, where is he?" She throws her arms to the side. She's wearing the same thing she had on earlier, except now her camouflage jacket is unzipped, revealing a white crop top that shows off her flat stomach and a belly button that sparkles with a little diamond.

When did she get that?

"Who?" I ask, genuinely confused. My brain is stuck on seeing the girl I've known for eleven years suddenly look like a woman.

"That drug dealer guy. The one selling the baggies from the party."

That's a bucket of ice water. In all my problem solving getting her in here unnoticed, I didn't come up with a story about him. Something tells me "soaking in a tub of acid" would be the wrong thing to say.

"Dunno."

"You do too. I saw you guys take him." For the first time, she scans the room. "This is where you live?"

I shrug and tuck my hands in my pockets. It's unnerving to have her in my space. No one comes in here except for Bridgette, and that's because she won't listen when I tell her no.

"It smells like dog in here." She scrunches her nose.

I gesture to the six or seven dogs roaming around. Of course it smells like dog, though my nose is dead to the scent now.

"Where's Karen?"

If getting my chihuahua out of bed will derail her line of questioning, I'm all for it. I motion for Truly to follow me, and I take her to the back where my bed is. There, asleep on the dog bed next to my pillow, is Karen. I point to her.

"Oh my God, she's so cute. I forget how tiny she is," Truly gushes and climbs on my bed, lifting the dog into her arms.

If I thought seeing her in my space was uncomfortable, seeing her in my bed is worse. She leans back against my headboard and snuggles into the blankets, cooing and stroking the top of Karen's head.

Women don't get in my bed. Not since I got back from the war, at least. Not that Truly is a woman in my bed. Not in that way.

I suppose she is growing up, though. It's getting harder and harder to see her as that sassy little girl, and easier to see the woman she's becoming. She doesn't even look like herself. Something's changed. There's no longer an innocent gleam in her brown eyes. She's more mature or something. I don't fucking know.

She pats the bed next to her, and I shake my head.

"Come on. We need to talk."

I push off the wall I was leaning against and sit down on the edge of the bed.

"Keep going. All the way back. I need to be able to see your eyes for this conversation."

Despite my better judgment, I kick my shoes off and climb onto the bed next to her. But I don't get under the covers like she did. That's too close.

"Tell me where he is, Roch."

My eyebrows raise at her use of my road name. She's never used it before. She's fought me on the use of it every time. What's changed?

"What?" she asks. "You've been trying to get me to use it for years. I thought you'd like it."

"I do."

"Okay, now that that's settled, tell me where he is."

"No."

"Seriously. I'm not leaving without an answer."

"No." I'd sooner go to pound-me-in-the-ass prison for murder than admit to her what I did to that fucker tonight.

"Then tell me this. What does the club do for money? What do you do for money?" She tucks a strand of hair behind her ear, revealing that heart-shaped birthmark. The spot where I have the beaded pendant she gave me all those years ago burns.

That first day we met changed my life. No one has ever been as interested in me as she was that day. I wonder what Ricky would say if he were looking down on us right now. Would he be disappointed I didn't walk out of her life the day I walked into the life of a biker?

"Can't say."

"Can't or won't?"

"Both." I meet her eyes, pleading with her to understand.

"Is he dead?"

My mouth opens, but nothing comes out. I can't find the right words in the best of times, let alone now, while she's looking at me like our entire future is hanging on the balance of my answer.

She assumes the truth. I know it because tears well in her eyes, and she hands Karen over to me.

"Does Mom know what you do?"

"No." That I can answer honestly. She may have assumptions, but she doesn't know with certainty.

"I see." She climbs off the bed, sniffling. "I don't know what to do with all this. It's unfathomable. I don't know what he did or if he deserved it, but killing someone makes you a bad person."

"Tru."

"I don't want to see you anymore. I won't tell anyone your secrets. You don't have to worry about that." She turns on her heels and jogs to the front door, but when she opens it, she runs right into a smiling Bridgette. She takes one look at the crying girl, and her face falls.

"Hi, Truly. I didn't know you were in here."

"I was just leaving." She pushes past Bridgette and runs off.

"Everything okay?" Bridgette asks. She's known me long enough to see that no, it is not fucking okay. "I'll go talk to her."

She chases Truly down the side yard. I should follow them. I should be worried everyone is going to know Truly was out here. But I'm too shocked to do anything but hold Karen to my chest and wonder how the fuck I can fix this.

Chapter

SIX

Truly

I run.

Everything I thought I knew is wrong.

In my mind, Will's a quiet, indrawn man. Every time I look at him, I see his mind churning, and even though he doesn't express his thoughts or feelings verbally, they're there. I see it in his eyes and in the way he takes care of Mom and me.

I never imagined he was a cold-hearted murderer.

"Truly," Bridgette calls after me.

I have a big enough head start that I think I can get to my car before she catches up. Until I reach the closed gate. I wrap my hands around the steel bars and rattle them. It's no use, though—the gate is securely locked.

Bridgette's breathing heavily when she reaches me. "I'm so out of shape."

"How do I get out of here?" I ask.

"You can ask Ford to open the gate. You're not a prisoner.

He'll let you out." She lifts her chin at the man standing to my left, who I didn't see before now.

"Open it," I demand.

He nods and pulls his phone out. It must be remotely controlled. Bridgette holds a hand out, halting him.

"Or you can have a chat with me. Maybe get some questions answered. Talk it out with someone who might understand."

"Honestly, I just want to get as far away from here as possible." There's no telling what could happen if I stay. I don't know any of these people, including Roch.

"You'll be safe here. I promise."

I take her in. She could be a sorority girl with her hourglass shape and blond hair curled into perfect loose curls. How did she get mixed up with these guys? Curiosity gets the better of me.

"Fine, but I don't want to see him."

"You don't have to. I'll take you back to mine and Loki's room. We have our own house near Tahoe, but we keep a room here for when there's a party, and we don't want to drive home." She winces. "Keep an open mind."

"What do you mean?"

"Come on." She guides me through the front door, and I realize why she wanted me to keep an open mind.

Half-naked women are milling about a large room with a bar on one side. On the other side are couches and a pool table. Some men are perched at the bar or playing pool, while others are groping or making out with the half-naked women. On the wall-length projection TV, a porno is playing. Hard rock blares through the speakers, but the movie's moaning and wet sex noises can also be heard.

Heat creeps up my cheeks. I've seen pornography the way everyone with the Internet has. But never like this. And never with thirty other people around who apparently see nothing weird about a man shoving his dick down a chick's throat while they throw darts.

"Come on. This way." Bridgette grabs my hand and leads me down a hallway to our left. She removes a key from around her neck and unlocks a door.

Inside there's a bed, TV, nightstand, and dresser. But there's also what looks like a giant dog kennel that looks big enough for a person.

Fuck this.

I flip around, ready to get my ass out of here.

"Wait. It's not what it looks like," she says, and then mumbles under her breath, "I forget not everyone is a kinky motherfucker."

"What?"

"It's for private use, if you know what I mean." Her gaze drops to the ground.

"I don't know what you mean. Like, at all."

"I'm not going to shove you in there if that's what you think. Pretend it doesn't exist."

"I don't think that's possible."

"Sit down on the bed with your back to it," she says, as though that's going to make me forget.

"This is the weirdest night of my life," I mutter and sit down with her next to me.

"Tell me what happened."

I contemplate how honest I should be. Maybe she doesn't know what goes on. What if I say something I shouldn't, and it gets both of us in trouble?

"I know most everything there is to know about this club. Nothing you can say will be a surprise," she assures me. "But can you start with how you know Roch? He's a little tight-lipped, and I've been dying to find out."

That part is easy, so I take a deep breath and let it all out. I tell her about how Will and my dad were held captive in Afghanistan. I tell her how Will brought Mom a blood and dirt-stained letter that was like every other goodbye letter — saying he's sorry, he wishes he could be there to see me grow up, and he loves us.

Then I tell her about how Will has taken care of us over the last eleven years, doing repairs on the house, taking in dogs Mom knows will end up being put down, and, more recently, saving me from trouble.

Then I switch from saying Will to saying Roch. I explain about the party tonight. About spying from behind the dumpster. She cringes when I tell her how I saw Roch beat the shit out of the guy and shove him in the van. It's that look on her face that tells me she does know what they do.

"I came here to confront him, expecting him to tell me I'm crazy. That he dropped the guy off at home after roughing him up, or something."

"But that's not what he said." It's not a question. She gets it.

"No."

"And now you're questioning if you ever knew him at all and what kind of guy would do something like that."

"Kind of. Yeah." I wring my hands together in my lap.

"I'll save my story for another day, but I'll tell you this much. Those guys out there aren't upstanding citizens. They do bad things. So much worse than you're imagining."

"Wow. Some pep talk," I sass.

"Hear me out because they're also loyal. They won't admit they have a conscience, but the Royal Bastards don't touch women or children. They don't go after innocent people. The people they harm," she says carefully. "They're scum."

"Like that makes it better." I stand up, not believing she's defending them. We're talking about murder. The ultimate sin. The very worst thing a human can do to another.

"It doesn't make it better, but it does help. Especially when you're a good girl who's in love with a bad man."

"I'm not in love with him. He's like an uncle to me."

"Are you lying to yourself or just me?" She points at my face. "I know that look."

"What look?"

"The look of a girl in love with someone she has no business loving." She smiles softly. "You're me."

"You can't tell him."

"Cross my heart." She draws an X over her chest.

"He doesn't see me like that."

"I wouldn't place any bets just yet. I've never seen him more upset than I did a minute ago."

"He still thinks I'm a kid."

"You'll just have to make him see you as the woman you are now, not the little girl you were when you met." She motions for me to rejoin her on the bed.

I plop down. "It doesn't matter. Maybe you're okay with what he does, but I'm not. I've been taught to respect life, not take it."

Mom has made sure of that. She always brought home animals on the verge of death. Sometimes she was able to save them, sometimes not. But she always tried. This motorcycle club does the opposite of that. Roch included.

"It's completely understandable to feel that way. Especially when you still see the good in the world. I'm not going to get into it, but I will say this. I've seen the dark and evil of this world. Looked the devil himself in the eyes. Those guys out there"—she hooks a thumb over her shoulder—"aren't that. They're no angels either, don't get me wrong. Brace yourself, because I'm going to be blunt. They kill people for money, and they do it without a speck of guilt. But in the world they live in, it's not innocent people they take out. They're people you don't want to share space with on this earth. They say they'll take on any job, but it's macho bullshit. I know them."

"Do you even hear yourself right now? We're talking about murder."

"No, we're talking about taking out the trash." She rests a hand on mine. "And trust me when I say it's better to have someone on your side who'll fight for you and protect you, at any cost, than to have someone who does the right thing for the sake of doing the right thing. I'd choose a decent man who does bad things any day."

I think about that, chewing on the inside of my mouth. If it's true and Roch's not harming innocent people, do I care? How do you measure the worth of a human life?

Fuck, my head hurts. I didn't expect to have an existential crisis tonight.

"It doesn't matter anyway. They're out of the game. Tonight was their last job like that," she says.

"What?" Couldn't she have led with that information?

"They're going back to their roots."

"Which is?" I gesture for her to continue.

"I think that's enough storytime for one night." She pats my knee. "You have enough to chew on."

"You're right. I don't think I can handle much more."

"Do you want my advice on making Roch see you as a woman?"

What a loaded question. A yes would mean I'm okay with what he's done and I believe Bridgette. A no would mean I can't accept this life. Even if I fail at making Roch desire me, it means I've accepted it. And that feels like an important decision, not only for my love life but also my life in general. It's admitting not all lives are worth saving.

"Yes," I say confidently.

"Well, okay then. We have a goal." She hands over her cellphone. "Put your number in there."

"Why?"

"Because you're about to become my new best friend."

I eye her skeptically. But she's so confident and seems to have a plan. What harm could it do? I plug my phone number in and hand it back.

"Perfect. I'll be in touch." She flashes me a devious wink.

I think I like this girl.

"How was the rest of your weekend?" Max asks in class on Monday.

"Relaxing. Didn't do much." Whatever plan Bridgette had in mind wasn't an immediate one, because I haven't heard from her.

"Awesome." He eyes me like he has more to say, but is either collecting his thoughts or building courage. "I was wondering if you wanted to study tonight. Finals are coming up, and I thought it'd make things easier for me if I had someone to go over the materials with."

"Sure. Should we go to the library?"

"We could, but then we'd have to keep quiet and couldn't discuss things. How about my place?"

I briefly wonder if this is a ploy to get me alone, but I could use a study partner, and Max has been my friend.

"Fine by me. 6:00?"

"That works. We can order in."

"Okay, I'll be there."

He smiles big, and I take a minute to study him. He has to be Italian with his rich complexion and dark hair, but we only met this year, so I don't know much about him at all. I have no business going to his house when I don't know where he lives or who he might live with. I hear Roch's voice in my head telling me not to go, but this is for school.

That night, I pull up to a large house in the hills, overlooking the entire valley. It's a beautiful Tuscan style home with a façade made up of brickwork and stucco. The windows have rounded arches and are framed with mustard-colored shutters. It's beautiful and definitely not the home of a college student. He must live with his parents.

I knock on the door and am greeted by an older woman in an all-black uniform.

"Hi. Is Max home?" I ask.

"You must be Truly. He told me he had a friend coming over." She gestures for me to enter.

The foyer alone is the fanciest thing I've ever seen. A large bronze and crystal chandelier hangs from the vaulted ceiling, catching the light and making every reflective surface sparkle. A grand staircase is laid out before me, splitting and winding up all three floors on both sides. There's an entryway table with Madonna Lilies in an antique lime green Tuscan vase. Their floral scent fills my nostrils.

I become very self-conscious. One wrong move, and I could break something I'd have to sell my organs to replace.

"Max is in the kitchen waiting for you. Right this way."

I follow her, whoever she is. I'm assuming a housekeeper or maybe cook, but hell if I know who rich people keep around to do their dirty work. Mom and I were never poor, but we weren't rolling in the dough either.

Toward the back of the house is technically a kitchen, in that there are a stove and fridge and everything else you'd expect to find. But it's also bigger than my entire house: there are grand, wooden built-ins along every wall, the island could hold an entire buffet, and the eat-in kitchen table would put any formal dining table I've seen to shame.

That's where I find Max, a backpack slung over a chair, a stack of books in front of him, and a pair of noise-canceling headphones on. I tap him on the shoulder, startling him.

"Shit. You scared me." He sets the headphones on the table.

"Sorry." I chuckle.

"Take a seat. Or we could go to my room. Whichever." He shrugs in a boyish way.

"Here's fine." I set my backpack down and pull out my laptop. "You didn't tell me you were a Rockefeller."

He laughs. "Not quite. My dad does pretty well for himself, though."

"What does he do for work? I might need to change my career plans."

"He's an investor, I guess. He and my uncle own a few businesses. *Owned* a few businesses, I should say. My uncle died not that long ago, so now it's just my dad."

"Sorry to hear that."

"Thanks."

We study for a while, quizzing each other, and going over the study guide. At one point, the woman who let me in the house brings in bags of Styrofoam containers with Italian food from a restaurant I've never heard of. I plate myself spaghetti, macaroni, and some kind of bow tie pasta with pesto.

"This is the best food I've ever had in my life," I mumble around a mouthful of food.

"I'm glad you like it." He smirks, amused rather than offended by my bad manners. "It's from one of the restaurants my dad owns."

"I could bathe in this cream sauce." I lick the back of my fork. He tracks the motion with a hunger of his own, and not for food, judging by the way his eyes become half-lidded. I set my utensils down and push my plate away.

"Want seconds? There's plenty."

"No. I'm stuffed. Thank you, though. That was the best meal I've had in a long time."

"I'll have to feed you more often then." He clears his throat. "So, did you go home after I dropped you off at your car?"

The change of topic throws me, and it takes a minute for my brain to catch up. He's referring to *the* night.

"I made a stop to have a talk with Will."

"Oh really?"

"Yeah. He was out of line, telling me to leave the party like that." I downplay the conversation that actually occurred.

"How'd he take it?"

"Fine."

"I remembered where I recognized him from," he says nonchalantly.

"Where?" I ask too quickly. If he knows Will's a Royal Bastard—or worse, if he knows what the Royal Bastards do—it could mean trouble.

"He's an asshole, Truly. He's had"—he shifts in his seat uncomfortably—"dealings with my dad and uncle."

"What kind of dealings?"

"Did you know he's in a motorcycle gang?" He completely ignores my question.

"It's a club."

"Semantics." He looks around the room, for what, I don't know. "You shouldn't be around him."

"Why would you say that?" I hang on his words, committing each one to memory, including tone and inflection, so I can replay it all later.

"They kill people. Did you know that?"

"No," I lie. There's not a chance in hell I'm telling him anything I know or don't know.

"Yeah, well, they do. You need to stay away from him and everyone else associated with him. He goes by the name Roch."

"How do you know all of this?"

"So, you do know who he is."

"No, I think you have the wrong guy. Like I said, he's a family friend. He was in Afghanistan with my dad."

"I've seen pictures of him. Of all the Royal Bastards." He brushes my hair off my shoulder, letting his fingers linger on my back. "I'm worried about your safety."

"Where have you seen his picture?"

"You're missing the point," he argues.

"You don't need to be worried. Will wouldn't let anything bad happen to me." Anger laces my tone despite knowing he's right. Hanging out with a bunch of contract killers is generally a bad idea.

"Okay, okay. I'll back off." He holds his hands up in a placating manner. "But I'm here if you ever need me. You have my number."

"Thanks." I close my laptop. "I should go. It's getting late, and all those carbs made me sleepy."

"Don't go. I'm sorry I brought it up. It's none of my business."

The sound of leather soles walking across marble floors echoes, and I peer down the hallway. A good-looking older man appears. His dark features match his son's, but he has a goatee and mustache framing a fake-as-hell smile.

"Who do we have here?" he asks in greeting.

"Dad, this is my lab partner, Truly."

"That's a beautiful name. It's nice to meet you."

I hold out my hand to shake, but he rotates it and kisses the top. It's not charming, it's uncomfortable, and it makes my skin crawl.

"You too. Actually, I was just leaving."

"That's a shame. I love meeting Max's friends," he says. "Maybe we'll see each other again."

The words themselves are benign, but they feel loaded, and almost threatening. I quickly pack my stuff away, ready to get out of here.

"I'll walk you out." Max stands to his full height and accompanies me out the front door. "Sorry about my dad. He can be a little much."

"Oh? I didn't notice." I open the passenger side door and toss my book bag inside. "Thanks for the study session. I think it was helpful."

"I agree. We'll have to do it again sometime." He opens his arms for a hug, and I reluctantly lean into him—anything to get out of here quicker.

"Yes, we will. See you Wednesday."

I rush to the driver's side and slide in. I have to focus on not slamming on the gas and screeching my way out of the driveway.

I don't know who Max's family is, but they're somehow connected to the Royal Bastards, and not in a good way. Rival gang, maybe? But Max's dad didn't look like a biker. An enemy of some kind? Possibly.

Whoever his dad is, I need to keep him away from me.

Chapter
SEVEN

Roch

The gavel slams on the table, earning the attention of the room. Loki's smiling, which doesn't always happen. He must have good news.

"Khan, Trucker, and I met with Miguel yesterday. We're set up to distribute weapons throughout the West Coast. He gave me half the first payment up front, the rest upon delivery of our first shipment." Loki slaps two huge stacks of rubber-banded cash on the table. "I need volunteers for the first run."

I lift my hand. I love being on the road. It's quiet, and I can be in my head all I want without someone trying to pull me out. Some of the guys play music through their Bluetooth while riding, but not me. I like the sound of my tires spinning on the asphalt. I like hearing the wind as it slaps against me.

Sly raises his own hand, along with Bullet.

"Roch, Sly, Bullet, you guys ride, and I'll have Ford drive the van," Loki directs. "Sly, here's the cash. Where does that put us?"

"Well within the black. We can start adding some livable space in the basement." Sly flips through the stacks of hundreds.

We've wanted to add a couple rooms and another party room down there for a while now. The more brothers we have, the more cramped this place becomes. We can do the work, just needed the funds to buy supplies. Guess we have that now.

"Khan, I want you to run point since you have a background in construction. Coordinate with Sly on money," Loki says.

He nods. The big motherfucker was in construction before he patched in, but he had to retire after a hand injury. He got hooked on pain meds and almost lost his life to it. That is until he found the club. He's been around longer than I have, but not by much. He and Loki became close right away, so it wasn't a surprise when Loki chose him to be Vice Prez.

"Anyone hearing anything about the Corsettis?" Loki lights up a smoke.

"I got word Anthony is opening the club and restaurants back up. Did a drive-by this afternoon to confirm," Goblin grumbles.

"And? Are they open?" Loki asks.

"Yeah, they are."

"Fuck."

"That's not all. I heard a rumor he's getting into a new line of business." Goblin taps his fingers on the table in a random beat that grates on my nerves.

"What's that? Drugs?" Moto asks.

"No, they traded gun trafficking for the human variety."

Saliva pools at the back of my throat, and vomit threatens to come up. I swallow it forcefully, not wanting to show my brothers what the mention of trafficking does to me. It's too close to what I went through. Taken, abused, tortured, starved, made to do unthinkable things to survive.

I need to get out of here. Need to hurt someone. Preferably Anthony fucking Corsetti.

I feel a stirring from the back of my neck. Karen pops out of my hood long enough to nuzzle me. She must sense my impending panic attack. I reach around and scratch her head until she falls back into her cocoon.

"You're shitting me." Loki pounds a fist on the table, but the thick black walnut absorbs the impact and doesn't even wobble.

"We need to confirm, but that's what I'm hearing. Franco's been running a ring out of New York for a while. It makes sense Anthony would fall back on it." Goblin fishes a cig out of his pack, but doesn't light it. He just taps an end on the table, flips it over, and taps the other end. Again and again.

"Who's Franco?" Bullet asks.

"Dom and Anthony's dad," Goblin explains. "Dom tried his hand in the business, but he kept more women than he sold. Franco pulled the plug and told him to find a new way to bring in cash for the family. That's why he ended up stealing weapons from us."

"So where has Anthony been this whole time?" Loki asks.

"Tennessee, Oklahoma, I don't fucking know. My guy said somewhere in middle America." Goblin finally lifts the cig to his lips and lights up.

Everything in me wants to hunt Anthony down right now and take him out. Anyone who abducts an innocent person for their own benefit is a pile of shit and needs to be exterminated.

"But we don't know where he is now?" Khan asks.

"No. He hasn't been seen," Goblin says on an inhale.

"We were so caught up in Dom, we didn't even pay his baby brother attention. What do we even know about him?" Sly rests his elbows on the table.

"Fuck all," Goblin replies. "Never had a reason to."

"And we don't now. I'm not about to get mixed up with that fucking family again. We'll keep an eye on things, but that's it. Not our fucking circus, not our fucking monkey. Not anymore." Loki leaves no room for argument, except I have one. A big fucking one.

My teeth grind together, and I feel the muscles in my neck and shoulder tighten painfully as the meeting goes on. Everyone else is fine with our prez's decision. Except me. My situation was different, I wasn't a child or woman, but I was stolen from my life. I experienced horrors no one should have to go through.

Yeah, we've done the same to countless men. But none of them were innocent. They all deserved whatever punishment they got. What happened to me, I didn't deserve. And neither do those women and kids Anthony has decided to take and sell.

The guys joke and laugh, talking about additions they want to include in the basement. They've moved on. Meanwhile, my rage burns hot and furious. A five-alarm inferno I can't control.

I jump to my feet so fast, my chair goes flying and hits the wall behind me. The room goes quiet, but I don't stick around to explain myself. Couldn't even if I wanted to. I storm outside to be with my pack. They understand me. They were held against their will and forced to do whatever they could to survive too.

I sit in the middle of the grass and am immediately swarmed by wet noses, rough tongues, and waggling tails. They whine at me, begging for attention. I pet each one, focusing on them and not the darkness taking over my mind.

After my commander interrogated me for days on end, they sent me to a psychiatrist who diagnosed me with PTSD and selective mutism. They put me in cognitive behavior therapy and tried to drug me.

I didn't want any of it. I'd rather live in my head and cope the best way I know how to—with these dogs who I can relate to more than any therapist out there. I don't need someone picking my brain apart. I'm not a case study.

"Roch," Khan says from a few feet away. "Let's talk."

I reluctantly stand and follow him to the fire pit surrounded by plastic chairs. We stare each other down for long moments.

"What the fuck was that about? Is it Anthony? You got beef with him?" He adjusts his position, and I watch the legs of the cheap lawn chair bend. Despite breaking at least one of these things a week, he doesn't ever quit sitting on them.

"Kill him," I say with venom.

"You think you could do me a favor and write out your life story so I could fucking understand where you're coming from? Because I gotta be honest, ninety percent of the time, you leave us confused."

I shake my head. I've written things down before, but it's degrading, and makes me feel stupid. I'd rather not say anything at all and let people draw their own conclusions. I could give two shits what anyone thinks about me as long as I don't feel dumb.

"Whatever happened to you before you got here fucked you up, huh?"

I nod.

"It was Anthony, though, right? That caused you to flip out back there?"

I nod.

"You're gonna have to suck it up. Prez isn't joking when he says we're not to touch him. And I agree. We haven't even started back up with the guns, and we're not prepared for another war. You get that, right?"

I nod.

"You leave on the run north tomorrow. The ride'll clear your head."

Another nod.

"I'm here for you, brother. Whatever you need, but you gotta let this go. At least for now."

I scowl. They think assholes like that deserve to stay living? It ain't fucking right. If Anthony's willing to sell people, he's willing to do a lot of crazy shit that could blow back on us. We'd be better eliminating the entire Corsetti family. I can think of a lot of creative ways to do it too.

"Get some sleep. You ride at dawn. Need me to have Loki ask his old lady to watch the mutts?" He stands, done with the conversation.

I nod. Tabitha and Sissy can do it, and they have multiple times in the past, but they don't treat them like family. They treat them like a chore. I like it better when Bridgette's around.

"Okay, I'll take care of it." He squeezes my shoulder as he walks by.

Just like any family, we're not without faults, but they took me in despite my cold, brusque personality. To this day, they know fuck all about my past and don't give a shit about it.

I was lucky when I found Aiyana and Truly, but I have to hide the darkest parts of me from them. My brothers all have their own demons, so I don't have to shelter them from shit.

Later that night, I'm almost asleep when a knock sounds on my door. I click on the lamp on my nightstand, adjusting to the sudden brightness. Throwing my legs over the side of the bed, I feel for the pair of jeans I left on the ground. I tug them up my legs and move to the door. It's ten, and whoever the fuck it is better be ready to make it quick. It's seven hours until I leave for the coast. I need some sleep.

"Hey, you." Bridgette takes one look at me, and her bright smile falls. "Were you sleeping? You're normally up late."

"Run," I grumble and walk back inside to grab a shirt. Prez wouldn't be thrilled about me not being dressed around his woman.

"That's actually why I'm here." She follows me in. "Khan asked if I'd take care of the dogs while you're gone, but I can't."

"Why?" I ask, tugging a tee over my head.

"I have a lot of homework and won't be able to get away. But I came up with a solution."

I raise a brow, knowing she's lying. She's in culinary school. The only homework she could have is making a Bundt cake or some shit. And if it were that important, she'd be jumping at the chance to use the restaurant-style kitchen here at the clubhouse.

"I asked Truly to do it. She's going to stay here in the casita for a couple days. Isn't that great?"

"No," I say with as much venom as I can muster in a one-syllable word.

"Hear me out. I cleared it with Loki, and he said he'd warn the guys off her. She has finals to study for, so she said it would actually help her to have some private space to study."

"No."

"She has my number, and I'll pop in to check on her. It's the perfect solution."

"No."

"Well, it's too late. It's already settled, and like you said, you're leaving on a run. You can't stop it from happening." She quickly spins on her heels and runs out, slamming the door after her.

Coward.

I can't let Truly be at the clubhouse. Especially not without me around. What if she ventures out and one of the hang arounds hits on her? Fury courses through my blood at that thought. I'd fucking break anyone's neck who tried to get near her. She's too young to be anywhere near here.

Yeah, lots of younger women like to come sniffing around, hoping to bag a biker, but they're not Truly. She's sweet and innocent.

And mine.

Not mine like that.

Just… mine.

I pace around my room, the dogs barely lifting their heads up to witness my meltdown. Apparently, this freak out isn't worth their attention.

I could go talk to Loki. Tell him it ain't happening. Tell him his old lady has overstepped. But it would expose how much Truly means to me, and I can't have that. I hit the problem from the other end and pick my cell off up my nightstand.

Me: No

Her reply is instant. Like she was waiting for my reaction.

Truly: I take it Birdie told you the exciting news?

Me: Stay home.

Truly: Not gonna happen. I'm looking forward to a weekend of not having Mom hovering. Don't take that away from me.

Truly: I promise not to leave your tiny home and to take excellent care of your babies.

Me: Tough dogs.

Truly: Yeah, yeah. They're more likely to lick someone to death than eat them.

She's wrong. They're tame as fuck around people they trust and like. She's never seen them attack before. They mauled one of Corsetti's men when he stepped into the backyard looking for more of us to kill the night Loki's mom was murdered. The guy had no fingers or face left by the time I got them off him. Wasn't even worth torturing the blubbering asshole for stepping foot on our property. Shot him in the head to shut him up.

Me: Stay home.

Truly: You said that already. And I told you, it's not gonna happen.

I chuck my phone across the room and growl loudly. I fucking hate being ignored. People have two reactions to my inability to communicate. They think I'm crazy enough to murder them and give me a wide berth, or they think it means I won't do shit about it and ignore me. Men tend to go with the first one, but the women in my life fall solidly on number two.

Giving up on sleep, I flip on my TV and strip back down to my underwear. I'm too wired to relax now. I find an old western playing and flip the light off.

I won't be able to stop this from happening. There's no time. I'll have a word with Goblin in the morning. Out of all of us, he's the most responsible. He looked after Bridgette when she was being held here, I'm sure he'll do the same for Truly.

That's what I tell myself anyway.

Chapter
EIGHT

Truly

I pull up to the clubhouse with a smile on my face. There's a new guy at the entrance, but he must be expecting me because after I wave at him, the gate slowly opens, and he points to a parking spot.

When Bridgette, who asked me to call her Birdie now that we're friends, called to tell me her plan, I didn't get it. What was the point of me staying at the clubhouse if Roch wasn't there? Then she filled me in on her devious ploy.

I know Mom wouldn't agree to me staying here, so I told her my new friend from college was housesitting and wanted company. She gave me the side-eye but didn't object. I played up how excited I was to finally have a friend who's a girl. She knows what a big deal that is for me, so I'm sure that helped my cause.

I get out of the car and am met with a very large, very tall, and, much to my dismay, very sexy man. I immediately regret ever thinking this was a good idea. No matter what Birdie says, I know who these guys are and what they do.

What the hell am I doing?

"Truly?" His deep voice strikes a note my eardrums weren't prepared for. My nipples pebble at the sheer masculine energy he exudes.

I hurry and cross my arms to cover the unwelcome response while nodding my head frantically.

"I'm Khan. You know where you're going, girlie?"

"Yeah. Yes. Yep. I do."

"Where's your bag?"

I fold the driver's seat down and produce my duffle.

"Is this a clown car?" He ducks his head in the car, nearly having to fold himself in half just to fit.

"It's a normal-sized human car," I defend.

"Shit," he drawls. "Take out the driver's seat, and I still wouldn't fit."

"You're not a normal-sized human," I note.

He rumbles a laugh. "Guess you're right. Follow me. I'll give you a tour."

"It's okay. I know where the casita is. I don't need to see anything else." I think back to the one time I saw the inside of the clubhouse. My cheeks heat, remembering the porn and half-naked women.

"Don't be silly. You'll need to know where the dog food and shit is." He takes my bag from my hand and starts toward the front door.

Guess I'm following him.

"Truly, this is Tabitha. She takes care of us." He loops an arm around a voluptuous, dark-haired woman. She has clothes on, so I'm already feeling better about being here.

"Truly, huh? You Roch's girl?" She melts into Khan's side, patting his chest affectionately.

"No, it's not like that." My gaze drops to the ground.

"What's it like then?" she asks.

"Oh, um. He's a family friend." I'm not used to having people be so blunt.

"Sure, honey." She pulls away from Khan. "I better go. I need to start dinner."

"Tabby's an angel and cooks for us all. You're welcome to join us."

"Thanks, but I brought a few things." I do not want to eat with these people. I'm not here to make friends.

"Well, if you change your mind…" Tabitha saunters off, her curvy hips swaying to a beat only she hears.

"Okay, this is the dining area." He motions to space where some wooden tables and chairs are sporadically placed. "And that's the bar. Help yourself to whatever you want. There are all kinds of alcohol and beer."

The long wooden counter is worn and beat up but polished. At least ten barstools line its length, one of them occupied by a man reading a paper.

"I'm nineteen," I deadpan.

"And I ain't the cops," he says. "This is Goblin."

"Truly, right?" Goblin folds the paper and sets it down. He must be in his thirties, but he has a much older vibe. His short hair is graying at the temples but is trimmed neatly, and he wears a stylish pair of black-rimmed glasses. If it weren't for the leather cut and worn jeans, I'd think he belonged on Wallstreet.

What is it with this club and the sexy as hell men?

"Yes," I say.

"I got a glimpse of you that night in the vet's office. Your mama saved our asses. I'm forever thankful to her." Goblin lifts my hand and kisses the top of it. It's such a gentlemanly thing to do. I wasn't expecting it.

Unlike when Max's skeevy dad kissed my hand, Goblin's gesture feels genuine and kind.

"She was glad to help." She wasn't, but I don't want to be rude.

"And this is where we hang out and blow off steam." Khan's arms open to the great room.

I know this space well. This is where I saw the debauchery the other night. In the daylight and with no one around, it looks impersonal. Like the shared space you can rent when you live in an apartment complex. The only thing that gives it away is the smell of stale cigarettes, spilled liquor, and something else I can't put my finger on.

"Back through that way is the kitchen. You'll find the dog bowls on a shelf and the dog food in giant blue trashcans." He points to a swinging door behind the bar. "And through the slider is the backyard where Roch's place is."

He doesn't know I've been here before and I'm not about to tell him.

He guides me out back, where we're immediately swarmed by almost a dozen dogs. They know me. Not just from the other night, but also because I helped Mom rescue them all.

Eager to be left alone by the behemoth of a man acting as my tour guide, I ignore the dogs and walk across the yard to the small house where Roch lives. Khan trails behind me and sets my duffle on the doorstep.

"Your man must've been pretty nervous about you being here alone. He's made us all promise not to party while he's gone, so feel free to come and go. It'll be a couple quiet nights around here," he says in disappointment.

"Don't hold back on my account. I have studying to do, so you might not even know I'm here."

He bellows out a full-bellied laugh. "Do you even know Roch? He'd flay us alive if he found out we had a party with you here."

Despite the humor in his tone, something tells me he's not joking. And after seeing the brutal way Roch beat up the drug dealer, I fully believe he's not. Roch's got a dark side I don't ever want to see again. At least not if it's directed at me.

"Thank you for the tour. Maybe I'll see you around."

"Better believe it." The jolly biker giant stomps away, leaving me alone.

Finally.

Butterflies fill my belly as I step inside Roch's space. I didn't get to inspect it too closely before, and I plan to rectify that. I won't snoop. At least not a lot. But I'm tickled to be able to roam around without him watching me.

A high-pitched growl comes from further into the space, and I pad back to the bedroom, where I find Karen standing on the edge of the bed. Her whole body shakes with excitement, and I scoop her up in my arms, allowing her to lick my face.

"You must be so sad without your daddy here," I coo.

I've never seen anything like the bond Roch and this dog have. They're such an unlikely pair. Karen is loud but couldn't hurt a fly, while Roch is… well, Roch. He's like an earthquake. Scarily quiet, but shakes you to your core. His ice-blue eyes make you think he's cold and unfeeling when in reality, I think he feels everything.

My first day at college, I was so excited. It was a chance to be around people who weren't Mom's friends or customers at the clinic, and I was getting to do it without her supervision. But then I was met with snide comments about having a baby in the class, and I came home crying that first day.

Mom must've told Roch, though, because he showed up on his bike to take me to school on my second day. He held my hand and walked me to my class, glaring at anyone who dared look my way. As embarrassing as it was, I look back at that day as one of the best of my life.

I've always known I love him, but it was that moment that made me realize I *love* him.

Knowing Karen's preferred method of getting around, I was smart and wore a hoodie today. I tuck her in the hood and take my time walking around the casita. There's nothing personal on the walls, or anywhere for that matter. At first glance, you'd think no one even lived here, but I know him, and he's written all over every item.

From the way his bed is made, tucked tight like he learned in the Army, to the way every loose object is lined perfectly. One coffee cup, one glass, one plate, and a set of utensils lie straight along a shelf over the hot plate on the small kitchen counter. A TV remote, a pad of paper, and a pen sit neatly on his nightstand. In his fridge, there's a perfect row of bottled smoothies, a row of water bottles, and a row of equally sized apples.

I grab a beer because, why not? Khan's right, there are no cops or people who will call the cops. The Royal Bastards are lawless. Might as well fit in. Then I crawl into Roch's bed, set Karen in her bed, and lay down. I roll onto my belly, unashamedly pressing my face into his pillow and deeply inhaling.

Roch isn't a cologne guy. He smells of motor oil, the outdoors, and soap. One time, I spent an hour going up and down the body care aisle trying to pinpoint his soap brand until I came across Irish Spring. I secretly bought a bar, and to this day, I keep it in my underwear drawer like an obsessed stalker.

Zero regrets.

I open my book bag and pull out my laptop. Finals week is coming up, and I have a lot of studying to do.

After nearly an hour of reading through my material, music turns on in the back yard. Some kind of old school rock. The kind where the men have teased hair held back by a bandana, no shirt, torn jeans, and eyeliner.

I look out the window and see Khan in front of a barbecue, Goblin sitting in front of a fire pit with a bunch of men in leather vests, and then Bridgette. Tabitha and another blonde woman are setting bowls of food out onto a picnic bench. A few of the dogs start sniffing around, and the blond-haired woman shoos them away.

I realize it's their dinner time. I'm going to have to walk out there in front of them to get the dog food. I dread it. It'll be awkward. But the dogs have to eat, and I am here to dog sit.

I breeze past the group, keeping my eyes on the backdoor Khan said connected to the kitchen. A hush falls over the group, but no one stops me. I fill ten dog bowls, stacking them into two sets of five, and carefully carry them back out the door. They teeter precariously, but I somehow manage to get them over to the far side of the yard, hoping the bikers will get the hint I don't want to talk.

The dogs hear the clank of the bowls hitting gravel and rush over.

I pad quietly back to the casita to not draw attention to myself when I hear Khan call out, "Truly, come meet everyone."

Shit. Damn. Fuck.

I turn around and make my way over the group. Everyone's eyes are on me, and I tug at the hemline of my crop top. Yeah, I'm nervous because of how dangerous these guys are, but there's something else. I'm nervous because I realize that I want these guys to like me. They're essentially Roch's brothers. I need to impress them.

"This is Truly." Khan wraps an arm around my shoulders. Which isn't hard because the top of my head barely reaches his armpit. "Truly, this is Moto, Miles, Trucker, Loki, Sissy, and you know Bridgette, Tabitha, and Goblin."

Moto looks like one of my favorite sexy Japanese anime villains, Komuro, with his shaggy hair, swimmer's body, and dangerous vibe. Miles is around my age with a prospect patch sewn where his name should be. He's cute, but he doesn't have that well-worn look to him like the rest do. Trucker is clearly the oldest of the bunch. His hair is gray and slicked back, and he has a full gray beard. But his body doesn't say old man at all. His shirt stretches tight across his firm midsection, and he fills out his jeans in all the right places.

Loki is a younger version of the old man, except his hair and beard are still brown. Trucker must be his dad. The resemblance is too strong. Bridgette beams at me in a strapless sundress that she's practically spilling out of. She's the prettiest woman I've ever met in real life. Goblin tips his beer at me in a casual gesture, but his eyes scrutinize me in a serious manner. I don't know what he's looking for, but it's clear he's searching for something.

"Nice to meet you all." I lean forward and stop myself. Was I about to curtsy? What the hell is wrong with me? "I should get back to my studying."

"No, stay!" Moto gestures to the chair next to him. "Have some steak with us."

"That's okay. I have some ramen calling my name." I mentally facepalm. Turning down steak for ramen isn't even believable to me.

"Don't be dumb." Khan pushes me forward. "Take a load off. Dinner's in ten."

"What're you studying in college? I have a mechanical engineering degree, myself." Moto drapes an arm on the back of my chair. Not in a creepy way, it's friendly and confuses me even more about the type of men they are.

"Veterinary science so I can help my mom out at the clinic," I say proudly. "Legally anyway. I've been helping her since I could walk in some way or another."

"That's where I know you from. I was trying to pinpoint it." He chuckles lightheartedly.

"Yep."

The night goes on, and slowly I become more and more comfortable. It might have something to do with the three beers I had, but I think it's more to do with the fact that they're all cool people. Moto is interesting and excitable, Goblin is intense and smart as hell, and Khan seems slightly insane. Okay, exceedingly insane.

Loki and Bridgette are absolutely adorable and have an undeniable sexual chemistry between them. Just being around them makes me wish I had someone to grab my ass or make me feel desirable. And Trucker is, I don't know, wistful maybe? I caught him watching everyone's animated storytelling, looking proud at the people in front of him. But there's also a sadness there.

Around midnight, Loki and Bridgette take off for home,

and Trucker leaves soon after, leaving me, Khan, Moto, and Miles.

"I better go take over for Duncan. He's been guarding the gate all night," Miles excuses himself.

"Yeah, I should get to bed. Since I slacked off tonight, I have a lot of catching up to do tomorrow." I stand up and stretch.

"Hold on one more second," Khan says and lifts his long neck to his mouth. He drinks half it down in one gulp. "Are you and Roch together?"

"Awfully gossipy of you to ask," I say.

"Yeah, this place can be a hen house sometimes, but I'm curious, and I can't ask him."

"No."

"But you wanna be, huh?"

"No," I repeat, but my eyes dart away.

"Liar," Moto chimes in.

"Even if I were lying, it wouldn't matter. I'm just an obnoxious troublemaker to him."

"Can I give you some advice?" Khan asks, tossing his now empty bottle into a bin.

"I can't stop you."

"Don't go there." His easygoing tone from before is gone, and now there's a hard edge to his voice. "You're a sweet girl, but this club, everything we get into, it's not safe for someone like you."

"I'm not that sweet," I defend.

"You are. And you should stay that way. You stick around here long enough, all that sweet will get sucked right out of you. Bridgette used to be like you—"

"She's still sweet," I interrupt.

"On the outside, she is. But darlin', spend the night in the room next to her, and you'll change your mind. If it's not Loki fucking her while she's caged up, it's her screams from the nightmares she has. You think she was that way when she came to us?"

I think back to the tall kennel in hers and Loki's room. I was confused, but knowing it's not to lock prisoners in actually makes the situation a whole lot better. I'm sure that isn't the reaction Khan was hoping for, so I keep it to myself.

As for the nightmares, that does scare me a bit. I wonder again how she got mixed up in the club, or how she ended up with Loki.

"Trust us with this one, okay?" Moto chimes in.

"You don't need to warn me off him. He doesn't want to be with me. He won't ever want to be with me." I stare at the ground, not letting them see my disappointment in the situation.

"That's good. I hope it stays that way. Night, darlin'," Khan says.

My intoxicated self stumbles back to the casita, calling the dogs inside. They clammer onto the sofas, dog beds, and some of them join me on Roch's queen-sized mattress. It doesn't bother me, I welcome the snuggles.

I lie awake for a long time thinking about everything that's happened today. Some positive, some negative, but the one thing that blares loudly in my mind is Khan warning me off Roch.

I know Roch has issues, but my fear of that side of him is slipping away the more I'm around the club members. They aren't a gang of evil murderers. I think Birdie was right, they're good people who do bad things. Roch included.

I already knew this in the back of my mind, but and seeing it firsthand dispelled any doubts. Spending time with the Bastards tonight helped to put things into perspective.

Roch and I have more differences than we can count, but I also know we need each other.

His dark world needs my light, or someday, he'll lose his humanity completely. He needs to be reminded he's not the monster he thinks he is. And I need the confidence he gives me. No one makes me feel as smart and interesting as he does.

We're polar opposites, but doesn't that make us perfect?

Chapter
NINE

Roch

Everything was going as planned.

The ride up was smooth, and we transferred the guns over with no problems. It was too late to head back home, so we hit up a motel to crash for a few hours. But the second I climbed into bed, I get a video message from Moto. I press play and see Khan with Truly. They're holding hands and racing over hot coals on bare feet.

I jump out of bed and redress myself. Can't sleep knowing she's interacting with my brothers. Especially because Khan's known for stupid challenges that usually land someone in the hospital. How will I explain away third-degree burns on the bottom of Truly's feet to Aiyana?

And what was Truly thinking? She knew I wanted her to stay in the house and away from all of them. She's young, smart, and pretty. Sexy, if I'm honest with myself. Her natural beauty and confidence drive men crazy. I've saved her from enough bad situations to know I'm not the only one who thinks so.

I hop on my bike, shooting a text to Sly so he knows I left early. I speed down the freeway at midnight, trying to get home and make sure no one gets the opportunity to hit on her. She's naïve enough to believe the flowery talk I hear Moto spew at chicks, getting them to do all kinds of shit, including threesomes with Sly. And she's tiny enough to be Khan's type. He likes girls he can throw around in bed like a rag doll.

Truly has me all fucked up, and I don't know what to do with her. If she were my old lady, she'd be off-limits, and no one would dare touch her. But she can't be that. Not when I've known her since before she grew those perfectly round tits of hers.

It's her fault I'm thinking this way. She planted the seed in my head months ago after I rescued her ass from some party in Lake Tahoe. Whatever asshole she went there with didn't tell her the point was for everyone to drop E and fuck. Of course, she called me. After I got there, she made me take her for a walk before she'd leave.

She held my hand, just like she did when she was younger, as we strolled along the lake. The moon was full and bright, reflecting off the lake and lighting up the shore. She prattled on about school and how she ended up on this date. Then she stopped, turned to face me, and said, "I'm going to throw this out there because if I wait for you to notice, I'll die a disappointed old woman. I like you. I know you're going to say no, and that's okay, I just had to tell you."

She was wrong. I didn't say no, but I also didn't say anything at all. I was stunned stupid. I'd honestly never thought about her like that. *Until that moment.* Now it's all I think about. It was about to be a nonissue when she found out the truth about my involvement with the club, but Birdie stopped that from happening. I don't know whether to be mad or grateful.

It takes five hours, instead of the normal six, to get home. When I glance at my cellphone, it's three in the morning. I'm thankful to find the backyard empty, at least they're not still partying. But that could mean she's in Moto or Khan's, or hell, even Miles/Mikey's bed right now.

I try to sneak into my home quietly, but when you have ten dogs excited to see you, it doesn't happen. I try to shush their whines, unsuccessfully.

"Roch?" Truly asks groggily, rubbing her eyes. She's standing by the bed, dressed in an RBMC T-shirt that hangs to the middle of her thighs. Her very bare thighs.

"Sorry," I mumble, standing to my full height and tucking my hands in my pockets.

"You're home early. Khan said you wouldn't be back until tomorrow around noon," she says with a yawn.

She's beautiful with a rat's nest on the side of her head and wearing my clothes.

Why is the one girl I can't be with, the only one I see?

"Couldn't sleep."

"Well, I guess I can pack up and go home," she says but makes no move to do so.

"Sofa," I say and tug off the sheet that protects the cushions from the dogs.

"Don't do that. Your bed is big enough for both of us."

This is a bad idea. A very bad fucking idea. But after unloading the guns yesterday and riding all the way back to town tonight, I'm exhausted. And too big for the small sofa.

I nod and follow her back to my bed. I toe off my boots and remove my cut, but that's as undressed as I plan to get.

If I'm not careful, I'll forget the repercussions and convince myself I can be with her. I'm a strong man, but I'm still a man.

She crawls under the covers, but I stay on top with Karen between us.

"So what did you do on your run?" she asks.

I ignore the question. For one, I can't tell her. For another, I don't want to talk. I need sleep. I cover my eyes with an arm, shutting her out.

"Whatever it was, it made you grouchy." She moves Karen to the other side of her and scoots closer. "Was it dangerous?"

"Yes," I say, mostly to give her something to chew on so she'll let me sleep.

"I had fun with your friends. Khan taught me how to walk on hot coals without burning myself. It was crazy." I hear the smile in her voice, and it warms a place in my chest that normally feels so cold.

"I know," I mumble.

"I figured someone would tattle. Is that why you came back so soon? Because you were mad I didn't stay locked up in here?"

I sigh and roll onto my side. In a lot of ways, she's much different than she was at eight-years-old. But in some ways, she's the same talkative girl who overshares until she gets a reaction.

I shrug.

"I don't know why. Everyone's so nice, and we had a lot of fun."

I grunt.

"No one was inappropriate. Not even the club whores." The corner of her mouth tips up while mine drops open. "Don't look so scandalized. They taught me all about club life."

"Tru," I warn, using her nickname.

When she sits up, my T-shirt stretches across her chest, showing me the outline of her pebbled nipples through the fabric. She's not wearing a bra. My cock thickens along my thigh. I can only hope my jeans are bunched up in a way that'll hide it. If I adjust myself, she'd no doubt notice.

If her end goal with all this bad behavior was to get my attention, she has it now.

"It's been months since I told you I like you, and we still haven't talked about it. But I've seen the way you look at me and the way you try to hide it. You think I'm too young? Or off-limits because you knew my dad? That's stupid. He'd want me to be with someone like you. Someone who would run into the enemy's territory to save his best friend." She smacks the bed on either side of her in frustration when I don't react. "Mom too. She knows you and trusts you."

"Trusts me," I repeat her words. Aiyana trusts me to rescue her daughter when she makes juvenile decisions, she doesn't trust I won't break her little girl's heart if I hooked up with her. Two very different meanings.

"Yeah, it might take her a minute to come around to the idea, but she would. Or we could hide it from her." She's grasping at straws that aren't there.

"No."

Her eyes well with tears, and guilt smacks me in the chest. Never could stand her tears. I place a hand on hers. I don't know if it's comforting or not, but it seems appropriate.

"Well, this is embarrassing. I'm going to go now." She stands up to collect her things. I watch in stunned silence. I try to conjure sweet words that'll make her feel better, but they don't come to mind. Or out my mouth.

"Stop." I jump up and block her from stuffing some clothes into her bag.

"What?" Her eyes are trained on the ground, and I tip her chin up to look me in the eyes.

"Stay."

"Why?"

"Sleep."

"I'm humiliated. I can't sleep next to you knowing you think I'm repulsive."

I still have her chin pinched between my fingers, and I lower to her level, brushing my lips against hers before releasing her. I don't know why I did it. To shut her up, to see how it would feel, or maybe I did it because I'm exhausted and too weak to fight this thing brewing between us.

"Wow." She reaches up and touches her lips.

"Sleep," I repeat.

"Yeah, okay." She gets back into bed, and I follow her. This time, she snuggles herself into my side. I don't stop her, and I'm shocked at how well she fits.

Touching is one of the things that I don't do anymore. When you've been violated in every way possible, human contact becomes something that makes your skin crawl. But ever since she was a little girl, holding my hand and dragging me all over the place, Truly has been the exception. Only right now, our touches mean a whole lot more than it did back then.

I feel her breasts smashed against my arm, I smell her fruity shampoo, and her breath tickles along my bicep. I can almost forget who I am, who she is, and all the reasons this is wrong.

She looks up at me, her dark eyes even darker with only

the moon lighting up the room. I wrap an arm around her, testing how it feels. I don't feel trapped. Memories from years ago don't flood my memory. I don't want to fight or kill someone.

I want to stay here. With her.

She lifts her head off my shoulder, bringing our mouths inches apart. I stare at her pouty lips, wanting to taste them again, but knowing a kiss isn't just a kiss when you're horizontal.

"Sleep."

She makes a frustrated sound, but her head falls back onto my shoulder. I don't know what the fuck I'm doing here. I kissed her, then encouraged her to get in my bed, and now I'm forcing her to sleep. I know I mess up a lot, but even for me, this is bad.

I keep her close all night, almost in awe of how much I like it. A few times, I start to pull my arm out from under her, but I don't like the thought of not having her there. My hand's gone numb, and sharp prickles run up and down my forearm, but still, I don't move.

At one point, I even bring my lips to the top of her head and kiss her. It's harmless since she's asleep and won't be able to read anything into it. So I do it again. And again. Each time inhaling her shampoo before pulling away.

I can almost make-believe this is real. That I found someone who knows I'm fucked up and doesn't give a shit. That I could go to sleep every night with a woman who'll give me her body and make me feel like a king.

It's a fucked-up fairy tale, though. Aiyana would have my balls if she knew I was snuggled up to her daughter. Truly thinks she can handle me, but even she'd get tired of me not talking back. All the quiet nights would drive a girl like her crazy.

But for right now, I'll lie awake and burn this moment to my memory. It's enough.

I get up before Truly does. Probably because I never fell asleep. I gather the dogs and get them out of the house. They trot off to hunt down the best place to piss while I go inside the clubhouse and do the same since my toilet is next to my bed where Truly's sleeping.

After that, I head to the bar where Miles/Mikey has a fresh cup of coffee for me. I give him a nod and take a seat on the barstool, spinning it around so I'm facing the TV where the news is playing.

"Miles, can I get a refill?" Goblin asks from the stool next to me.

Miles. I need to remember that.

"You're back early," Goblin comments while taking a sip from his steaming mug.

I nod.

"But Sly, Bullet, and Ford aren't back yet." His voice is deep and rough from too many years of smoking.

I take a sip of coffee. He doesn't need me to confirm what he already knows.

"One might wonder why a man would leave his brothers behind."

I glare over at him.

"Not me." He holds his arms up in defense. "But someone else might."

I roll my eyes.

"One might also wonder if it's because of a girl. Obviously not me. But I do have to admit the situation points that way." He pretends to watch the news for a long minute. "I'll say one thing about this, and then I'll butt out. She's a nice girl. Sweet on you and pretty fucking naïve. But she's also brave and strong. She fit right in last night, and no matter what Tabitha and Sissy blabbered on about or how gruff Khan got, she didn't flinch. I like her."

I growl, deep in my throat. I don't want to talk about this. Not with her or him.

"Like I said, had to say it. You don't deserve to be alone if you don't want to. If anything, get your dick sucked so you aren't such a miserable bastard." He slaps my back, sending me flying forward, my coffee sloshing over the edges.

"Fuck," I mutter.

"Sorry about that." He grabs his newspaper and coffee and moves into the living room. "Remember what I said."

I set my cup on the bar, and Miles is immediately there to refill it and wipe up the mess. I take the coffee back into my house, thinking Truly might want some.

I find her sitting up in bed, Karen snuggled up on her lap. But I left that dog outside to do her business like I do every morning until she comes to the slider at the clubhouse, and I let her in to have breakfast with me. She didn't do that today.

"She was clawing at the door when I woke up. The second I got her into bed with me, she passed out."

The bitch chose Truly over me. Jesus. You adopt a dog thinking they'll always be loyal to you for rescuing them. Guess I can't blame her, morning Truly with her hair in a knot on her head and sleepy eyes is way better than a mean biker who shoves you in his hood.

"Is that coffee?" Her nose twitches as she sniffs the air. "Hand it over, and no one gets hurt."

I pass her the mug and watch as she inhales the aroma before taking a sip.

"This isn't bad. I expected a biker clubhouse to have terrible coffee." She moans with her next sip.

It's a sound I like a lot.

"So, biker boy, you busy today?"

I nod.

"Do you have some time today to take a girl on a ride?" Her eyebrow quirks.

My mind goes right back to last night, with her so close I could taste her breath. How it felt to kiss her and have her in my arms.

"A motorcycle ride," she clarifies. "Get that appalled look off your face."

She climbs out of bed, still only in my shirt, and slowly approaches me. She rises to her tiptoes and presses her chest to mine. I don't know what to do. My brain sends warning flares, telling me to back away, but every other part of me wants to see what she'll do.

"But I want the other kind of ride too. Just so we're clear." She smacks a kiss on my cheek and grabs her duffle bag off the floor. "I'm going to get dressed now. You can stay and watch."

Swear to fuck, I almost smile at her sass. I almost smack her ass as she passes me too. But instead, I hightail it out of there to get some fresh air.

I need to get her away from me. Out of my space and my

life at the club. It was easy to stay away when I had a place to go I knew she wouldn't be at. Things changed quickly, and now I'll never look at my bed again without wishing she was in it.

I'll take her for a ride, then I'll send her ass home and ignore her texts for a while.

At least until I remember why I'm fighting this so bad.

Chapter
TEN

Truly

I get home around noon after a long ride plastered to Roch's back. We rode to nearly the top of Mount Rose, only stopping for five minutes at a scenic pull-out. The sun was hot, and the views were incredible.

After that, Roch all but shoved me in my car and ordered me to go home. I know he's struggling with whatever's going on between us, but come on. It's time for him to get over that. I need another plan. Maybe Birdie has another trick up her sleeve.

Birdie's plan to make Roch jealous went better than both of us thought when he raced home after seeing a video of me doing something stupid. And God, that kiss. If you can call it a kiss at all. His lips barely touched mine, but it was more potent than any other I've had.

I walk inside the house I share with Mom, and find her in the kitchen making her lunch.

"You're back! I missed having you around," she calls over her shoulder as she chops vegetables. "Want a salad?"

"Yes, please. I missed you too." I drop my duffle off in my room and then plop down at the dining table.

"Tell me more about this mysterious friend." She sets a bowl of lettuce, carrots, cucumbers, and cabbage down in front of me, with my favorite goddess dressing on the side.

"Just someone I know from school." I hate lying to her, but I'm also not going to blindside Roch and tell her. She'd kill him before he knew what was coming. He doesn't deserve that, especially after I strong-armed him into the whole thing anyway.

"What's her name?"

"Rochelle."

"That's pretty. I hope you'll bring her by some time for me to meet."

"Sure."

She'll believe me when, after a month, I tell her Rochelle was a mean bitch. I'm an easy target since I have zero street smarts and tend to get taken advantage of by men and women alike.

I have a 4.0 GPA, but I'm also gullible.

"Are you ready for finals next week?"

"Almost. A few more things to go over, but honestly, my classes aren't tough this semester, so I'm not worried." I take a big bite of my salad.

"I'm proud of you."

"I know, Mom."

"I mean it. You're smarter than your dad and I ever were." She stirs her fork around her bowl, lost in memories.

"I wish I remembered more about him."

"I know. You were so young, and he was always away. It doesn't surprise me you don't remember much."

"How did you two meet? Because you were living in the colony, right?"

Mom is a full-blooded Washoe Indian. The tribe doesn't have a reservation. Back in the day, the Washoe Indians sued the government for taking their land and were awarded a ton of money. Instead of buying up land for a single reservation, they bought ranches, neighborhoods, and what they call colonies, but are really just a few acres of land they live on. The tribe is spread out among all the different properties.

"I was until I met your dad. Your grandfather didn't want me to marry him, but I was young and in love. I had to give up my family for him."

"That seems like a big price to pay."

"It was. But when you meet the right person, you'll move mountains to be with them. And your dad was the right person for me." Her eyes water through her smile.

"Do you ever regret it?"

I didn't realize I was asking because if Roch ever decides I'm worth the risk, I might have to walk away from my own family. Mom is understanding and supportive, but not when it comes to being with an older man who's known me since I was a kid and happens to be a biker.

Not any mother's dream.

But Roch's it for me. I knew it when I was eight and gave him my hummingbird pendant, and I know it now. I wonder what he did with that thing anyway. I never saw it again after I set it in his hand all those years ago.

"Never. He gave me my happiest years, and he gave me you." She boops my nose, and I brush her off.

"Good to know."

"Why? Are you planning on marrying some guy you

know I'm going to hate?" She chuckles, not realizing how close to the truth she is.

"But I love him," I singsong dramatically, not lying, but also not telling the truth.

"You better be joking." She stands up and collects our dirty dishes, setting them in the sink for later.

"Need me in the clinic?" I ask.

"Not today. It's been slow, which means tonight we'll get ten emergency calls. Save your strength for then." She grabs her keys off the counter and heads out the door.

Back in my room, I unpack. When I pull out Roch's T-shirt, I grin. I tuck it away in my underwear drawer with the bar of Irish Spring. I can't stick it in the hamper, or Mom will surely know something's up.

I check my phone for the hundredth time and notice I have a text waiting for me.

Max: SOS. I'm going to fail this final.

Me: That bad, huh?

Max: Yes. Please say you can study.

Me: I can study. But can you come here?

I don't want to go back to that insane house with Max's creepy dad.

Max: Sure. I'll be there in a half-hour.

Me: See you then.

I rush through tidying up my room and take a shower. I hate to wash away Roch's scent, but after not showering yesterday, or this morning, and then going for a long ride today, I'm feeling dirty and gross.

The second I yank a clean shirt over my head, I hear the doorbell ring. My hair's a wet, soppy mess, but it's better than greasy and infested with tiny bugs from the ride.

"Hey." I open the door to a grinning Max. I can't deny he's cute, but in a respectable way. I wish I had feelings for him. My life would be much simpler.

"Hey, beautiful." He steps through the threshold and gives me a hug. "How was your weekend?"

"It was nice. Did a lot of studying."

"That makes one of us. My dad is convinced I'm going to take over the business one day, and he's had me at his side every weekend for months."

"I'm sure it'll pay off when you graduate and have a job to go to."

His eyes darken a hint. "Sure. Let's go with that."

"Well, come on in. We can study in my room." I motion down the hallway. "Second door on the left."

We make it to my room, and I watch as he circles around the perimeter, taking everything in. It's mostly pictures of Mom and me, but there are a few of Roch throughout the years and one of Dad during his time in Afghanistan. He's standing next to a Humvee. He has some sort of gun slung over his shoulder and so much PPE, you can hardly tell it's him.

I sit crisscross on my bed and offer him the Papasan chair on the other side of the room.

"So, what do you need help with?" I ask.

"Getting drunk, for starters. Maybe then I'll forget I'm not prepared for the final."

"I'll do you one better. I'll help you study so you don't have a wicked hangover and fail."

"Fine. We'll do it your way. But if I'm not prepared by the time you're done with me, we're going with option two."

"Deal."

For the next few hours, I go over the study guide with him, and we take turns quizzing each other. It's nearly dark when I decide to call it. My brain is mush, I'm tired after hardly any sleep over the weekend, and I need to go check on Mom.

A loud bang sounds on the door, causing me to jump to my feet. My first thought is something happened at the clinic, but then I realize it's the door.

"You expecting someone?"

"No." I jog out of the room and toward the front door.

"Truly, let me answer it if you don't know who it is." Max shoves past me and manages to get his hand on the door handle before I can.

"Who the fuck are you?" a deep and loud voice asks. I know that voice. It belongs to Khan.

"Max. Who the fuck are you?"

I yank on Max's arm, pulling him out of the doorway so I can see what's going on. Standing on my doorstep are a frantic looking Khan and a stoic looking Roch. Instantly I know something's wrong. Roch wouldn't bring his brothers here if it weren't an emergency.

"What's going on?" I ask.

"We need the Doc. Is she here?"

"She's at the clinic, but—"

They don't wait to hear the rest. They whip back around and jump back into the minivan that has—

Oh my God, the van is littered with bullet holes. They peel out of the driveway and cut through the lawn to the clinic instead of taking the road.

"I gotta go." I push my feet into my shit kickers by the front door.

"Wait, I'll come too."

"No, Max. This is family business."

"They're not your family. Those guys are criminals."

"I don't have time to argue with you about this. Please lock the door on your way out." I run across the lawn with a pit in my stomach. The last time the guys were here, they were dragging in a practically lifeless Bridgette. I wonder who they're bringing in now, and how mad Mom will be when she sees them.

The back door is wide open when I finally reach it. Thankfully, it's after-hours, so employees and patients have long since gone home. Unless those emergencies Mom was expecting came in, the place should be empty.

I stop short when I walk inside and see a trail of blood streaked down the hallway. I avoid the mess and follow the path of red to Room Two, where Mom performs surgeries. The door is closed, and I don't want to break the sterile field, so I keep going until I reach the waiting area.

Just like last time, the room is full of overgrown men with leather vests. The one I have my eye on is staring at the floor, resting his forearms on his thighs, and has his hands steepled together.

"Roch?" I ask, earning his attention.

The look on his face breaks my heart. There's worry and concern, but mostly there's sadness. Standing at his side, with an arm over his shoulder, I turn to someone who can answer my questions.

"What happened?" I ask Loki, who stands by the front door with his beanie pulled low on his head.

"Lots of shit, darlin'. Lots of shit."

"Are there people out there looking for you? Are you putting my mom's life at risk?"

"They ain't looking for us because they already found us. That's why we're here," he rasps out.

"Do you think she needs my help?"

"Most likely. There're two guys back there and only one of her."

"Who's hurt?"

"Sly and Ford," he replies. The handsome prospect and the man Roch was with at the party.

"I'll go see if I can give her a hand." Before I make it too far, Roch grabs my arm. I turn to look at him, but wish I didn't. He wasn't this distraught when he brought my mom that letter from my dad, and he wasn't even this distraught when he showed up here with Birdie.

He opens his arms, and I step into him.

Whatever happened is bad.

Chapter

ELEVEN

Roch

I'm so fucking stupid. I left my brothers up north while I drove all night because I was jealous. I saw Truly having fun with Khan, I let my dick do the thinking, and now Ford and Sly are half-dead.

The entire ride and the meet-up went so smoothly, I was sure the ride home was the least of our worries. They didn't have anything illegal on them, so we were safe from the cops and anyone looking to take the product. There was no reason for them to get ambushed on the highway.

"Explain it to me again," Loki demands.

Bullet runs a hand through his hair. "We were following Ford on our bikes. Nothing was out of the ordinary when the tires on the van blew. But it was crazy 'cause all four went at one time. That's when a bullet hit Sly in the leg. He went down, hard. I pulled up behind the van and got in the back. Ford was on the floorboard, but there was a lot of blood coming from his shoulder. I told him to stay there, and I dragged

Sly to the van, but by that time, the gunshots had stopped. That's when I called you."

"Did you see anything?" Khan barks.

"No, bro. Nothing. I didn't even look around. I'm a fucking idiot. I should've paid more attention."

"You were saving Sly and Ford. That's exactly what we would've done." Moto claps a hand on Bullet's shoulder.

We all wait in silence after that.

If I had been there, I could've told them where the shooters were located, what kind of gun they were using, and known how many there were. But I wasn't. I was kissing a girl in my bed. A girl who's too young and innocent to understand why we can't be together. But after this, maybe she'll get it.

What feels like hours pass before Aiyana walks into the room, Truly right behind her.

"Gotta stop meeting like this," Aiyana says to me. Her tone made it sound like a joke, but the look on her face says she's serious.

Once again, I broke my own rules and brought my problems to the clinic. But the second I saw Sly and Ford, barely clinging to life, I had to make a decision. Sure, I could take them to the hospital, but with that comes questions we can't answer.

Plus, we're just getting back in with guns. If Miguel knew something like this happened on our first run, he'd second guess his decision to let us back into the game. I don't want to go back to killing assholes for cash every other weekend, so there wasn't another option.

"Sorry," I say.

"How're Sly and Ford?" Loki interjects.

"They're alive. But barely. I had to call in a favor to get

some blood. One that's going to cost me the price of a hip replacement on a golden retriever."

"We'll pay for whatever it costs." Loki pulls out his wad of bills. We all follow suit, holding out thousands of dollars each.

"I don't want your money. I'm a nice person, and I love Will like he's my brother, but please hear my words this time. Don't come back. I can't be your personal hospital. I worked too hard for this place to get involved with what it is you guys do."

"Sorry," I repeat, because what the hell else do I say?

"We're leaving the cash," Loki says, tossing the bills on the counter. "Thank you. We won't come back. I promise."

We all file down the hall to collect the wounded and get back to the clubhouse so we can figure out who the fuck tried to take us out.

Ford and Sly get tucked into their respective beds by Tabitha and Sissy. Ford looked awfully fucking happy to be doted on by Sissy. The girls don't usually get after the prospects. They save their efforts for the patched members.

Sly, however, still hasn't woken up. This is a good thing because, on top of the bullet hole in his leg, the entire left side of his body is basically ground hamburger meat from the road rash. Shit's gonna sting for a long time.

"Church?" I ask Loki. I'm fucking exhausted, but whoever did this is still out there.

"No." He takes his beanie off and scrubs a hand through his hair. "Let's get some sleep and come back to it tomorrow."

I nod and stumble back to the casita. My head feels heavy, and my legs are wobbly. I need some sleep, and I'm already pissed my bed will be empty.

I open the door and toe-off my boots. A throat clears, and I look up into a pair of beautiful brown eyes.

I stalk toward Truly. She takes one step back with each of my forward strides until she runs into a wall. I cage her in and crowd her space. Her eyes widen comically, but I'm not laughing.

Leaning down, I take her mouth in a bruising kiss. I part her lips, making room for my tongue to slip and slide with hers. She melts into me, her arms going around my middle and her fingers tickling across my lower back. I moan into her mouth, enjoying every second of this kiss.

Reluctantly, I pull away, resting my forehead on hers. Our heavy breaths mingle, and our eyes lock. I tell her what I need to say through a look alone. With anyone else, it wouldn't be possible to understand. But this is Truly, and she's been reading me for a long-ass time.

Pools of sadness leak down her face as she starts to understand.

"So that's it?"

My nod is almost imperceptible, but she sees it.

"Fine." She roughly wipes away the tears. "Get off me, please."

I take a few steps back, wringing my hands.

"I don't ever want to see you again, Will. Don't come around the house. Don't answer Mom's calls. Just disappear." Her tone is harsh and biting. I feel the verbal lashes rip apart what little soul I have left. "Do you understand me?"

I nod, and she flies out of the house in a torrent of fury. I'm left alone again, but it's how it should be. This is the life I was meant for, and to want anything more is stupid.

Karen prances over to the edge of the bed and stands on her hind legs, her front paws swimming through the air.

You're right, old girl. Not alone.

Cup of coffee in hand, we file into the Chapel for church. Ford makes an appearance, but Sly isn't here. It's a reminder of the shit that went down.

"Listen up," Loki calls out, and the room goes quiet. "Corsettis are taking credit for what happened. Apparently, Anthony hasn't forgotten we killed his brother."

"And he waited until now to retaliate?"

"He isn't used to running things. He's a disgusting fuck who spent his days beating the shit out of his human pets and not learning the family business. But now his dad has sent him more minions, and he's ready to fight."

"What are we going to do?" Moto asks.

"What we always do. We go to war." Loki stands up. "As soon as Sly is feeling better, I want him finding out who they're working with. We need to know as much as we can about how they're running their business. Moto and Roch, find out where Anthony's living these days. Go to the clubs, the restaurants—he has to pop up somewhere. Then follow him to wherever the fuck it is pricks go at the end of the day."

"I can hit up Miguel. Find out if he knows anything," Khan suggests.

"Okay, do that." He sits back down and scrubs a hand over his face. "One more thing. I can't believe I have to get mad about this shit, but rule one is do your job. If you're on a run, you stay together. I'm looking at you, Roch. Things might've ended differently if you'd stuck around."

He's right. I know he is. But it doesn't stop the bitter anger from flooding my body. My nostrils flare, and I get the urge to beat the smug out of him. He's done some dumb shit for Birdie, and no one said anything. I plant my feet to the ground, not willing to go to blows when I know it's just defensiveness I'm feeling.

"Keep me updated. We should strike soon. Before Anthony has another chance to hit us." Loki bangs his gavel, and I jump to my feet, rushing out so I can cool off.

I go straight to my bike, slap my helmet on, and tighten the strings of my hoodie, so Karen stays safe. Not giving anyone the chance to catch up, I tear out of the parking lot and jump on the highway.

I cruise for miles, clearing my head, and feeling my blood pressure lower. When I got home from Afghanistan, the doctors drugged me up. Had me on all kinds of shit. They stopped me from feeling the lows, but they also took away the highs. I quit putting that shit in my body the day I got back on my bike. Fuck pills, and fuck therapy. All I need are the road and my bike.

That's my religion.

I was supposed to do surveillance with Moto, but since I'm heading toward downtown, I decide to drive past a few of the Corsetti family businesses. It's too early for the restaurants or clubs to be open, but if luck's on my side, Anthony will be at one of the locations.

The parking lots are empty on the first and second stops I make, but I find who I'm looking for on the third—a blacked-out Maybach parked by the back door of a club. I pull over at a taco stand across the street and order lunch. Sitting down at a picnic bench, I settle in.

The tacos aren't bad, and the owners don't seem to mind I'm taking an hour to eat. I've almost given up, when I see an oily bastard slide into the back seat of the Maybach and a driver get behind the wheel. I toss my trash, but wait to get back on my bike until after the car pulls onto the street.

Keeping a distance, I follow until we get to the outskirts of town. They end up in a ritzy neighborhood that's set high on a hill to appropriately look down at all the people they think are beneath them.

I'll stand out like a sore thumb up here, so I flip around. At least now I know the general area. Won't be hard finding out which house is his later on. Especially when I have a less conspicuous mode of transportation.

I pull over for long enough to drop a pin in my location and send it to Loki with the words, **'Got him.'** His return text tells me to get back to the clubhouse, followed by a second text that says, **'Good job.'**

In biker talk, that's the same as him telling me I'm forgiven. I cruise back home to find Loki, Khan, and Goblin looking at aerial maps of the area around where I told them Anthony was.

"This one was just purchased a month ago. The buyer is hiding under a shell corporation and bought the place as a real estate investment. I'd put money on that being our house." Goblin jabs a finger on a plot of land.

"Probably. I'll borrow Birdie's car and do a drive-by, see if I can get confirmation," Loki says, walking backward as he heads to the front door.

I leave them, deciding it's time to go check on Sly. I've been avoiding it because I feel guilty, but I need to make amends. I knock twice on his door and open it.

"S'okay?" I ask from the doorway.

"Hell yeah, it's okay. Get in here, bro. I'm bored as fuck." Sly's perched on his bed, with a laptop resting on his legs. If it weren't for his leg propped up on pillows and wrapped up in gauze, you'd never know he was injured. "I was just doing some digging on who Anthony has got himself mixed up with."

He turns his laptop to me, and I see a picture of a giant motherfucker with a ski mask on. It's no surprise this is Anthony's contact.

"This is Victor Knight, otherwise known as Night Giant. He's been laying low after the Feds took down most of their operation, but he's popping back up, finding new contacts. I'm assuming that's how Anthony got hooked up with him."

"Asshole."

"Yep. Anthony used to be one of Victor's best clients, so it makes sense."

"This?" I point to another photo.

"Our man Anthony also has a family." He clicks on a photo of Anthony with a much younger woman and a kid who looks about college-aged, bringing it to the front of the screen. "It was dumb of us not to ever find out more about this creep, but he seemed like the least of our worries at the time. This is his wife and kid. The wife keeps herself pretty medicated, probably because her husband buys young women, uses them, beats them, and then exchanges them for a new model."

"Son?" Something about the kid is familiar, but I can't place him. I could be wrong. All the fuckers his age look the same these days.

"He's in college, being groomed to take over the business. That kind of thing."

Sly closes the laptop and rests his head on the pillow stuffed behind him. He looks suddenly tired.

"Oh hey, wanna see my rash?"

I shake my head, but it's too late. Sly uncovers the leg that wasn't shot and lifts up the white gauze covering the entire length of it. His mottled skin is red and irritated, chunks of flesh are missing, and there's puss oozing from various parts of the wound. It's gross, but healing.

"Hurts?" I ask.

"It's more itchy than anything else. Your doc hooked me up with a painkiller that is making my life right now. I'm pretty sure the prescription is for a horse." He tosses me the bottle that has the name Misty on it. "Mistys are always strippers, horses, or cats."

I nod. It's true. One of the foster homes I was in had a cat named Misty, and during my career in the Army, I met plenty of strippers by the same name. I toss the bottle back.

"Sorry," I mumble.

"No sweat, bro. I heard why you ran back, and I don't blame you. If I had a bitch, I'd freak the fuck out if she were left alone with these horny idiots."

Speaking of horny idiots, Moto barges into the room with a tray full of drinks and food.

"Time to eat so you can take more pain meds." He places the tray across Sly's lap and all but tucks a napkin into his shirt.

I've never been able to figure these two out. They fuck chicks together all the time, but over the years, it's become more. Like they're in a relationship or some shit. Not that they'd ever admit it. I think they're worried what everyone would think. I personally don't give a shit who they fuck.

"Gonna go," I say.

"Next time you see Loki, send him in. I need to update him on Victor."

I nod.

On my way back to the casita, unwelcome thoughts of Truly pop into my mind. I wonder how she's doing, and if she hates me. It's probably better if she does. I think about texting Aiyana, but I don't for two reasons. One is I think it would raise red flags about mine and Truly's relationship. For another, Truly asked me to disappear from their lives, and I don't go back on my promises.

I need to close that chapter and be done with her.

Chapter

TWELVE

Truly

I cried all night and woke up with eyes so swollen, not even sliced cucumber could bring it down. When Roch caged me in and kissed me, I thought it was his way of telling me he wasn't going to run from this anymore. Then I saw the look in his eyes and knew I was heartbreakingly wrong.

It wasn't a forever kiss. It was a goodbye kiss.

I'm bitter and spiteful. I want to nail his nuts to the wall and use his dick as target practice. I want to go out and hook up with a random stranger and send him pictures. I want to crush his heart the way he crushed mine.

All of these are poor coping mechanisms, so instead, I go to my classes, take my first final, and come home to mope. Except now, I'm lonely and need someone to talk my shit through with. So, I call Max. I need a friend.

"Hello," he answers.

"Hey. How are you?"

"Okay. Just got home after suffering through two finals today. My brain hurts."

"Poor guy. You want to hang out?"

"Uh, yeah. I can do that. You want to grab dinner downtown or something?"

"Can we order in? I had a shit weekend and need a male perspective."

"Boy trouble, huh?" There's a twinge of disappointment in his tone.

"Kind of."

"Did you have a breakup? I didn't even know you were dating anyone."

"No, not a breakup, and I'm not dating anyone," I admit.

"Well, then my answer is yes." He chuckles. "Can you come over?"

My lip curls at the thought of running into his dad again.

"How about here?" I offer.

"I have to stick around the house tonight. My dad's out of town for a few days, and he doesn't like my mom left alone."

"Oh, okay. Yeah. I'll come over. Give me an hour?"

"Perfect."

"Bye," I say and hang up.

As long as his dad isn't home, I don't mind hanging out in a mansion.

I take a walk over to the clinic to let Mom know where I'm going. The place is busy today. The vet techs I've known since I was a little girl are running around frantic, barely having time to say hello. I peek into exam rooms until I find Mom sticking a thermometer up a shaking chihuahua's bum.

I jerk my head in the direction of her office, letting her know to meet me there. She nods her response. I take a few minutes to stock some of the things the techs use all day, but rarely have time to refill. I move laundry from the washer to the dryer and take the dried towels to Mom's office.

I've almost folded them all when she strides through the door and plops down in her office chair.

"It's been insane today."

"I see that. Sorry I wasn't around to help."

"It's fine. You will be soon enough. Then we'll be working side by side. I'm so excited for that day." A broad smile takes up half her face. She would've been happy with whatever I decided to do, but she didn't hide the fact that she wanted me to be a vet like her.

It was never a choice for me, though. I love animals and wouldn't want to do anything else with my life.

"Me too. And not just because that'll mean no more finals."

"How'd today go?"

"Pretty sure I aced it."

"I expect nothing less." She sits up straight. "So, what's going on? I know you didn't come over to fold towels and stock finger condoms."

"I wanted to let you know I'm heading over to a friend's house for a while."

"This same mysterious friend who keeps popping up?"

"No. That one turned out to be a dickhead. This friend's name is Max. Remember my lab partner?"

"Gotcha. Sorry about the dickhead. You want to talk about it?" she asks.

"No, I'm fine. And not all that surprised."

"Okay, well, I better get back to work." We both stand up, and she hugs me tight. "Hey, have you heard from Will?"

"What? No. Why would I?" I close my eyes, mentally berating myself for being so defensive.

"He never called after they left. I thought maybe he'd want to update me." She walks out of the office, and I follow. "Oh well. Everything must be okay if they didn't need any more help. I swear that man will be the death of me. I love him, but his life decisions are questionable."

"I'll be back later tonight," I say.

"Love you." She waves as I leave.

"Hey, Tru," Max greets me at the door, pulling me in for a hug. "Come on in."

"Thanks."

"I didn't know what you'd want for dinner, so I ordered a shit-ton of Taco Bell." He leads me back to the dining room.

On the table are at least seven bags of food. I look behind me, wondering if there's an unknown Army he's planning on feeding. There's no one there. It's only us two.

"Expecting the football team?"

"Sorry." He smiles, showing off his deep dimples. "My dad doesn't allow fast food in the house, so when he goes out of town, I get carried away."

"Your mom doesn't care?"

"Nah. She has a strict diet of vodka and tonic, but sometimes she'll splurge and add pills to the mix," he says with derision, and I regret saying anything.

"Sorry. I guess that's why your dad didn't want you to leave."

"Exactly." He grabs plates and hands one to me. "She didn't use to be like this. She's not my real mom, but she's the closest to one I've ever had. Everything was great for a while, then her nighttime drinking became daytime. Now she's drunk more than sober."

"I hate that for you. I'm sorry."

He shrugs and changes the subject. "I thought we could load up and take it to my room. It's less sterile up there."

His house is pretty cold. None of the furniture is inviting, and I haven't seen a TV yet.

"Sure."

I collect a couple of my favorites and follow him up the stairs. While everything on the main level is elegant and expensive, Max's room is like every other college guy's room. Large flatscreen, three different gaming stations, a nondescript black comforter, and clothes littering the ground.

I much prefer Roch's bare-boned and organized space.

I take a seat in one of the gaming chairs, and he sits on the bed before we dig into our food. It's been so long since I've had Taco Bell, I actually moan when I crunch into a taco.

"Wow, Tru. Did you just come?"

I blush. "No. It takes a lot more than a taco to get me off."

He bursts out laughing, and I smile too. This is nice. I needed to be around someone who likes me and actually talks to me. All the nonverbal communication with Roch is exhausting.

That's what I'm telling myself anyway.

"You ready to tell me about your guy troubles?"

I sigh and set my food down. I give him the Cliffs Notes version of my history with Roch, leaving out any incriminating details.

"Why did they show up that day at your house? It looked tense."

"There was an accident, and they're allergic to hospitals," I explain.

"But a veterinary clinic is better?"

"I think they like the privacy aspect of seeing my mom."

"Right," he draws out. "Because they're outlaw bikers and don't want cops nosing around."

"Something like that."

"Then what happened after that?"

"I went over there to tell him I didn't want to hide anymore." I pick the shreds of lettuce off my taco.

"And…"

"And he kissed me then told me to leave."

"Wow. I'm no expert on relationships with dudes, but that was a jerk move." He sticks his burrito into his mouth, swallowing half the thing in one bite.

"Right? So what do I do?"

"There's nothing to do. For a reason I can't begin to understand because, well, look at you"—he gestures up and down my body—"he's not interested."

"Guess not."

"You need to move on. Find someone who thinks you're worth the risk."

I get the feeling we're not talking in hypotheticals anymore. I study Max again. His black hair is a curly pile on the top of his head while the sides are closely shaved. His face is always smooth, never with any stubble. He dresses impeccably. There's no reason why I shouldn't choose him.

Except he's not Roch.

"I'm sure I will one day," I say carefully.

"I'm sure you will." He brushes the crumbs off his fingers over his plate and then sets it aside. "So, you weren't surprised when I told you that club is full of murderers."

"I wasn't." It may have been a surprise to me when I found

out, but since Max knows, it must be some kind of an urban legend around town.

"And you're okay with that line of work?"

"Definitely not okay. But I think they might be like Batman or something, only stepping in when the law can't." I chuckle.

"They're not the good guys," he says humorlously.

"No, you're probably right about that."

"I heard they're moving back into guns. Did anyone fill you in on that while you were there?"

What started out as a light-hearted conversation has turned weirdly specific and serious.

"No, no one said anything. They don't discuss their business."

"Sorry, I just hate them. Remember how I told you my uncle died recently? They were the ones who killed him."

My head snaps up. "What? Why?"

"They wanted the gun business. That's what my family did. They ran guns. The Bastards took it from them and killed my uncle in the process."

"I-I'm sorry. I don't know what to say." I'm not dumb enough to think there aren't two sides to the story, but I don't doubt the club killed his uncle.

"Just stay away from them. It's not safe. The way they run their business is borderline homicidal, and they don't care who they hurt," he spits out.

"Considering the way things ended, that's not even an issue."

"I'm glad."

It's awkwardly silent for a long minute. I don't know what to say, and he appears lost in his thoughts.

"I should probably go." I stand up, collecting my plate to drop off in the kitchen because Mom raised me with manners even when it's uncomfortable.

"Don't go. I'm sorry. I told myself I wasn't going to bring it up, but then I did. Stay," he pleads.

"Okay, maybe for a little longer."

"Nice!" He rubs his hands together in excitement, the tense moment forgotten.

"What do you want to do?" I ask.

"How about we go swimming?"

"I didn't bring a suit."

"Are you wearing underwear?" He quirks a brow.

"Yes."

"That's the same as a bathing suit. Come on." He grabs my hand and yanks me down the stairs and into the backyard. The pool is ridiculous. There's a waterfall with a grotto underneath, beautiful glasswork, and even a slide that looks carved from rock.

Side by side, we strip and jump into the pool. The cold water sucks the air from my lungs, but it feels refreshing. When we resurface, we're both gasping and laughing.

After an hour of playing Marco Polo and splashing around, we pop out of the pool and lay on lounge chairs.

"I'm glad you called me, even if it was because a guy hurt your heart."

"Me too."

"Should we get changed? We could watch a movie."

"I don't think so. I'm tired, and I have two more finals this week." I stretch lazily.

"Always so studious."

Over the next few days, Max and I hang out often. Since

his dad is gone, I end up going to his house more often than not. We watch TV, play video games, and usually end up in the pool. It's a sound distraction, and I find myself only being sad at night when I'm alone.

Maybe this thing with Roch was bigger in my head than it was in reality, but when you know your heart belongs to someone, who's to say it's too early, or too soon, or even too late?

As long as I can stay busy, I'll be okay. I don't need Roch to do all the things I had planned for my life, it just would've been better if he could be part of it. At least that's what I tell myself.

Then the weekend arrives, and everything goes to shit.

Chapter
THIRTEEN

Roch

"**U**pdate me," Loki says during church.

"I'm still trying to name all the people Anthony has been taking meetings with," Sly says. "But a lot of these guys are unknowns. Not in any governmental database anywhere. It's like they're ghosts."

We've been taking turns surveilling Anthony and snapping pics to bring back to Sly. We've been forced to be on the defense since my brothers were run off the road and shot at. It fucking sucks to not be the attackers, but we need more information before we can go on the offense.

"Keep trying," Loki orders.

"I don't understand why we aren't blowing shit up. I could break into the restaurant he's been using for business, and set something up that'll take him and whoever these scumbags are he's meeting with out," Khan says. His natural instinct is always to kill first and ask questions later. He's not rational in the slightest.

"We don't know who those guys are or who they're connected to. And the last thing we need is any more enemies. Not when we've barely started back up with Miguel." Loki lights a cig and takes a long drag. This room has no ventilation, so the smoke settles on the tobacco-stained ceiling when he blows out.

"No one will know it was us. Trust me." Khan cracks his fat knuckles loudly.

"And they'd never piece it together that it would be the guys who not only recently killed his brother, but were on the receiving end of an attack from him a few days ago. That's not suspicious."

"What about his house? We can get him there."

"Goblin, do we have confirmation of the wife living in the house?"

"We spotted a woman looking out of the third story window, but we've never seen her leave."

"Then blowing up his house isn't an option. We don't fuck with women," Loki says.

"How long are we going to wait? He could strike us at any minute. I don't know about you, but I'd rather kill him first." Khan drags a frustrated hand through his shoulder-length hair.

"I hear ya loud and clear. It won't be much longer, but we need more information before pulling the trigger."

"Anyway, it doesn't matter right now. Anthony flew out of town yesterday morning," Goblin says.

"Where did he go?"

"Still trying to figure that out," Sly jumps in. "It was a private plane with incredible security."

"What you're telling me is, you can't find out?" Loki quirks a challenging brow.

"Oh, I can find it. It'll just take me a little longer."

"Great. Let me know. As for everyone else, we have another run on Sunday. Who's up for it?"

I raise my hand, and Loki gives an appraising stare. I know he's wondering if I'll see everyone else home safely, but he doesn't have to worry. Despite how much I hated doing it, I made certain there won't be any more distractions. I haven't heard from Truly or Aiyana in days, and I doubt I will.

Miles offers to drive the van, giving Ford more time to recover. Goblin and Khan also raise their hands. With the three of us plus Miles, we'll be able to handle any trouble. Matter of fact, I hope Anthony does decide to come for us again. Everything that's happened lately has me on edge.

I need to feel my hands around someone's throat and squeeze until their eyes bulge. I need to slice a million cuts into someone and watch them bleed out. I need to take out all the shit on someone who doesn't deserve to live on this earth any longer.

"Okay. I'll let Miguel know you'll meet him at the border Sunday afternoon for pick up. He'll give you half the cash and the address of where you're going. Drop off is central Oregon, so you'll be gone a week and a half," Loki instructs.

Goblin and Khan groan. I know what they're thinking— long rides leave you with a stiff back, sore ass, and achy muscles. But I welcome the pain and distraction.

The gavel pounds, and the guys rise to their feet, ready to shuffle out.

"I got an idea," Moto says, rubbing his hands together. "There's no work until Sunday, and Anthony's out of town, so there's no current threat against us. Let's party."

"Hell yeah," Khan cheers. "I'll get Tabitha and Sissy on board."

"I met a chick who works at Lusty Lady. I'll give her a call, tell her to bring some new talent." Sly smiles mischievously.

"To do what with? You can't even walk." Khan points to the pair of crutches.

"Bro, if you need your legs to fuck a girl, you ain't doing it right."

"Burn!" Loki shouts.

"Maybe if you want to stay horizontal, but that's not how I get down," Khan boasts. "I like to throw my girl against a wall and feel her thighs wrapped around my waist. Can't do that with a bum leg."

"I can if Moto is holding her up from behind with his cock deep in her ass." Sly's smile is devilish.

"Fuck, it's been too long since we've had pussy around here," Khan groans painfully.

"I got you, bro. Making the call now." Sly stumbles out of the room on his crutches.

I make my way back to the casita to do some training with the dogs, wondering what it would feel like to be care-free. I barely remember what fun is. It seems too far out of reach to grasp, and the closest I've felt to any kind of happiness was the night Truly slept in my bed.

Maybe I'm meant to be so bogged down with bad memories and worries for the future that it's impossible to enjoy my life. Maybe this is all I can hope for.

Sure as fuck feels like it when the only person who makes me feel anything, I have to keep far away for her own safety.

Later that night, the party is in full swing. From my window, I see at least twenty women walking around, nearly naked, and all vying for the attention of a biker. Or, if things get desperate, a hang around. Of which there are plenty to choose from. Apparently, they opened the gates wide and let anyone walk through the door.

Moto has a girl sitting on his lap while her legs are draped across Sly's. His bum leg is stretched out to the side, out of the way. Khan is manning the meat smoker with a chick tucked into his side. Loki and Bridgette are at a picnic table making out.

And I'm in here. Hiding from everyone.

I'm hungry, but can't wrap my head around joining the party to get some food, so I tuck Karen into my hood, and sneak up the side of the house to my bike. It's dark out, and the weather is cool. Perfect riding conditions. I need a long ride.

I'm so in my head, I don't pay attention to the car parked on the corner that flips its headlights on, and follows me as I veer onto the main road. I still don't notice them when I turn onto Mount Rose Highway.

The only thing running through my mind is Truly. I wonder what she's doing right now. I hope she's staying out of trouble. But probably not. That girl is so smart, she gets bored. And when she gets bored, she does stupid shit I have to bail her out of.

Except I'm not her savior anymore.

The guardian bell hanging on the underside of my bike begins to jingle aggressively, warning me of danger. All my senses go on high alert. Especially considering the road is straight and my speed is even. The hairs on my arm stand on end despite the warm evening.

Something's wrong.

I look in my rearview, but nothing is out of the ordinary. There's a set of headlights in my rearview a few hundred feet back, but no one else is on this road. I slow down a bit to give the car a chance to pass me. I'd much rather be behind someone where I can keep an eye on them.

But their speed decreases with mine.

What the fuck?

I lay on the throttle instead, hoping to lose them. I veer around a bend and check to see if they're right behind. But the road behind me stays dark. I ease up and slow to a more respectable speed. I blow out a breath.

My heart hasn't even slowed its rhythm when I see a car coming toward me. The high beams burn my eyes, and I'm forced to avert my gaze from the road ahead. I lock my eyes on the outside line of the road to make sure I stay riding straight. I flash my own brights at them, and instead of them catching a hint, I hear the engine rev as they speed toward me.

It's too much of a coincidence that this truck isn't connected with the suspicious car behind me. I glance over my shoulder quickly to see that car is now gaining speed and has almost caught up to me.

Instead of panic, excitement courses through my veins. These fucks want to play? I'm game.

If I can get around the truck without being hit, then there's no way they can catch up to me. I know this route and all its many turnoffs like the back of my hand.

The truck gets closer and closer. When they've almost reached me, they swerve into my lane, playing a deadly game of chicken. But that's what I was expecting, and I veer in the opposite direction at the same time. They miss me, but barely and I almost lose control.

I look in my side mirror and see the truck is on the shoulder now, turning around and giving me plenty of time to get the fuck out of here. Except the car continues to gain speed until they're a few feet from my rear wheel.

That's when I see a spark hit the road next to me. I'm not sure if it's residual floaters in my vision from the headlights or what.

It happens again and again, fiery particles hitting the ground around me. I realize they're bullets ricocheting off the road. If I don't get out of here fast, I'll be dead for sure. I speed up, zigzagging around so they don't know where to aim. It's dangerous because I could lose control, but I'm more worried about getting shot right now.

I speed-dial Loki and listen as it rings and rings. No answer.

I dial again, and this time he answers.

"Are you calling me from out back? I'll come—"

"Under fire," I say.

"You're being shot at?" He snaps his fingers, and I know he's trying to get my brothers' attention.

"Mount Rose."

"Can you drop a pin for your location?"

"No."

"How far up are you?"

"Ten miles."

"That's too far for us to catch up. Can you flip around?" His bike roars to life in the background.

"Yeah," I say, even though I'm certain it's a death wish.

"Okay, we're heading that way. Stay alive until we get there." He hangs up.

Stay alive.

With no other options, I brake hard. Chances are, they don't want to kill me. I'm worth nothing to them with my guts splattered all over the road, but if the goal is to wipe out the club, I'll make for some enticing bait.

My tires squeal, and the acrid chemical smell of burning rubber permeates my nostrils. I hear the engines of the vehicles behind me getting closer and closer at an alarming rate.

When I'm nearly stopped, I throw a foot down to the side and spin around. I quickly gas it and take off again, except this time, I'm heading right for them. Bullets hit the road on either side of my bike, giving me my answer. They want me alive.

They fan out, blocking both lanes of the highway. On one side of the road is a mountainside. On the other is a guardrail and at least a five-hundred-foot drop to the ground below.

Shit.

Truly and I stopped here not that long ago, so I know there's a scenic pull-out right around here somewhere. If I can turn off there, they'll miss me, and it'll leave them scrambling long enough for me to get away. It's hard to see in the dark, but the reflector on the guardrail shows me the spot where the shoulder widens for cars to stop and take in the views.

I speed up, having two seconds to get to where I need to be.

Everything happens so fast, my brain has a hard time keeping up. The truck realizes my plan, and before I can clear the space, he makes a hard left. The truck clips my back tire, and my bike tips over, sending me flying through the air. My singular thought is of Karen, who is still in my hood, so I twist my body to land on my front. I grit my teeth as my shirt is torn open, and my stomach meets the asphalt, knocking the air out of me.

My bike crashes into the guardrail in a sickening crunch, but I slide right under it. With my fingers digging into the ground, desperate to stop, the ground first disappears under my feet as I begin to fall off the cliff. Then my legs. Then my torso. Then my shoulders.

I'm dead. Game over.

Except, my helmet doesn't quite fit under the guardrail. With a painful jolt, I'm stopped in my tracks. I don't have time to feel relieved, though, because the strap under my chin is both choking me and keeping me from plummeting to my death.

I hear the screech of brakes, followed by a screaming sound of bending metal to my left. The guardrail holding me in place jerks my head painfully. Someone's crashed into it.

I can't see shit being face down. My dome prevents me from seeing out my periphery, but I don't dare try to turn my head, worried it would unwedge me from my precarious position.

I listen as something big collides violently with the guardrail and goes over the edge, followed by a deafening explosion. Heat from the inferno below warms my legs.

I reach above me, feeling around to see just how securely I'm wedged in. Not enough to make me feel safe. Black spots fill my vision, alerting me to the lack of oxygen in my brain. The plastic buckle and braided nylon of my chin strap are all that's keeping my helmet on. It digs painfully into my throat, cutting off my air supply, and acting as a noose.

Despite the stinging in my fingers, I claw at the ground above, trying to get hold of anything to pull myself up. I'm in shape. I do pull-ups, sit-ups, and push-ups for entertainment at night. If I can just find anything solid…but there's nothing except loose gravel.

Shoes crunch on the rocks and stop near my head. I should've known this wasn't over. Sweat drips down my forehead and stings my eyes as I continue to find a way out of this.

"I wasn't supposed to kill you, but fuck. That was my brother that just drove over the edge, and it's your fucking fault."

The last two things I hear before I black out are sirens and an ear-piercing gunshot that echoes through the valley below.

Then everything goes dark.

Chapter
FOURTEEN

Truly

With everything going on with Roch and then spending time with Max while his dad was out of town, it's been a while since Mom and I have had a chance to hang out. Tonight, we're changing that.

We've settled into a Twilight marathon when Mom's cell phone rings.

"Ugh. That better not be an emergency. I was looking forward to a night off." Mom huffs and then answers. "Hello?"

It's silent, but the look on her face tells me the call isn't about a bulldog who ate rocks and needs emergency surgery. Her eyes are wide, and her mouth falls open. She's panicked and worried.

"Who is it?" I whisper shout.

"Yes, this is she." She pulls the phone away from her ear and presses the speaker button so I can hear.

"Do you know a William Pellman? You're marked as his emergency contact."

Mom and I share a look of dread.

"I do. He's my husband's best friend," she says as though Dad is still alive.

"Can you come to Renown Medical Center? We have Mr. Pellman here in the ICU."

I feel as though my heart has flown out of my chest and splattered to the ground. Tears burn my eyes and leak down my cheek. I don't know what happened, or how bad it is, but I know the ICU is the place where people go who need help to stay alive. Not people who broke a toe or have a cold.

"What...?" Mom's voice is barely audible. "What happened?"

"He was in an accident. That's all I can say over the phone. Can you come?"

"Yes."

"Okay. Park on the emergency side of the building. When you walk in, ask reception how to get to the ICU."

"I'll be there in ten minutes." Mom ends the call and stands up to push her feet into her Birkenstocks. I jump up and do the same.

"I don't know what we're walking into. Maybe you should stay home until I find out." She brushes the tears from my cheek. She's always protecting me from things.

"No. I'm going."

"Okay. Let's hurry."

We rush to her truck, an older Ford F-250 that was Dad's before he died. She never could part with it, despite it breaking down all the time.

After we're belted, she starts the engine and peels out.

"I told him the club would get him killed one day. Why the hell doesn't that man listen to me?"

"They're not what you think, Mom. They're decent guys," I defend without realizing I wasn't supposed to be around them. Ever. That was the one rule about mine and Will's friendship.

This is going to get ugly.

"How would you know? I swear to God, if you tell me you've been hanging out with those thugs, I'll kill you."

I stay silent, trying to figure out how to get out of this conversation. She smacks my arm, hard.

"Truly, answer me."

"It wasn't a big deal. Roch—"

"Roch? So you're using his stupid nickname now?" she interrupts, her tone venomous.

"Road name, and yes. He was going out of town and needed someone to watch the dogs. The girl who normally does it, Birdie, wasn't available, so I offered." I leave out the first time I was there. She doesn't need to know everything.

"He asked you to?"

"No. Birdie did."

"How in the hell did this woman know about you?" Her voice rises to a shout.

"You've met her. The one you treated the first time the club showed up."

"You mean Bridgette?" She slams her hand down on her steering wheel. "Goddamn it, Truly. I have so many questions, and you're going to answer them all, but right now, I can't focus. I'm too worried about Will. Trust me, when he's healed, and out of that place, you *both* have a lot of answering to do."

I rest my forehead against the window, watching the world pass by in a blurry haze. I knew this is how she'd react, but I'm almost grateful to be rid of the secrets I've been keeping. Some of them, at least.

Mom parks outside the emergency entrance, hops out, and slams the door shut after her. I don't think I've ever seen her this mad. But with Roch being injured, it's the last of my concerns. I'll gladly let her rip both our heads off if it means he's alive to share in the verbal lashing.

I jog to keep up with her. After a quick stop at reception, we take the elevator up a few flights, and step into a very sterile smelling hallway. We follow the placards that lead us to the ICU.

"I'm the emergency contact for William Pellman. Someone called to tell me he was here."

"Yes, ma'am. Go have a seat in the waiting room, and I'll tell the doctor you're here." She points to an open area with TVs playing softly, lots of cushy chairs, and a wall of magazines. It's also completely full of large, burly bikers who look distraught.

Birdie spots me and leaps to her feet. We hug for a long time, both of us sniffling in each other's ears, but neither of us caring.

"What happened?" I ask, pulling away.

"Gonna have to talk about that later, darlin'." Loki wraps an arm around Birdie's waist and tucks her in tight to his side.

Mom stands a few feet away, scowling. Her arms are folded across her chest, and her eyes are wide. I'm not helping my situation with her.

"Mom, come here." I wave her over, and she reluctantly complies. "You know everyone, right?"

"Unfortunately. Who's going to tell me what happened?" she demands.

"He was in an accident on the highway, heading toward Tahoe. Someone ran him off the road," Loki voice lowers to a whisper and adds, "and then shot him."

"What?" Mom shouts, bringing a hand over her mouth.

That's when Trucker stands up. The older man is calm and collected when he approaches and holds a hand out to Mom.

"I don't think we've met. I'm Trucker."

"Aiyana." She gives him her hand for only a second.

"It's nice to meet you. Would you like to go get a cup of coffee with me?"

"I-I don't know. Will I be safe?"

Trucker's mustache twitches in amusement. "Baby, there's no one else you'll be safer with."

Mom narrows her eyes at the endearment, but Trucker motions for her to walk, and she does.

"Did my dad just put moves on your mom?" Loki says with amusement.

I wave him off. I can't care about that right now.

"Who did this to him?" I whisper.

"Can't tell you club business."

My face turns red. I'm sure of it. How dare he keep secrets from me when Roch's in the hospital.

"Come on, Truly. Let's go sit down and wait for the doctor." Birdie leads me away from the men and into our own private corner of the room. "I don't know what happened, but I know he's in bad shape."

"Is he going to live?" I gulp down the hysterics wanting to pour out of me.

"I don't know." She takes my hand and covers it with both of hers. Her brown eyes are sympathetic.

We wait quietly for a few minutes until Mom returns, a drink carrier full of cups of coffee in her hands. Trucker trails behind her, a smirk on his face.

What is he playing at?

146

"Here." She hands me a cup before offering one to Birdie.

"Thank you," she says politely and takes it.

"It's black. I didn't know what everyone likes."

"Black is fine." She takes the carrier away from Mom. "Why don't I go hand these out?"

Mom takes one before nodding and grabbing the seat next to me.

"You *know* these people, don't you?" she asks.

"Not well. I met the guys, but Birdie and I are friends."

We've become close over the last few weeks. Even after Roch crushed my heart, she called or texted daily. We even met for coffee one afternoon. We click more than I ever have with another girl.

She even confided in me how she ended up involved with the club. She was abducted, raped, beaten, and nearly killed. She also explained the cage and how it makes her feel safe to be locked up, knowing Loki is the only one with a key.

It's fucked, but I also think there's beauty in their ugly.

"I see."

I watch seconds tick by on the digital clock mounted on the wall as I sip my coffee. My mind races with reasons why it's taking so long. Maybe he's in surgery, or they're putting him on life support. Maybe he's dead, and they're wasting time until one of them has the balls to tell a room full of bikers they've lost one of their own.

"Aiyana Reid," a woman in a white lab coat calls out.

"That's me." Mom's chin lifts as she walks across the room, wanting them all to notice how the doctor is asking for her. Not them.

I follow and hook my arm with hers, hoping she won't make me go sit back down.

"I'm Dr. Barnaby. I've been working on your—"

"Family friend," Mom supplies.

"Right. William is in critical condition. It sounds like he was run off the road, which sent him careening off the cliff. The only thing that stopped him was his helmet getting wedged between the guardrail and the ground. It prevented him from falling, but the strap around his neck cut off his air supply. Luckily, he was rescued before any lasting damage could occur, but he injured his vocal cords and has a nasty abrasion around his throat. As far as the gunshot—"

"Gunshot?" Mom gasps.

"Yes, he was shot, but it was a through and through in his bicep. It didn't hit nerves or his bone, so we stitched him up and gave him a tetanus shot and a round of IV antibiotics."

"So, he's going to be okay?"

"Yes, he'll be okay. We'd like to keep him overnight for observation, but he's fighting us on that point. Maybe you could talk to him?"

"Yeah, sure."

"Right this way."

I give the room of bikers a reassuring nod and follow the doctor as he leads us to a small, dark room. Roch's sitting on the edge of the bed, dressed in a hospital gown, with one arm in a sling. He's fidgeting with his IV, ignoring the protesting nurse next to him.

"Mr. Pellman," Dr. Barnaby says, startling Roch. He looks up, and his shoulders slump. "I have a couple guests who would like to talk some sense into you."

"Will," Mom scolds and helps him back into bed, begrudgingly by the look on his face. "You need to listen and do what the doctor says."

"Wanna go," he chokes out, the injury to his vocal cords must be bad. Every syllable sounds pained and harsh.

"Not tonight."

"We'll leave you to talk." The doctor and nurse file out, clearly hoping we have more success than he did.

My lower lip quivers, and I approach cautiously. The last time I saw him, I was so damn angry. But seeing him in a hospital bed melts the anger away.

"Do you need anything? Some water?" Mom holds up a mug that was sitting on a bedside table.

Roch nods and opens his mouth for the straw Mom brings to his lips. But his eyes are on me, and mine are on him. I study his features to get a read on how he's doing.

When he's mad, his lips purse tightly. When he's sad, the corners of his eyes turn down. When he's annoyed, his head rolls back, and he closes his eyes. I don't see any of that. He's blank. Expressionless.

Mom sets the water down and fusses over him, covering him up and muttering about how she doesn't understand why he stays in this silly club if it's going to get him killed.

I take a seat next to him and rest a hand on his arm.

"Are you okay?" I bite down on my lower lip to stop it from quivering when I see the blood-stained bandage across his throat.

He nods.

"The doctor told us what happened. You're lucky to be alive."

Another nod.

"Do you want to see the guys? They're all in the waiting room."

He shakes his head.

"Why? They're anxious to hear how you're doing."

"Weak," he croaks.

"Um, you were run off the road, you dangled off a cliff by your helmet, and then got shot. It's okay to look weak."

He shakes his head again.

"Well, I should go tell them you're awake and okay then." I move to stand up, but he grabs my hand, stopping me. "You want me to stay?"

He nods.

"Okay."

Chapter

FIFTEEN

Roch

"**W**ell, someone should tell them," Aiyana eyes us speculatively. "I'll be right back."

The second she's gone, Truly flings herself over me. It hurts like fuck, but it's also exactly what I need. I wrap my functional arm around her and clutch at her shirt, keeping her close.

She feels like every amazing thing a man like me doesn't deserve but craves. Like happiness and home.

"I was so worried. Are you okay, really?" She doesn't leave me, but lifts her head.

I squeeze my eyes shut. My mind is a jumbled fucking mess. I've pieced together that the cops showed up before my brothers could get to me, considering I woke up in the hospital and not the clubhouse. The second I came to and realized where I was, I tried to leave. I tore out my IV twice and even made it down the hallway once. Then they stuck me with a needle full of something strong, and it was lights out.

When I woke up the second time, my arm was in a sling, and the IV was back in.

The nurses kept firing question after question at me. I wanted to shout to leave me alone, to get the fuck away from me, that I don't like to talk, but my lips wouldn't move. I tried to tell them no, which is usually easy for me to say, but my throat was too swollen and painful.

They stood over me, giving me pitying looks, like I was stupid or some shit.

When Aiyana walked in, I knew I'd fucked up. Ten years ago, I made the mistake of putting her name down on my emergency contact list because I didn't know anyone else. If something bad happened to me, she'd be the only person in the world who might care to know.

After that, I forgot about it. Fucking dumb decision because that's who they called while I was unconscious.

Then I saw Truly, and I was glad that's who they called. Coming that close to death has me rethinking my priorities.

I open my eyes and push her head back down on my chest. Don't give a shit if it feels like a thousand nails driving through my road rash covered chest, I need to have her close and our time is limited.

"S'okay," I mumble, and feel her relax into me.

I have no business encouraging this closeness between us. Nothing's changed. If anything, it's more dangerous for her to be associated with me now than it was a few days ago. There's no doubt in my mind those assholes were sent by Anthony. I push all of it away for right now, though. It's been a hell of a day, and this right here is all I need.

"Mom will be back any minute." Truly sniffles and sits down in the plastic chair next to my bed. "Who did this?"

My eyes flash with anger, but not at her. I'll find the asshole in the sedan and make him pay. Then I'll find Anthony and do the same. If Loki still isn't on board with taking him out, I'll go nomad. Take care of it myself or die trying.

"Don't do that." Truly reaches over and smooths the wrinkles between my eyes. "Don't plan your vengeance while you're hurt in the hospital. I need you safe."

The door swings open, and Aiyana breezes into the room.

"Well, they're not leaving. At least not all of them. Trucker, Loki, and Khan are still here. They said they need to talk to you, but I told them they can wait. It's their fault you're in here in the first place."

"Not… their… fault." My words are barely audible and take way too much effort to get out.

"Ever since you started hanging out with them, bad things have happened to you. You can't tell me it's not their fault."

She doesn't know bad shit's been happening to me my whole life. Starting with parents who were more concerned with their next fix than taking care of their kid and continuing with the foster homes who looked at me like a paycheck and not a human. The Army treated me like a commodity. The men who kept me locked up for six months used me as a punching bag, a cum dumpster, and then a bargaining chip.

The truth is, the only people, besides Aiyana and Truly, who have treated me like a goddamn human are my brothers.

"Mom, you can't say that. You have no idea who they are. You only know rumors," Truly defends.

"Don't think I've forgotten how much you suddenly know about club life."

My eyes widen, wondering what the hell she's talking about.

"Don't look so innocent," she says, directing her attention on me. "I know all about you leaving town and my daughter staying at your clubhouse with no one there to watch out for her. Do you know how dangerous that was? For Christ's sake, look at you. This could've been her."

Truly shakes her head imperceptibly, telling me Aiyana doesn't really want answers.

"You're being dramatic. This didn't happen in the clubhouse." Truly motions to my battered body. "I'm safe there."

It's like watching a tennis match between mom and daughter. Each of them spewing their own opinions, but neither listening to the other. It's going nowhere, and my head is throbbing.

I clear my throat, silencing them both.

"Tired." I do my best to look pathetic.

"You're right. We should go. The doctor said you'll be able to leave tomorrow, so I'll come back to pick you up. You can stay with us until you're feeling better." Aiyana collects her purse and slings it over her shoulder.

"No," I say.

"What do you mean, no?"

"He doesn't want to go to our house, Mom. He has his dogs." As if realizing the dogs are home alone, she bolts upright and covers her forehead with her hand. "Oh my God, the dogs. Do I need to go feed them? Take care of them?"

I lift up the hospital blanket and show her Karen, who's snuggled up against my calf. From what the nurse said, the paramedics discovered her sleeping away, still in my hood, when they brought me up off the ledge. They don't normally allow pets, but they said she could stay until someone else could take her since she's so small. Truly scoops her up and tucks her under her chin, cooing softly.

"What about the other dogs?" she asks.

"I'm sure someone else can watch the dogs," Mom says with aggravation lacing her tone.

"Birdie," I agree.

"I'll text her." Truly whips out her phone and starts tapping out a text.

That cold spot in my chest warms at how she steps in to care for me, even without me asking.

"We can take Karen home for the night." Aiyana does the same thing her daughter did, scoops the dog out of Truly's arms and tucks her under her chin. They're so much alike, but neither would agree.

"I'll take care of Karen. I'm not going anywhere." Truly coaxes the dog—whose wide eyes are begging me to rescue her—from her mother. "With his sore throat, he can't talk, and who knows what the doctors and nurses will read from that."

She's being kind. Even without the injury, everyone in this room knows I don't communicate well. Jesus Christ, she's too perfect. Too pure. Way too sweet for an asshole like me. Doesn't stop me from wanting her. Strike that, fucking needing her.

"Can I talk to you in the hallway, please?"

"Sure."

Aiyana hands me Karen and escorts her daughter out of the room. I blow out an exhausted breath. I should tell Tru to leave with her mom. It's not right for her to stay in a hospital all night. But having her here is calming the noises in my head, and fuck if I don't need a little comfort right now.

I've almost fallen asleep when Truly comes back in. This time instead of her mom, she brings in Loki, Trucker, and Khan. I guess she got her way.

I'm sure there'll be hell to pay for that later. For right now, I'm grateful.

"What the fuck happened, bro?" Loki holds up his fist, and we bump knuckles. The other guys do the same.

I look from them to Truly. She shouldn't hear any of this. It's too dangerous.

"I'll take Karen for a bathroom break and find her something to eat." She takes my dog and bends down to kiss the top of my head, stunning me and everyone else in the room. Goddamn, if that didn't make my heart skip a beat. I shake the emotion off, I need to remember I can't keep her.

"She's a good kid," Trucker says.

"She reminds me of Birdie, tough as fucking nails, but still sweet. Everyone likes her." Loki shrugs like he's telling me something I don't know. "So what happened? By the time we got up there, place was swarming with cops, and you were being loaded into an ambulance."

"Anthony."

"How do you know?" Khan asks.

I shrug. It's a gut feeling. No one else has a reason to come after the club.

"Sly's getting more information on the truck that took a dive off the cliff. The asshole inside is a goner, but we're hoping to get an ID on him." Loki checks his phone. "Birdie's back at the house. She fed the mutts."

"Thanks."

"Well, we better head out. You shacking up here for the night?" Khan asks.

I nod.

"All right, man. See you tomorrow. Need a ride home tomorrow?"

I nod, assuming Truly came in the same car as Aiyana.

"Text when they spring you." Khan wiggles my foot, and I kick him in return.

A few minutes after they leave, Truly returns. She tucks Karen back under the blanket, and then sits down on the edge of the bed.

"You need anything?"

I shake my head.

"Some water?"

I shake my head.

"Do you need another blanket? It's cold in here."

I shake my head again and rest a hand on her knee to stop her from asking any more questions. Her head lulls forward, and she places her hand on mine, rubbing her thumb back and forth. When she looks up, her eyes are brimming with tears.

"I was so scared."

I give her arm a yank, and she collapses on top of me. Her whole body shakes with her sobs. I pat her back, hoping it soothes her, but not sure I'm doing it right. My hand hits a strand of her hair, and an idea hits me that might be better than the back-patting thing. I comb through her hair with my fingers. It's so silky and soft. I don't know how I never noticed how thick and smooth it is. I love how it feels running across my skin.

Her tears soak through the stupid ass gown they have me in. I hate to see her cry. I remember how comforting her kiss to my temple felt, so I lean down and place my lips on her head. She sucks in a breath, and her head pops up from my chest. Her eyes are puffy and red-rimmed, while her cheeks are damp and tear-stained.

She's never looked so beautiful.

I cup her cheek and bring her mouth to mine. I can't help myself. It's probably the drugs, or maybe the near-death experience that has me making bad choices.

Her salty tears settle deliciously on my tastebuds. I lick the seam of her lips so I can get more, except her lips part, and instead of tears, I suddenly taste *her*. I become intoxicated, desperate for more. Our tongues twist together. The slip and slide sensation sends pleasure straight down to my cock, which is hard as stone now.

I want to touch her, feel her, climb inside of her and figure out what makes her tick. Close isn't close enough, but with my arm bound to my side, there's no way I can do all the things to her I want to do.

I break the kiss and tilt her head so I can lick and draw the flesh of her neck into my mouth. Fuck, she's mouthwatering here too. Not like cherries or vanilla, but like sunshine and happy endings. Things I never even dreamed I'd experience, but here she is, panting and moaning at my attentions.

"Knock, knock." Someone enters the room, and we bolt apart.

Truly's lips are swollen and red, and there's a bruise forming on her neck where I'd been sucking. I did that. I marked her. I should be embarrassed I'm reacting like a horny teenager, but I'm not. I like the idea of leaving her with something to remember me by.

"Sorry to interrupt." The nurse gives us her best side-eye. "Time to check your vitals."

Truly slowly removes herself from the bed and slides over to her chair. She tries to hide her smile by biting down on her lower lip, but it's no use. She's beaming.

She waits patiently while the nurse goes through her

checklist. Thankfully, her questions can all be answered with a nod or a shake of my head.

"Okay, I'm going to go now. Just so you know, we stop by every hour, and the doctor won't be in until morning." She winks at Truly, causing her cheeks to pink up, then she's gone with a soft click of the door closing.

"Oh my God." Truly covers her face. "I can't believe that happened."

"Come 'ere," I rasp out.

She moves back to the bed, still unable to show herself to me. I pull her hand down and kiss the back of it. One moment of weakness was all it took for me to completely forget all my rules. Don't think anyone would blame me.

Except maybe her mom.

"Roch, I swear to God. If you're going to kick me out like you did after our last kiss, I'm going to punch you in the junk and never talk to you again."

I shake my head and scoot to the edge of the bed to make room for her. She lies down next to me with her head on my functioning shoulder. I can almost see the swirl of thoughts swarming around in her head, but I don't want to talk about any of it right now. My arm's throbbing, my head is pounding, and I need some sleep.

She must pick up on that because she keeps them unsaid, shocking the hell out of me. This girl doesn't know how to contain her words, so I appreciate her effort.

"I'm going to say one thing and one thing only," she starts. "I love you, William Pellman. I loved you as a dumb kid with a crush, I loved you as an angsty teenager with a fantasy, and I love you as a woman with a dream of being your forever."

Chapter
SIXTEEN

Truly

After Roch falls asleep, but before the hour is up when the nurse is due back, I climb off the bed and move over to the very uncomfortable chair that reclines. I want to stay close and allow him to hold me all night, but I know he'll sleep better without me there.

He didn't say anything after I told him I loved him, but I didn't expect him to. For someone so emotionally unavailable, it's no surprise. Plus, he's had an eventful night with being run off the road, almost dying, and then finally giving in to his feelings for me.

I can only hope it's not a temporary thing. All this back and forth between us is making me lose my mind. I know myself, though. It doesn't matter how many times he changes his mind, I'll be there, broken-hearted and waiting until the next time he forgets he doesn't want me.

I watch him sleep for hours. He's the most beautiful man I've ever seen. I love the way his floppy, blond hair has a slight curl on the ends, just enough to give it volume and style without him paying any attention to it.

His daily anxiety is written all over his face. Despite his chin being covered in scruff, I can still make out his sharp jawline that no doubt stays strong from all the clenching he does. Then there are the deep grooves between his eyebrows, a result of the permanent scowl that scares others, but makes me smile.

Even in his sleep, he looks grumpy.

My favorite thing about him, though, is his arms. I've spent hours studying every inch of them from where I sit on the back of his bike. The way the veins on his arms protrude as he accelerates and steers does something to me. I know they have nothing to do with masculinity or virility and more to do with his low body fat, but fuck if my body missed the memo.

"Here, hon. I brought you a blanket. These rooms can be chilly," a nurse whispers, handing me a blanket.

"Thank you."

"No problem. Do you need anything else? Something to drink?"

"No, I'm fine."

She quickly checks his vitals without disturbing him.

"He's a lucky man."

"I know. If he didn't have that helmet on, he wouldn't be here." A shiver runs up my spine.

"There's that, but I think he's lucky because he has a girl who'll sit here and watch him breathe all night." She places her hands on her hips, studying her patient.

"Thank you," I say in a hushed tone, smiling, though I can't imagine being anywhere else.

"Well, I'm off. Be back in a bit. You should try and get some sleep too."

I don't know how long I keep myself awake, but eventually, exhaustion wins out, and my eyes close.

It's light in the room by the time I wake up, and Roch is sitting up in bed, a plate of neon yellow eggs and plain toast in front of him. His features are pinched in disgust as he pushes it around his plate.

"I can't believe I slept through you being served breakfast." I stretch my arms wide and yawn.

Roch grunts and tosses his fork onto the tray.

"Why are your eggs glowing?" I joke and move to sit on the edge of his bed.

"Gross." The word sounds choppy, like it was shoved through a meat grinder before it left his mouth.

"Do you know when they're going to let you leave?"

He hands me his discharge papers.

"Just need the doctor to sign off," I say after reading through them. I dig Karen out from under the blankets. "I'll bet she needs to go out. I'll be right back."

He gives me a nod.

I pass the waiting room on my way and see that Ford is already here, slumped in a chair with his phone out. He's attractive, with his shaved head and dark features. Just not as handsome as the man poking at his eggs in the other room. He catches me out of the corner of his eye and gives me a chin lift. I hold Karen up and point to the exit. He nods in recognition, and I walk outside.

I set Karen down and glance at my phone. There are a few texts from Mom ranging from passive-aggressive to outraged.

Our little talk outside of Roch's room yesterday wasn't exactly cordial. I know she suspects my feelings for the badass biker are more than platonic, but she's too afraid to ask.

I ignore all her questions about why I insisted on staying and tell her I'll call her later. She doesn't know it yet, Roch either, for that matter, but I plan on seeing Roch home and, if he lets me, staying by his side until he's feeling better.

Karen lifts up on her hind legs and paddles her front paws. I scoop her up and kiss her face.

"Put in a good word for me with your dad, would you?"

She yips, tongue lulling out to the side, like always, ever since her teeth were pulled all those years ago.

This time when I walk past Ford, he hands me a brown paper bag.

"Change of clothes," he says in explanation.

"Smart. I'm sure the ones from last night aren't wearable."

"Everything but his vest, from what I understand."

"I'll give them to him."

"Great. I'll be here when he's ready to go."

I take Karen and the clothes back into the room and set the bag next to Roch. He's since pushed his food tray off to the side. The only thing gone is the apple juice box that's now crumpled on top of his eggs.

Big strong man likes apple juice. *Noted.*

"Ford brought you clean clothes."

He holds up his discharge papers, now complete with a signature scribbled next to the X, then holds up his hand, showing me the cotton ball with tape over it—no more IV.

"Thank goodness. Let's blow this joint."

I think the corner of his mouth tips up, but it's hard to tell from under his mustache.

Someday I'll see you smile, tough guy.

He stands up and shuffles to the bathroom. With his back to me, the hospital gown parts and gives me a brief glimpse of his rounded, boxer-brief clad ass. He's a vision in a pair of worn jeans. But in tight boxer briefs, he's a gift.

He glances over his shoulder, totally catching me checking him out. He shakes his head, but he's amused. There's no tightness in his jaw, and there's a twinkle in his eye. Then the door shuts, and I'm cut off. Damn.

Minutes pass, and he doesn't emerge. I set Karen down on the bed and knock on the door. No answer.

"I'm coming in," I announce before turning the door handle. Thankfully, it's not locked.

What I see has my heart sinking. He's sitting on the toilet seat, in his underwear, with his jeans down around his calves, struggling to pull them up with one hand. My heart sinks seeing his chest mottled with oozing wounds, and I kick myself for basically lying on top of him last night. I had no idea.

"Let me help," I offer.

"No." He stands up, trying to shimmy them up, and almost falling on his ass in the process.

"Stop being so stubborn. Sit back down."

Seeing no other choice, he does as I ask. I kneel down in front of him and pull his jeans up his thick thighs covered in light brown hair.

Goddamn it, even his leg hair is sexy.

"Stand up."

He rises to his full height, his eyes locked on the ceiling. I work his pants up his legs and over his butt. Which only leaves his zipper and button left. Oh boy. This is not how I envisioned my first time being this close to his dick. I need to button them first, I'd hate to snag something in the zipper.

"We're about to get a lot closer, you and me," I say while bringing the top of the jeans together and pushing the button through the hole.

Okay, halfway there. All that's left is reaching in there and pulling up the zipper. I shouldn't be so nervous, right? This is productive. Like a meet and greet with his penis so we can become acquainted. That's progress, right?

I shake out my hands, then grip the hem of his crotch with one hand as I reach beyond his fly to grab the zipper. I gasp when I not only feel the metal zipper, but I also feel *him*. He's hard. His dick is hard.

I look up to see him not staring at the ceiling anymore. His eyes are half-lidded and lust-filled eyes are now on me.

My fingers rub and down before I realize what I'm doing. He's long and thick. My pussy clenches, and my breathing slows. God, I'm so turned on.

Before I sink back to my knees and attempt my first blow job, I zip him up.

I clear my throat. "Okay, shirt's next."

I unclip his sling and slip his T-shirt over his head. His shoulders are broad, and he has a light dusting of chest hair between his hard pecs, as well as a happy trail leading down. My mouth goes dry, and I bite my bottom lip.

He clears his throat, breaking the spell his bare torso put me under. I blink a few times before carefully guiding his injured arm through an arm hole. He slips his good arm in the other side by himself, but looks to me for help to secure his sling.

"There we go." I scan him from top to bottom. "Oh, shoes. Do you have shoes?"

He nods and guides me out of the bathroom with a hand on my lower back. He opens the hutch in the corner of the room and pulls out his black leather boots. Unable to put them on himself, he hands them to me and sits down. I push his big feet into them and lace them up. I don't miss the pitting and scratches down the side of them. I cringe. It's a reality check of how bad the accident was.

"It must've been scary. To be skidding across the ground and then dangling off a cliff." I run my fingers across the imperfect leather.

"Little," he says.

"I'm glad you're alive." I stand up and step between his legs. His uninjured arm automatically goes around me, resting on my lower back. I lean down and kiss him. I don't know where we stand, so I shouldn't take liberties. But he kisses me back, reassuring me we're okay.

He pats my ass twice and ends the kiss.

"Go," he says with a hoarse voice.

"Yes, let's. Wait. Where's your vest?"

"Cut." He nods at the hutch.

"Right. Cut. Biker boys and their lingo." I walk over and take the leather out from where it's folded on a shelf. It's more beat to hell than his boots. I trace along the patch on the chest that says "Roch." I once Googled the nickname, knowing there must be meaning behind it. I was right. Roch is the patron saint of dogs.

That made me smile—such a tough name for such a sweet thing.

I shake it out, ready to help him into it, but the light catches on something sewn inside. I turn it inside out to inspect it. I nearly drop the thing when I see it's the hummingbird pendant I gave him all those years ago.

It's a tribal symbol, something my mom gave my dad when she knew he was the one for her. Dad left it behind for safekeeping, and never returned. Mom gave it to me the day we learned he wasn't coming home. She told me humming-birds represented love, and when I meet the man I'd be with forever, I should give it to him.

Being eight years old and meeting a beautiful, stoic man seemed like my best option at the time, so I gave it to Roch. Mom didn't have the heart to ask for it back, so she let it go. But I knew. Someday I was going to be with the grumpy man who never smiles.

A tear streaks down my cheek at seeing the red, orange, and yellow beaded pendant again. I can't believe he kept it, let alone sewed it into something he wears every single day. My eyes lift to where he's standing awkwardly, waiting for my reaction.

I hold it up and help him into it, then I pat the place where it rests against his heart.

Goddamn, this man.

Chapter

SEVENTEEN

Roch

"**I**'m coming home with you and staying until you can at least dress yourself," Truly says from the front seat of the minivan.

"No."

"Roch, you can't even put on your own shoes, and I'm on summer break."

I sigh. I'm too tired to argue, but not tired enough to remember the threat against us. After last night, I want nothing more than to have her tucked in next to me, but if anything happened to her… well, I wouldn't survive that.

"Give me one night. If you want me to go home after that, I will." She whips around to face me, where I'm slumped on the bench seat in the back. "Please. I'll worry."

"Fine," I say, but I don't recognize my own voice. It sounds like I chain-smoked my way through an entire decade. My throat's swollen on the inside, and all cut up on the outside.

If you thought a gunshot wound would hurt worse than near strangulation, you'd be wrong.

"Thank you." She reaches back and rubs my knee.

Ever since our kiss, she's been doing that. Touching me whenever she wants, and fuck if I don't like it. I didn't think I'd want someone doting over me. I'm not the kind of guy who enjoys sympathy or pity from anyone. But with her, it amuses me. I know in her misguided heart, she thinks we're meant to be or some other fucked up romantic notion. It's not true, of course. People aren't fated, they make a choice.

She's got her head in the clouds, and I have mine rooted in dark reality. I'd never tell her that, though. I like her floating above me.

Ford parks in the lot at the clubhouse, and we unload. Truly fusses and tries to help me out of the van, but I brush her away. I hurt my arm, not my legs. Plus, the girl weighs a hundred and ten pounds soaking wet. I more than double that. I'd crush her if she tried to stop me from falling.

We go inside and find the place packed. My brothers, a bunch of hang arounds, some patch pussy, and who knows who else, all gather to welcome me home. I should feel something other than annoyance at the gesture, but I need to rest so I can start plotting Anthony's takedown.

I go through the motions of nodding at everyone, even allowing a few bro hugs, but my agitation grows by the minute. I don't like parties on the best of days, let alone when I'm the center of attention.

"Sorry, guys. Doctor's orders, he needs rest." Truly take my hand and leads me out the back door.

She's useful in more ways than one.

"Thanks," I mutter.

"No problem. I could see the deer in headlights look. And I wasn't lying. I saw your discharge instructions, and you're to stay in bed for at least a few days."

The second we're in the backyard, the dogs rush over, and calm settles over me. I crouch down so they can smell my wounds. Dogs are intuitive and rely on their instincts and senses. I don't have to say jack shit for them to know I'm injured. It's why I relate to them so well. We're the same.

After giving them some attention, we make our way into the casita. Truly's take-charge attitude has her roaming around like a mad person, getting Karen settled and stacking pillows up for me. It's cute how serious she's taking the role of caregiver. Yeah, it's a little immature, but she's young, and everything is so new to her. I'd never begrudge her that.

"Want to lie down for a while? Take a nap?" she asks.

I nod, and allow her to help me out of my vest and boots.

"Want your jeans off?" She toys with the button of my pants, while eyeing me.

I shake my head and scrub a hand through my hair. After feeling her hand on my dick earlier, I know if I strip down, there will be no nap. I haven't had the urge to fuck anyone in so long, but that ended the first time I felt Truly's lips on mine. Now, if I'm not imagining all the ways I'm going to kill Anthony and his Army, I'm thinking of all the things I want to do to her body.

"Right." A look of rejection crosses her features.

I tip her chin up and kiss her sweet.

"Right," she repeats, only this time she's smiling.

That smile belongs to me.

We both climb into my bed. She stays seated while I rest back against the pillows.

"Can we talk?"

I nod.

"I don't know much about what your life is like here. Not the daily stuff." She motions around us. "But I want to. I know you think I'm too young, and the complications aren't worth it, but you sewed my hummingbird into your vest. You can't tell me that meant nothing."

I wrap a hand around her thigh, loving how much of her skin my palm covers. She's so fragile and delicate. She feels like something I need to protect, and if there's one emotion I know well, it's protection.

"I don't ever ask for words from you. Ever. But I need to hear them now. Do you want me in your life?"

This means something to her, and I know when I say the word, that'll be it. I can't push her away. I can't tell her to live her own life and only let her come around when it's safe. Because it'll never be safe. Right now, it's the Corsettis, but even if we wipe that crime family from the face of the earth, someone will always be around to take their place.

Despite all of that, I say yes.

She beams at me and tucks herself in my side. "I knew it."

I don't know what time it is when I wake up, but judging by the sun's placement low in the sky, it's afternoon. Truly's still sleeping, so I carefully maneuver out of bed.

I'm sore and achy. My body tells me to stay here and sleep for the next month, but my mind knows I have shit to do.

I push my feet into my boots, not bothering with the laces, and walk across the lawn into the clubhouse. Thank fuck, it's not full of people anymore. Only a few brothers are hanging around the common areas.

"Hey, bro. How are you feeling?" Goblin's at the bar, like always, watching the news with a tumbler in his hand.

I shrug.

"Wasn't sure I was going to see you tonight. Thought your girl would have you busy." He waggles his brows, causing me to roll my eyes.

Not even almost dying stops their minds from going right to sex.

I scan the area and find Loki and Khan sitting at a table, talking. I walk over and take a seat with them.

"Glad to see you up and moving," Loki says. "You ready for an update?"

I nod.

"You were right. It was the Corsettis. The truck was registered to a man with known ties. Still not sure who was in the car, but we're working on it." Loki nods to where Sly is perched at a different table, lost in whatever's on the screen of his laptop. "Sly, come show Roch those pics."

Sly holds up a finger, bangs a few more keys, then unplugs his laptop and brings it over to our table. On the screen are surveillance pics of five men. Anthony, Luke, his second, Anthony's kid, Anthony's dad, Franco, and one other man. A big, ugly motherfucker.

"We think this is the guy that goes by Night Giant. He's basically the king of human trafficking," Sly says. "They were giving him a tour of a storage unit Anthony purchased. My guess is they'll be starting construction on making the units semi-habitable. Or at least livable for long enough to be a holding cell for their victims until they can make a sale."

A growl escapes my throat. My skin crawls thinking about women and children locked up in a fucking storage unit.

"They have to be grooming the kid, right?" Khan points to the image of Anthony's son.

"Looks like. He was there every time these assholes met up." Sly blows up the image of the kid.

I swear to Christ, I've seen him before. It could've been from before when we took out Dom, but that doesn't feel right. It was somewhere else.

"With him hitting us twice now, I'm done playing games, and I'm not going to ignore him any longer," Loki says.

"Kill him." I slam the laptop closed, done looking at their disgusting faces.

"We've got some plans to make, but we can't make them until next week when the guys get back from the run. You can't ride with your arm, and everyone else has shit they're working on, so it'll be Khan, Goblin, and Miles going."

I nod. I want to argue because I'd ride through the pain, but if shit went down, I'd be a liability and get us all killed. There's also the fact I don't have a bike right now. I don't know where mine went after the accident. Even if I did, it's not driv-able. That thought depresses me more than my injuries.

"You need to heal up, bro. We need you." Khan squeezes my working shoulder.

"I think the girl Goblin's chatting up might be able to give you some sexual healing." Sly tips his chin behind me, a stupid grin on his face.

I look over my shoulder and see Truly standing next to our enforcer. He says something to make her laugh, and she slaps his arm. The gesture makes my eye twitch, and I have the sudden urge to punch one of my closest friends.

I jump up from my chair and walk over to them. Without realizing what I'm doing, my arm wraps around Truly's waist, and I tuck her into my side. The same way I've seen Loki do when he finds Birdie talking to me. It's a possessive move I didn't understand until now.

"I wasn't sure if it was okay for me to be in here." She peers up at me.

"S'okay."

"Truly was telling me about how you two met." Goblin's brow lifts.

"Well, only that we met when I was a kid," she clarifies, making me sound like a damn pedophile. She realizes how it came out and slaps a hand to her forehead. "That sounds bad, huh? Let me reword. He's a longtime family friend."

"You're a brave girl," Goblin says. "Most chicks run from this bastard."

I scowl at him. When the fuck did this place turn gossipy?

"Oh, he's a big teddy bear once you get to know him." Truly pats me on the chest, and I redirect my scowl to her.

"Teddy bear, huh? This whole time, all you needed were snuggles to not be such an asshole? You could've asked me to spoon you if you were feeling deprived of love, Roch."

Fuck my life. This conversation is irritating the shit out of me.

"Dogs," I say and drop my arm from around Truly's waist. If she and Goblin want to sit around and talk shit, they can do it without me.

"I think we hurt his feelings," Goblin jokes, sending them both into laughter.

I've taken two steps before Truly calls after me, "Wait. Let me help."

We go behind the bar and into the kitchen. Since she knows the routine, she reaches for the bowls on the top shelf and lines them up on one of the long, stainless-steel countertops.

"Sorry for teasing you. It's kind of fun having people around who know you."

I slide a stack of kibble filled bowls off the counter and carry them outside. Truly does the same. I watch in awe as she puts the dogs in a 'sit and wait' before setting bowls in front of them. It fills me with pride that she's been accepted as a pack leader. She fits into every part of my life with ease.

"You look tired," she comments, rubbing a hand down my arm.

I nod. I've been asleep more than awake today, but I'm still wiped out.

"Come on. Let's get you back in bed."

Inside, she feeds Karen her soft food. After she's done, she takes her to the sink and gently wipes her face off without direction from me. Warmth fills me, consumes me, swallows me fucking whole. My chest squeezes painfully with emotion.

Fuck me.

I don't just love Truly. I'm in love with her.

We both move to the bedroom, where she tucks Karen into her bed.

This time, I don't argue when Truly helps me out of my shirt and pants. It's a bad idea, but I don't care.

I slip under the blankets and sheets and watch intently as Truly turns her back to me and slips out of her pants and T-shirt, revealing a tiny tank top underneath that leaves her entire midsection exposed. She wraps her arms around herself before circling back around. She's bashful, and something about it turns me right the fuck on. Exhaustion wanes slightly, and I get the urge to feel her lips on mine again.

She flips the light off and slides into bed, wedging herself between me and Karen's dog bed. I wrap an arm around her and bring her closer, feeling the soft skin of her abdomen against my side and her bare legs entangled with mine.

"S'okay?" I ask.

"Yeah." She props herself up on her elbow.

I rub along the smooth skin of her lower back and then move lower to the top of her ass. My dick twitches, feeling the two swells of her ass cheeks. She's so fucking sexy. I push down, bringing her forward so I can take her mouth.

Before Truly, it'd been thirteen years since I'd kissed a girl. I'd convinced myself I didn't need it. That women bring problems, and I was fine without connection or touch.

I was so fucking wrong.

Chapter

EIGHTEEN

Truly

He deepens the kiss, drawing my lower lip into his mouth and releasing it with a scrape of his teeth before placing featherlight pecks all over my face.

I've never had a kiss like this before. I've never been this turned on before. My clit is throbbing, practically begging for attention. I squeeze my thighs together, desperate for an ounce of relief, yet it doesn't help. Nothing will until I have Roch between my legs.

He pulls his arm from under me and palms one of my breasts. I arch into the touch as his thumb swipes over a nipple, and I feel a gush of wet soak my panties.

This can't go far, at least not as far as my body wants to take it. He's injured and in pain, but I'm going to take whatever he gives me, and if that happens to be an orgasm, that's even better.

He reaches under the blanket and hoists me, one-handed, on top of him. My panty covered pussy comes in direct contact with his boxer covered dick. When I rock my hips, seeking friction over his long and thick erection, he groans.

"Am I hurting you?" I whisper.

"No."

"Then what's wrong?"

"Feels... good," he says through a clenched jaw.

I lean forward, careful not to upset his arm, and kiss his neck. Slowly, I move down, planting open-mouthed kisses around the scabbing on his chest. With him in this condition, sex is off the table. I wouldn't be able to enjoy it while also worrying he's in pain, but that doesn't mean I can't do things to him. Even if my only qualification is enthusiasm.

I've never had sex. I've never even given a guy head. I can't say why because Mom taught me about birth control when I was fourteen. She assured me she would take me to be put on the pill with no questions asked. She's always told me I'll know when it's right, and I should be prepared.

It never did feel right with anyone, so I never let anything more than kissing and over the clothes touching happen.

But with Roch, everything feels perfect. I want him to be my first and to share that with him, and him alone. Someday soon. The sooner, the better.

"I've never done this before."

He tries to pull me back up, not understanding why I'm telling him this.

"No. I want to. More than anything. But you should know, in case I'm terrible at it."

He tenderly brushes a strand of hair off my face, then traces along my lips with the tips of his fingers. Words mean nothing to me anymore. Through Roch, I've learned actions really do speak louder, because that one gesture reassures me that he doesn't care if I figuratively suck at this. As long as I literally suck at this.

I smile and rub up and down his length, still covered by his tight, black boxer briefs. His eyes narrow on me, half-lidded with lust. That one look makes me feel sexy, and gives me the confidence I need to pull down on the waistband of his underwear.

His heavy cock springs free, slapping him on the stomach. Just like on his forearms, he has protruding veins running along his length. I take him in hand and stroke down to expose his spongy head. It feels different than I imagined. All of Roch's other skin is weather-worn and work-roughened, but his dick is velvet-covered steel.

A curious clear drop of pre-cum glistens along the slit, and I duck my head to taste him. It's not altogether unpleasant, but knowing it's the physical embodiment of his arousal is intoxicating and makes me want more.

I lick him from base to tip, tracing his veins with my tongue. I'm unsure if this is what I'm supposed to do, but I shut off the doubts in my mind. I need to be in this moment. His expression is pure bliss, making me brave, so I wrap my lips around him and suck. His hips leave the mattress, and his eyes squeeze shut.

I moan around his rigid cock, flattening my tongue along the underside of him as I bob up and down the way I've seen online. With my other hand, I cup his balls and roll them in my palm.

I build a rhythm, pumping and sucking. He reaches down and moves the hair that curtains my face to get a better view. My ears burn knowing he's watching my every move, but it also has me soaking my panties. I take him further down my throat, swallowing around him. He lets out a guttural sound, and I know he's going to come soon.

I jerk him faster and suck him harder. Seconds later, his cock pulses under my touch.

"Fuck," he curses as thick, hot cum shoots down my throat. I work to swallow every drop without gagging. Drops of it spill out the corner of my mouth, but I don't let up.

When I feel him soften, I place one last kiss on his tip and release him, wiping around my lips. I try to roll off him, but he grips my arm, stopping me. He tugs me back down and kisses me hard. I assumed he wouldn't want to taste himself on me, but apparently, that's not the case because his tongue sweeps into my mouth like I didn't just have his cum in there.

I don't intend for there to be reciprocation. Yes, I'm wet and turned on, but I'm not worried about myself. There's time for more when he's recovered. This was all for him.

Roch has different ideas, though. He grabs a handful of my ass and encourages me to keep moving up his body. I don't know what he wants, so I look at him questioningly.

"Sit." He points at his face.

My cheeks heat. I don't know if I can do that. Can I?

"Now," he orders with his dominant tone that only makes an appearance when I've been bratty to him, and I scramble to obey.

I don't know how to do what he wants without hurting him, so I stand up and step up higher on the bed while he scoots down lower. Excitement and desire pool in my belly at the thought of his mouth on me.

"Naked," he says, pointing at my tank and panties.

I freeze while I process his words. He wants me to take my clothes off, but I've always been insecure about my naked form. I don't have big breasts or a big ass. I'm not sexy.

I'm flat-chested and have the stick figure of a twelve-year-old boy.

"Truly," he bites out.

Slowly, I divest myself of my tank top and panties while he gets comfortable underneath me. I'm grateful for the low light so he can't see my blush or the tremble of my hands.

After I'm fully nude, he yanks on my calf, pulling me from my self-conscious thoughts. I lower myself until I'm on my knees above his shoulders, hovering my nearly bare pussy above his face.

His eyes lock on my core, and licks his lips as though I'm his favorite meal. He wraps an arm around my thigh and pulls me down the rest of the way until his mouth is on me. With a flattened tongue, he licks from my asshole to my clit, guiding me with a hand on my ass. Electric pleasure shoots through my body, and like a drug, I want more.

He repeats the motion, and I tumble forward, gripping the headboard to steady myself. I can't trust my wobbly legs to not collapse completely when he does things like that.

He works me over with his mouth. Probing in and out, flicking my clit, and swirling his tongue all over my flesh. Then he presses a finger inside, curling it against my G-spot, while he eats me like a man starved.

Before long, I lose myself. Grinding against his mouth and throwing my head back in ecstasy. I lose myself in the moment, feeling something building deep inside. I release the headboard to massage my achy breasts, and I pinch and tug at my nipple.

That's all it takes to send me spiraling over the edge.

I scream his name as I come, barely able to stay upright. Tingles spread throughout my body, and my pussy clenches tight around his finger, thankful to have something to grip onto. I ride every wave of pleasure as it rocks through me until I finally come down.

I fall to the side, in a heap of boneless limbs, and laugh. A perfectly happy, love drunk, post-orgasmic laugh. I can't believe I'm here, in Roch's bed, recovering from an orgasm he gave me. It's too good to be true.

That thought sobers me up some.

I look over and find Roch watching me. I scratch my fingers through his beard and kiss him, our tastes mingling between us. He looks as content as I feel, reassuring me I'm not in this alone.

"That was amazing," I say against his lips.

He nods in agreement.

"But now I'm hungry." I get out of bed and throw on my panties and his T-shirt. "Think there's food in the kitchen?"

"No." He gets out of bed, too, his cock limp between his legs. Another jolt of arousal tickles my core at the sight.

Not now.

"What did the guys have for dinner? I'm going to check it out and see what I can scrounge up."

"No," he repeats, pulling on his underwear awkwardly with one hand. "Naked."

"I'm not naked. Your shirt hangs to my knees."

He stalks over to me and pushes me back onto the bed.

"But I'm hungry," I pout.

He huffs and tugs his shirt off me, exposing my breasts, which I cover with a hand. He eyes me like I'm an idiot because he just had his mouth on my cunt, but I don't care. This whole naked thing will take some getting used to.

He pulls the shirt over his own head, ignoring the fact it's inside out. He opens a drawer in his dresser and produces a pair of sweatpants. I watch him struggle to put them on for three whole minutes before I roll my eyes and help pull them up his legs.

Standing in front of him topless, he cups my breast and ducks down to give me another searing kiss, leaving me breathless. He taps the tip of my nose and walks out the door, hopefully, to bring back food, though I don't know how he's going to carry it.

I find my tank top on the ground, put it back on, and then sit down on the bed to cuddle Karen. She all but ignored our earlier activities, too tired to pay us any mind.

Ten minutes later, someone kicks the door. I rush to open it, revealing Roch, with a tray of food. I take it from him before he drops it, and carry it inside.

We make a bed picnic, sitting cross-legged facing each other. He hands me a paper plate with a sandwich he clearly made himself, judging by the fact that peanut butter and jelly are spilling off the bread. In addition to the sandwich, he also brought a bag of chips, a bowl of blueberries, and two grapefruit sparkling waters.

"This is my favorite flavor," I say, popping the top off the water and gulping half the can down. "Thank you."

He nods and takes a bite so big, half the sandwich disappears in his mouth. Of all the things we've done together over the years, we've only shared a couple meals. Once, the first day we met when we had pizza, and maybe a total of three times since, whenever Mom could talk him into staying for dinner.

For some reason, it feels even more intimate than what we were doing twenty minutes ago. I have him so high on a pedestal, sometimes I forget he's a regular human who does normal things. Like eat a sandwich.

The dogs gather around the bed, strings of drool hanging from their mouths.

"Gross," I giggle.

Roch takes notice, snaps his fingers, and points to the front room. With lowered heads, they all obey, leaving us alone again.

"Aww, now they're sad."

He tilts his head and gives me a pointed look that says, "They're dogs. They'll be fine."

"I'm still going to give them treats when we're done."

I toss a handful of blueberries in my mouth, savoring the mix of tart and sweet. An idea forms, and I pick up a single berry.

"Open," I say.

He shakes his head.

"Open, please."

He huffs, and then his mouth forms an O. I toss the blueberry, but I'm a terrible shot, so it bounces off his head. I giggle and hold up another one. He's obviously annoyed, but he lets me have my fun. Ten blueberries later, I make it in his mouth, and I jump up and cheer.

When I look over at him, I nearly fall over in shock. He's not smiling, but the left corner of his mouth is tipped up ever-so-slightly. It's such a small change, I don't think anyone else would notice. But since my favorite hobby over the last eleven years has been studying him, I see it.

My heart thuds in my chest with love.

Chapter
NINETEEN

Roch

A knock wakes me up in the morning. Rays of sunlight stream in from a slit in the curtains, illuminating Truly's face. Her deep brown skin glows, making her look like a goddamn angel.

My angel.

She's been staying with me for days now under the guise of needing to help me. At least that's what she tells Aiyana. She also told her she has her own room. It's a bald-faced lie. She's been in my bed with my dick down her throat and her cunt in my mouth.

The knock sounds again and I jump out of bed before it wakes her. I can't pull up my own pants without straining myself, so I don't bother and answer it in my underwear.

"Need you next door," Goblin says with a serious tone and a frown on his face.

I stare him down, folding my arms over my chest.

"The guys were attacked on their run again. We're whole,

but..." He trails off, looking behind me to make sure Truly isn't within hearing distance.

"Asleep," I reassure him.

"They killed one of 'em and captured two others. They're in the basement."

Moving back into guns didn't mean my killing days were over, it meant I'd now be doing it for free. Any of us could take care of the assholes, but I'm better at getting information than the others.

I nod and close the door, scrubbing a hand down my face. For the last few days, I've been cocooned in a bubble with Truly. She consumed me, made me forget who I was. Being called to the basement is a sobering reminder. Darkness clouds around me in a black smoke that I breathe into my lungs, accept into every pore, and the old me emerges.

I should send Truly home. She's become comfortable around here, and although she knows never to enter the Chapel and never to go downstairs, it doesn't mean she won't.

Instead, I let her sleep. It's less suspicious to disappear for a while, than to kick her out.

I don't bother with a shirt and barely manage to pull a pair of sweats on. I cross the lawn, tossing my sling into the yard, and enter the clubhouse. I'm done with this injured bullshit, and I can't look weak in the kill room. Goblin meets me at the door and walks with me down the stairs.

"One of the guys is Antonio Rinaldi. He's up high in the Corsetti chain of command. The other is no one important, but he might still have information."

I nod. Knowing those facts, I know who will die first.

Inside the kill room, I find Khan with a bloody apron on, standing in front of two men who are tied to metal folding chairs. Each of them are sporting swollen eyes and cut lips. Khan prefers brute strength, while I prefer to make them bleed methodically.

I go straight to the tray that has my obsidian knife on it. I hold it up, more for our guests than me. The handle is made from polished elk horn and joined to the blade with sinew. The obsidian itself has been ground, abraded, and pressure flaked to ensure it's sharper than any other knife you could purchase. I order them custom from a whack job in Arkansas who doesn't trust the government and therefore will never tell cops shit if questions get asked.

"Have you met Roch, Antonio?" Khan asks nonchalantly. "Scary motherfucker."

"I'm not saying shit, Khan. Might as well kill me now," the greased-up Italian says defeatedly.

"You want a clean death, you gotta help us out a little."

Antonio hocks a bloody loogie onto the cement floor. It's a disrespectful gesture I don't appreciate. I move behind him and tilt his head back until he's looking at the ceiling. I fight through the pain of moving my arm and make line after line of small cuts to his face, covering his forehead and cheeks.

His brow furrows as I methodically slice into his skin. The thin cuts themselves feel as benign as a paper cut, so I understand his confusion.

I set the knife down, toss Khan a face mask, and turn on the air vent. We're going to need ventilation for this next part. I open one of the cupboards, finding the industrial sized bottle of ammonia.

"No. No. No," Antonio cries.

"Ouch. That's going to sting a little. You sure you don't want to tell us what Anthony is up to? Maybe his plan for that storage unit and why he's been talking to Victor Knight. I mean, we can assume, but the confirmation would be nice." Khan drags a hand down his face, opening the thin cuts wider.

His eyes widen comically.

"Oh, you didn't think we knew? That's cute." He gives me a nod.

I tilt Antonio's head back again and pour the ammonia over him. He screams loudly, which was a mistake, because not only does it get into his wounds and in his eyes, now it's in his mouth. I set the ammonia down and watch as he sputters and retches.

"Maybe you want to save your superior?" Khan grips the chin of the other guy and squeezes. "I'll let him go if you give us more information."

"I-I don't know anything, man. I'm just a soldier," he stutters.

Khan nods to me again and I pick back up my knife. This time, I cut Antonio's shirt off his body and then slice longways across his chest and abdomen. He makes pained sounds that annoy the fuck out of me. I pick the ammonia again.

"What's your name?" Khan asks the frightened man who just pissed himself.

"Louis," he answers.

"I'm going to let you live, Louis."

The man looks almost relieved. Clearly, he hasn't thought about what that means.

"You can go back to Anthony, tell him everything that happened here and let him know you failed to keep one of his top guys alive. What do you think he'll do to you?" He asks, pacing the room calmly. "Or you can tell us what you know and we'll kill both of you quickly."

"I'm not lying. I don't know shit. Anthony told us where and when to go. That's it. That's all I know."

"That's unfortunate. You should've asked more questions."

I dump the caustic liquid down Antonio's chest, sending him into another fit of screams. I trade the ammonia for a roll of duct tape and wrap it around his head a few times until his mouth is covered, muffling his cries. I can't fault him for acting like a fucking pussy. Not only does it sting the cuts, but he's also got the beginning of a chemical burn going on. It's not a fun way to spend a morning.

"Think harder, Louis."

"Fine, okay. I overheard him saying he gets his first shipment in two weeks," Louis spits out.

"Human shipment, right?"

"Yeah, but they're all crack whores and prostitutes. Victor doesn't want to send him anyone valuable until he sees how he does with his trash."

He barely gets out the last word before I'm reaching for my knife and dragging it across his throat, hitting his jugular, causing blood to spray down the front of Khan.

"What the fuck, Roch? Warn a guy next time." He jumps back and holds his arms out to his sides.

I watch Louis bleed out, savoring every second of it. The way he spoke about those women had me seething. People aren't fucking trash. Well, maybe these assholes are.

"I guess we were done with him, huh?" Goblin steps into the room, appraising the mess. "Now what do we do with this one?"

"Let's send him back. Maybe it'll be warning enough for Anthony to stop fucking with us," Khan says. "Goblin, go get Ford and Miles. Have them dispose of this one and dump

189

Antonio at the restaurant. Preferably before he dies, but maybe wait an hour. Give this asshole a little more time to think about his life choices."

"On it." Goblin leaves the room.

"Thanks for coming down, bro. I know you've got your girl out there, but your whole silent but deadly vibe tends to get people talking." Khan kicks the foot of the corpse. "You can leave all this. I'll have the prospects clean it up."

I nod and walk over to the sink. No one cleans my blades but me. They may be sharp, but they're delicate. By the time I'm done, Ford and Miles are walking in, both of them wearing black trash bags. I eye them up.

"What? We're sick of our clothes getting ruined. If it's not the blood, it's the ammonia." Ford points to the moaning man with his head lulling forward.

I shrug. I guess they have a point. My sweats are ruined. I'll be burning them later.

Upstairs, I hit the shower. Someday I hope to have a bathroom built into the casita instead of a freestanding toilet and sink. Now that Truly is in my life, it's time to start thinking about it seriously. Or maybe moving. I don't fucking know. How soon is too soon for those thoughts?

After I'm clean and changed, I plan to see if Truly's awake. Probably is by now, but Loki stops me before I can walk outside.

"Church."

I look out the back door at the casita. I should go tell her to stay put and that I'll be back, but if she ventures this way, she'll figure it out.

I take my seat at the table, wishing I had a cup of coffee. This definitely isn't how I pictured my morning going. I'd hoped to spend some time making Truly scream my name. Now that we've started this relationship, or whatever the fuck it is, I can't get enough of her.

Now that I've ditched the sling, I'm hoping she realizes I'm healthy enough to let me fuck her. She's worried about my injuries, but my throat feels a shit ton better, and my arm is achy at best. I'm good.

"In case you didn't hear, Antonio is being shipped back to where he came from and his friend is no longer with us," Loki says and everyone quiets. "The only information we got from him was that their first shipment is in two weeks."

I clench my jaw at hearing him call the women a shipment. I know it's his way of staying detached, it's the only way to survive this life, but they're innocent lives.

"So what do we do?" Moto asks.

"I think it's time to go on the offense," Loki says.

It takes me an hour to get back to Truly. Thankfully, I find her in bed still. She has her phone out and her thumbs are moving fast and furious across the screen.

I climb in next to her.

"Just one second. I'm trying to explain to Mom that you need me here." Seconds later, she tosses her phone on the nightstand and rolls toward me. "Your sling. Where is it?"

"Gone."

"The doctor said a couple weeks."

I'm still shirtless and she leans over, kissing around the bandage covered wound gently. She looks up at me with heat in her eyes. I should've known I wasn't going to have to do much convincing to prove I'm fine. She's a horny little thing. I know she's been counting down the hours the way I have.

"Kiss me," she whispers, crashing her lips to mine. She gently bites down on my lower lip and it's enough to drive me mad.

I roll on top of her, settling between her legs, and claiming her mouth with my own. I thrust my tongue inside to explore. She tastes minty, like she just brushed her teeth. Our tongues slide against one another, making me crave tasting her sweet pussy.

"You feel incredible." She rocks her hips, grinding herself on my erection.

I moan into her neck as I drag my tongue along her flesh. I tug her neckline to the side, and find a place at the base of her collarbone that makes her squirm. I suck her skin into my mouth, relishing in the hiss she lets out. I kiss my way across her chest and to the other side, where I repeat the motions.

She shoves at my good shoulder and I think she wants me to stop, but the second I pull away, she's tearing off her shirt.

Fuck me.

Her tits are perfection. Tiny handfuls with bitable nipples.

I cup one in my hand, loving the way her pebbled nipple feels against my palm when I squeeze her soft breast. I reach it and give it a little smack, loving the slight bounce of her supple flesh. I lower my mouth over the peaked tip and flick it with my tongue. She cries out in pleasure, her pelvis leaving the bed.

I give her other tit the same treatment, but this time, I cup her panty covered pussy with my other hand. She's soaked clear through the fabric with her arousal.

"Please, Roch. I need more. So much more," she whines.

I sit back on my heels, taking in her writhing body. Suddenly, I wonder if this is a smart idea. I don't know anything about how girls feel when they lose their virginity. Will she look at me the same way?

"Whatever you're thinking, forget about it. This is happening." She cups my hard cock. "I want this."

I pulse underneath her touch, my dick begging to let this happen.

Fuck it.

I hook my fingers underneath the string sized fabric at her hips and yank until those thin strips break apart. She's bare except for a patch of hair at the top of her pussy. I give it a tug, watching the scandalized look cross her face. My thumb drags along the seam of her lips, collecting the arousal that's seeping from her. I smear it across her lips and then lick and suck it off.

I kiss down her body, stopping again at her tits to give them more attention before going lower. I toss her legs over my shoulder and nibble at both of her inner thighs. It's the only place she has any meat on her bones. She tries to redirect my head, bringing my mouth to her pussy, but I'm not ready for that yet. She needs patience.

I press my nose into that sexy as fuck tuft of hair right above her cunt and inhale. She smells delicious. Like sex and sin. I grab a pillow and stuff it under her hips, positioning her like a meal laid out before me.

Using my thumb and forefinger, I spread her wide, exposing her clit. It's red and engorged, waiting to be played with. I swipe up the length of her cunt, collecting her arousal on the way and savoring her unique flavor. I flutter my tongue against her little bundle of nerves causing Truly's breaths to come out in harsh pants. She writhes underneath me, unable to hold still.

I hook my arms under her thighs and go to town on her. I fuck her with my tongue, I gently bite her puffy lips, and I flick her clit until she's screaming underneath me. I shove two fingers inside her to give her something to clench onto. I wait until her pulsating orgasm calms before pulling out and licking my fingers clean. Her eyes on me the whole time.

I was glad I had my own space before, but I'm especially glad now. I don't want anyone hearing her come apart like this.

She tosses the pillow and lifts onto her knees. With our eyes locked, she unbuttons my jeans and reaches down the front of my underwear, taking me in hand. She blushes and bites her lip.

"I want to have sex this time." She swipes a thumb over my leaking tip, almost making me come from that alone. I swallow hard, knowing I shouldn't be her first. She deserves someone gentle and who can spew nice words at her. "I need this, Roch. Please don't pull away."

I step off the bed and her shoulders fall. She thinks this is over, but instead, I strip in front of her. She realizes what I'm doing, and a wide grin spreads across her pretty face.

I push her back onto the bed and settle between her legs. Holding myself up with one hand, I grab my shaft with the other, guiding my cock into her wet heat. She gasps after I press in an inch, she winces at three inches, and she cries out when I'm fully seated. Her tears are so pretty to me.

"S'okay?" I grunt, forcing myself to hold still.

"Just a second," she says on an inhale. She wiggles around, adjusting to my girth. "Okay, better."

I watch the place we're joined as I thrust in and out slowly. A smear of blood appears on my shaft. Her innocence on my cock is fucking beautiful. I rub a finger through it and lick it off. I want to devour everything she gives me. Not just the pretty, the ugly too.

I want it all.

Chapter
TWENTY

Truly

I should be grossed out, but seeing Roch lick my blood off his finger is disturbingly hot.

I wanted to be brave when he took my innocence, but that shit stung as he stretched me to accommodate his size. My tears don't bother him though. Instead, they seem to spur him on.

I'm not surprised. He's unlike anyone I've ever met. He doesn't understand most emotions. Sometimes he'll pat my back or my hand when he knows I'm upset, but it's robotic and a learned behavior.

However, pain he understands perfectly.

Roch leans back on his heels, taking my body with him. I guess his arm must be feeling fine, or he's decided the pain is worth the pleasure. Something tells me the latter.

He fucks me hard and brutal, his hands on my hips, rocking me up and down his shaft. Each time I crash into him, it hits my swollen clit. Shooting zings of pleasure rocket through my body and have me climbing toward another release. I snake my arms around his neck, holding on tight.

His eyes bore into me, never leaving my face. It's intense. More so than I ever imagined sex with him would be. His expression is so telling, I can almost hear the things he would say if he were able.

Fuck yeah, right there.

You feel fucking amazing.

Give it all to me.

You're mine.

It's written, so clearly, all over his face.

He moves us forward, leaning over my body, but keeping his weight on his bent elbow. His opposite hand reaches between us and rubs circles over my clit. I never thought I'd come during my first time, but the things he's doing to me have me spiraling, hard.

"Oh my God, I'm coming," I call out, startling Karen, who until now has slept right through the bouncing and rocking of the bed.

"Now," he grunts out, breathy and demanding.

I do. I gasp and squeeze my eyes shut. My pussy contracts, thankful to have his dick there filling me up. My hips thrust on their own accord, needing him to speed up. He reads me so well and increases his pace. Every slide of his dick along my inner walls fills me with pleasure like I've never felt.

Before I've even come down, Roch comes too. It's silent, but I hear his breath hitch and I feel his hot seed spill inside of me.

Wait.

I feel him spill inside me.

He didn't wear a condom. I'm not on birth control.

He pulls out and kisses the tip of my nipple one last time

before jumping up. He grabs a washcloth from a hamper full of clean and folded clothes Sissy delivered to him like she's his maid. He dampens it in the sink. Then he's at my side, still fully nude, cleaning me up. He's gentle and careful with every swipe of the cloth.

I need to tell him about the condom, but I know he'll freak out, and I want this perfect moment to last longer. I don't want it to be ruined by reality. I'll tell him tomorrow and go to the pharmacy for a Plan B. Or maybe I won't tell him and just get the pill. Yes. That's what I'll do.

He gets up again and wipes himself off before pulling his underwear back on. I don't know what to do. Should I get dressed? I have to pee, but the toilet is out in the open. I can't do that in front of him. Once again, he sees the panic on my face and claps for the dogs to follow him.

I pad over to the toilet and do my business. Everything aches down there, but it only makes me happy because it means I lost my virginity to Roch.

I wash my hands and slip his T-shirt on. By the time I'm crawling back under the covers, he returns.

"Can we stay in bed for while?" I ask, feeling vulnerable.

He nods and gets in next to me. I snuggle into his chest and his arms wrap around me.

"Should you put your sling back on?" I ask.

He shakes his head.

"Are you in pain after…" I trail off.

He shakes his head again and kisses my forehead. "You?"

"I'm fine," I lie, ignoring the burning between my legs. "I'm glad it was you. I've only ever wanted it to be you."

He cups the back of my head and holds me in place while he kisses the hell out of me. I guess he feels the same.

My phone alerts me to a text message. I ignore it, but it goes off again. And again.

"It's probably my mom." I roll off the bed and find my phone.

Four text messages are waiting for me. All from Mom asking when I'm going to be home and reiterating how inappropriate it is for me to stay at a biker clubhouse. I need to have an honest conversation with her. The longer I try to sneak or pretend like nothing's going on, the angrier and more hurt she'll be when she finds out the truth.

"I need to go home," I say, searching the floor for my two-day-old clothes. "She's losing her mind. I think I need to tell her about us."

I watch him from the corner of my eye, waiting for him to object. But he doesn't. Instead, he stands up and gets dressed himself.

"You aren't coming with me."

His brows raise and he gives me a "wanna bet" look.

"Roch, she's going to lose her mind. You don't want to be there."

He ignores me, putting on his boots. He winces when he extends his injured arm. I knew he's hurting, but I don't know how much. I can't convince him to take it easy and heal properly, so I leave it alone.

"I mean it. She has guns," I warn.

I don't think either of us are at risk of being murdered, but Mom will feel attacked and put on the spot if he's there when I tell her. It needs to be her and I alone.

"Not scared," he retorts.

"Come on. Please let me do this on my own. I'll come back later and tell you how it went."

He slumps onto the bed and I take a seat next to him.

"Are you going to be around tonight?" I ask, resting my head on his shoulder.

He grunts.

"Do you want me to sleep here again? I know you're Mr. Tough Guy and don't need me anymore, but—"

"Always need." He pushes me onto the bed and pins me to the mattress with his body. Then gives me a bruising kiss meant to reassure me.

He succeeds.

I toss my bag in the back of my car and hop into the driver's seat. A prospect I haven't met yet, opens the gate for me and I drive away. I think Goblin said his name was Duncan.

Thankfully, Mom will be in the clinic for at least another hour before she takes a lunch, so I'm able to sneak inside. I'm still wearing Roch's shirt and my hair's a mess. She'd no doubt connect the dots and know what I've been up to, without me even saying a word.

I rush to the shower and strip. This time, when I take in my naked body, I see something very different. My nipples are puffy and red from Roch's attention, there's a red mark on my clavicle from where he sucked on my skin, and there's beard rash on my thighs from when he had his mouth down there.

I smile, thinking back on our lovemaking. I've had orgasms. I own a vibrator. But it didn't even come close to the full-body experience from this morning. His rough hands all over my body and the way he knew exactly how to get me off was hot.

If the last few days have been any indication about what a life with Roch will be, then I want it. I want his vulnerability, I want his possessive dominance in bed, and I want to be part of his family.

I rush through a shower before getting dressed. My stomach growls loudly. Mom would love for lunch to be ready when she walks in the door, so I find some veggies in the fridge to cut up and some left-over chicken to put in a salad.

I've just plated our meal when Mom walks in the door.

"You're home," she says.

"Not for long, I'm going back. But I wanted to talk to you about something." I set our salads on the kitchen table. "Sit. I made you lunch."

"Thank you. It's been a crazy day. You know Mr. Wilkinson's Australian shepherd, Snickers?"

I nod, taking a bite.

"Well, they were out for a walk today and came across a group of wild horses. Snickers ran after them and got kicked. Poor thing broke three ribs, but luckily there was no internal damage."

"Oh my God, that's terrible."

"I know. Poor thing. But I got her all wrapped up and feeling less pain." Mom gets up and pours a glass of water. "But I don't think you're here to talk about Snickers. Why don't you tell me what's on your mind?"

"It's about me and Roch."

Her posture straightens.

"I love him, Mom. You know I do. I have since before I knew what love was. He never gave me any hint he felt the same way until recently, and he fought me on it. He told me no," I explain.

"Then the accident happened," she fills in for me.

"Yes. Then the accident happened and maybe it was his life flashing before his eyes or whatever, but we want to be together."

"There are so many reasons why this is a bad idea, Truly." She rejoins me at the table.

"You think I don't know that? There's nothing you can say that I haven't thought about already." I start counting on my fingers. "Let me guess. He's too old for me."

She nods. "For one."

"He's messed up in the head. He's in a motorcycle club. He doesn't have his own home. He lives a dangerous life. What else you got?"

"Yes. To all of it and you can't deny any of those points."

"I can't deny they exist, but I can argue none of it matters."

"Your safety doesn't matter?" she asks incredulously.

"Do you honestly think Roch would let anything happen to me? He's been keeping me safe for years."

"Safe from yourself, maybe, but not from outside influences. Whatever that club is involved in is dangerous and by being associated with him, you're putting yourself in the line of fire."

"I hear you and I agree, to some extent. It's not ideal and I would much prefer him to have a job that doesn't require him to carry a gun or do illegal things, but it's who he is. And I think he needs someone like me in his life."

"You think you can save his soul? Make him choose the right?" Her voice pitches in irritation.

"I'm not an idiot, Mom. I know he's not going to stop what he's doing for me. I wouldn't ask him to do that anyway. I love him for who he is, the fucked-up parts included."

Mom rests her head in her hand, covering her eyes.

"I've spent my life making up for the fact you didn't have a dad. I felt responsible for bringing you into this world when I knew how risky your dad's job was. Then my worst fear happened and it left you at a disadvantage. I thought I was doing a decent job and raising you to be well rounded and stable—"

"You did, Mom. Falling for Roch has nothing to do with how I was raised."

"You have daddy issues," she says matter of fact.

I laugh at the absurdity. "No, I don't."

"You're looking for love from a man nearly twice your age. That doesn't happen with well-adjusted girls."

"Oh my God, I can't even believe you right now. Do you even hear yourself?"

"Yes. and I'm making perfect sense."

"You're being ridiculous. Roch isn't taking the place of Dad. That is a sick and twisted thought."

"Isn't he? Why else would you not try and date guys your own age?" she asks.

"I have, and no one has ever made me feel the way Roch does. We connect, Mom. You know this. You always have. From the day I gave him the hummingbird, we were inevitable."

"You were a kid when you gave him that. It meant nothing."

"Maybe not to you, but it did to me. It was no accident. It was fate."

"Fate?" she screeches. "You think the spirits sent you your soul mate at eight years old?"

"I do. And now that I'm an adult, I don't want to waste

time being away from him. If anyone knows how quickly someone can be taken from this world, it's you."

"It's not the same."

"It is. I'm sorry you can't see that." I stand up and dump my salad in the trash.

"I can't support this. I'd never forgive myself if I sat idly by and let this happen."

"I'm nineteen, Mom. You don't have a say in my decisions anymore."

"But that doesn't mean I have to watch the train wreck happen," she says quietly.

"Train wreck? Glad you have such confidence in me." I place my hands on my hips.

"It's not you who I don't trust."

"Roch? That's who you don't trust? The man who rushed into enemy territory to save his best friend? The man who adopted a dozen dogs, not because he needs that many dogs, but because he didn't want to see them put down? The man who has come to my rescue a million times?"

"There's more to him than a big heart, Tru. There are dark things living in him too. Evil things. I see it in his eyes."

"I can't deny that, but I also know that dark doesn't touch me. He wouldn't let it."

"He can't control that."

"So what are you saying?" I throw my arms out to the side.

"I'm saying if you want to ruin your life, I don't want to witness it happening." Her head lowers.

"You're kicking me out?"

"No. I'm saying you have a choice. You can live here and give up your rebellious streak, or you can leave and be with him."

"I can't believe you. Do you not see you're doing the exact same thing to me that your parents did to you?"

"It's not the same."

"Your parents tried to stop you from being with the person you loved. It sounds exactly the same to me." I storm to my room and slam the door. Tears prick my eyes, both in anger and incredulity.

It's fine. I'll stay with Roch until I find a job and can get my own place. I pause. Assuming he'll let me. He has his hang-ups about me being so close to the club. What if he doesn't want me living with him? Then what will I do?

I sink to the floor, crying. I knew Mom wouldn't be happy, but I didn't think she'd kick me out. It happened so fast, I didn't have time to consider the consequences. I wipe away the tears, feeling the sadness be replaced by anger. If she would rather me be on the streets than watch me be happy, fuck her.

I finish packing and load my bags into my car. I didn't see Mom in the house, so I'm assuming she had to get back to the clinic. I start the engine and take one last look at my childhood home.

It won't be the last. Mom and I will get through this like we do every time we fight, but it feels different with my car full of my belongings.

Chapter
TWENTY-ONE

Roch

I take a seat next to Sly in the dining room. Loki is finally taking Anthony seriously, but I still want to know everything about him and what's going on in case I need to step in and handle it myself. It's what I want to do anyway. I want to squeeze that motherfucker's neck so hard, his eyeballs pop out of his head.

"S'up, man?" Sly leans back in his chair and stares at the screens of the two laptops in front of him.

"News?" I ask.

"I'm trying to learn about this Victor guy, but he's like a ghost. Everyone knows about him, but no one knows him." He points to a picture of Victor talking to Anthony and his son outside of one of his clubs. "I guess it doesn't matter. Our beef is with Anthony, but I'm worried if we take him out, it'll piss off a whole new enemy. One we have no information on."

I nod. I see his point. I also don't give a shit.

"And the kid. If we take out his dad, won't he be the next

one we have to deal with? I don't know. Might need to get rid of him too."

I nod again. The less Corsettis in this world, the better.

"He's a college student." Sly clicks a few things on the screen. "Max Corsetti. Twenty-two. Sophomore at UNR. Would've been a senior, but took last year off. Not sure why."

Moto walks over and joins us.

"Are you talking about the kid?" he asks.

"Yeah. Trying to figure out if we include him on our Corsetti killing spree." Sly rests his hands behind his head.

"Looks like he's pretty comfortable around those assholes."

"Yep. Which is why I say he needs to go too."

I hear the floorboard squeak behind us and I look over my shoulder. Truly's standing there, a duffle bag over each shoulder. Her eyes are red and wide. They're also locked on the computer screen.

I stand up and move in her line of sight, shielding her from seeing more than she should. When I'm inches away, she shakes her head, coming out of the fog she'd been in.

"Sorry," she says, tucking her hair behind her ears, revealing that heart shaped birthmark I love. "Can we talk?"

I nod and we go back out to the casita. I lift Karen out of my hood and set her down on the bed.

Truly lets the bags drop to the ground before running right for me. I brace myself and catch her in my arms.

"She didn't take it well. She kicked me out and now I'm homeless."

I knew Aiyana wouldn't be happy, but I never imagined she'd go this far. Truly is her only daughter, and she's spent her life taking care of her and making sure she had everything she could ever need. Guilt socks me in the gut. I don't want to be responsible for tearing apart a family.

I also know there's nothing I can do to change it. I stopped fighting her. I took her virginity and her heart. She's mine now. My responsibility and my honor.

"Stay," I mutter into her hair.

"Are you sure?"

"Yes."

I lift her up and she straddles my waist. I take her lips with mine, claiming her. I walk us over to the nearest wall and press her into it. She lets out an oof, but doesn't remove her lips from mine.

I lift up on the hem of her shirt and she helps me to remove it. My cock throbs painfully. I had a taste of her tight pussy, and now I can't get enough. I want to be inside her as much and as often as possible.

She's not wearing a bra, so I'm met with the image of her bare tits. Her nipples are puckered tight. I dip my head down and suck hard. She lets out a high-pitched moan and flexes her hips against me.

I can't wait another second. I turn us around and carry her to the bed, tossing her on her back. I grip the waistband of the leggings she has on and yank them off her, panties included. Her pussy is already glistening with arousal.

I unbutton my pants and push them to the ground along with my boxers. I reach into my nightstand and grab protection. I was taking a chance the first time I came inside her. I didn't have condoms and was too caught up in the moment to stop and get some from the clubhouse. But today, while she was out, I stocked up. I barely let her into my life, I don't want to subject kids to it.

She watches as I roll it on and I shove into her in one fluid motion. Truly screams my name, a pained and turned-on sound. I wrap her legs around my waist and she hooks her ankles at my lower back.

She grips the blankets at her side, holding on for dear life as I fuck her with quick, short thrusts. My balls tighten, but I need to make her come first. I reach between us and press my thumb against her clit, making slow, small circles.

"Oh my God. That's it. Feels so good," she moans.

I wasn't sure she'd like a hard fuck, but the rougher I get, the more vocal she is, and the wetter she becomes. She's perfect. Everything about her.

She tightens like a vice around my cock and shudders. It's all I needed to come. I explode inside of her with a roar. Filling the condom with my cum.

Slowly, I bring us back to earth until I soften and slide out. I collapse on the bed next to her, both of us breathing hard.

"I didn't know sex was like this. How does anyone get anything done when they could be doing that instead?"

My lips curl into a smile as I gaze over her. She's so fucking beautiful with her hair fanned out all over, stark naked, and glistening with perspiration.

She reaches over and touches my mouth, a look of shock on her face.

"What?" I ask.

"You're smiling. I've never seen you smile. Not once. I didn't think you were capable."

The grin falls away and I narrow my eyes at her. She can't be right.

"You don't. Sometimes I see your lips twitch or your eyes twinkle, and I know you're amused, but never have you given me a full-on smile." She beams at me.

I scowl.

"No, give it back." She reaches over and pushes the corners of my lips up. She giggles and I lean away from her, causing her hands to fall away.

She rolls on top of me, her bare skin flush against mine. My cock twitches, gearing up for the next round. I can't regret being celibate for all these years when Truly was my prize at the end. I'll never tire of fucking her.

"So, you're okay with me staying here a while?"

I nod.

"It won't be forever. I have some money saved and I'll get a job."

I wrap my arms around her, palming her bare ass.

"Forever," I say. I don't want her leaving in a few weeks. I want to go to bed with her and wake up to her. I want to keep her close so I can keep her safe.

"Roch," she says, pushing off me and standing up. She scours the ground for her clothes, but gives up and throws my discarded T-shirt on. "I can't live here. I have to go next door to shower and I can't pee without kicking you out. This place isn't built for two people."

She's right, of course. But I've thought about it and it's an easy fix. The plumbing is already there, I only need to erect some walls and put on a door. Khan would help me and we could knock it out in a weekend.

"Besides, I don't want you to get sick of me."

I sit up and grab her by the hips, pulling her between my legs. Lifting my shirt up, I kiss and suck on the skin of her abdomen eliciting a moan. I pull the shirt off completely and pause to admire how fucking beautiful she is.

She complains about being too skinny and lacking curves

she thinks would make her womanly, but I have no idea why. She's long and lean, with the perfect amount of tits and ass. She's natural and sexy as fuck. Nothing like most of the women who parade around here with fake tits and injected lips.

I suck her nipple into my mouth, flicking the tip with my tongue. She arches her back and grips a handful of my hair, holding me in place.

She climbs onto my lap, straddling me. She's still wet from earlier. We need to talk about birth control so I can go back to feeling her bare around me. But not right now. Right now, I'm going to fuck her sweet.

Then I'll do it all over again.

"I'm meeting up with a friend from school for an hour," Truly says after returning from a shower. I'm still in bed, tired from our marathon sex.

I look at her questioningly. It's getting late and almost dark out. With everything going on, I don't want her to be out in the world without protection.

"Don't look at me like that. I'm only going for a coffee and I'll keep my phone on me." She scoops her cell off the nightstand and tucks it in her bag.

"Who?" I ask.

"My lab partner."

I get the feeling she's being intentionally vague, but I'm not her keeper and I want her to know I trust her.

"'Kay."

"I'll bring back some Chinese takeout if you want?"

I nod and reach for my wallet in my pants.

"I don't need your money. You're letting me stay here. I can pitch in for meals."

I grab a hundred dollar bill out and hold it out.

"What did I say? I don't need your money."

She might not need it, but I'll be damned if she doesn't take it. She's works part-time with her mom and I'm assuming that's over now. But I have few expenses and make a lot of money. My bank account is nicely cushioned.

I get up, still naked, and stalk over to her.

"Take it."

"No." She places her hands on her hips defiantly.

"Truly," I scold.

"Roch, you're not my sugar daddy. I can take care of myself."

I narrow my eyes at her menacingly.

"Fine. Whatever. Pay for Chinese if it makes you happy."

I bend to her level and kiss her pouty lips, tucking the cash into her back pocket.

"You're infuriating."

I nod. Can't argue that.

I trail kisses across her face, stopping at the heart-shaped birth mark. I pull away and trace it with my finger.

"My mom said most people wear their heart on their sleeves, but I wear mine on my face. No matter how I'm feeling, she can tell by my expression. That's why I was given the birthmark."

Looking at her now, all I see is love. I cover the mark with my lips, and cover her heart with my hand. It beats strong and fast, the same way it does every time I kiss her.

"Go," I say, releasing her.

"I'll be back soon."

She blows me a kiss as she walks out.

I miss her already.

Chapter
TWENTY-TWO

Truly

When I walked into the clubhouse yesterday, Roch was sitting with Sly, staring at a computer screen. Curiosity got the best of me and I didn't make myself known right away.

On the screen were multiple pictures. One of them was Max. The other showed Max's dad standing with a bunch of men I didn't recognize. From the way Sly was talking, they're responsible for all the attacks on the club. My jaw dropped.

Suddenly, all of the comments about Roch and the motorcycle club make more sense. Max tried to warn me away from them more than once, and I wonder what his dad has told him about the Royal Bastards, or if he was speaking from personal experience.

The evil and creepy vibe I got off Max's dad clicks now too. I could feel it from the first second I laid eyes on him and when he spoke, it only confirmed my suspicions. That man is dangerous and shady.

I should've fessed up, told them I knew who he was, but something in me said I needed to confront Max first. Maybe there's a misunderstanding I can help clear up. I don't know.

I get in my car and pull out my cell phone. As I drive away, I click on Max's contact.

"Hello," he answers.

"Hey, Max. It's been a minute."

"It has. I've been missing you. What's going on?"

"Are you busy?"

"Not at the moment."

"Can you meet for coffee?" I ask.

"Why don't you come to the house? I can have our chef whip us up some cappuccinos."

I'm not an idiot. If Max is mixed up with whatever his dad is involved in, I don't want to be alone in a mansion where no one will hear me scream.

"Actually, I've been craving a Frappuccino from Sunny Side. Can we meet there instead?"

"Sure."

"Great. Ten minutes okay?" I ask.

"Yeah, that'll work. See you then."

I disconnect the call and click on the 90s country station. Tim McGraw's voice comes through my speakers, singing a prayer for God to not take his girl. I belt out the lyrics, remembering the first time I heard this song. Dad was on leave at the time and I was playing in my room while Mom made us dinner.

This song was playing loudly from the kitchen and I snuck around the corner to see what was going on. I found them swaying to the music in the middle of the room. Dad was singing softly in Mom's ear and Mom had tears streaming down her face. When Dad caught on to her crying, he cupped her face and kissed her tears away.

I was young, but I recognized epic love in that moment.

I pull up to the café, and park. I don't see Max's Audi, so I go inside, order us both drinks, and claim a table in the back of the café. A few minutes later, he walks in.

Nerves bounce around in my belly, and I second guess my decision to meet with him. I remind myself he's a nice, normal, average guy. Unlike his father, Max is even tempered, funny, and charismatic. I'm sure he has no idea what kind of activities his family is involved in.

When he arrives, he spots me and I hold up his drink so he doesn't get in the order line. He smiles broadly and makes his way over to my table. I notice he's dressed fancier than normal in a black, tailored button down and slacks. His hair is slicked back and his short beard is brushed straight and trimmed from the last time I saw him.

"Hey." He holds his arms open and I stand up to give him a hug. We've hugged many times before, but knowing more about who he is, I don't like being this close to him. Not until I get more information.

"How are you?" I ask after we've settled across from each other at the table.

"Great. Happy summer is here so I can sleep in and not stress about essays and labs and finals anymore." He lifts his cappuccino to his lips and takes a sip.

"Same. It'll be nice to have some time off."

"Are you working at the clinic all summer?"

My stomach sinks thinking about the distance between Mom and I right now. We'll get over it, I know we will. She'll see this isn't a game I'm playing with Roch and that he's going to be in my life forever.

Hopefully forever.

"I don't think so. My mom and I are kind of fighting right now."

"Uh-oh. What happened? You guys are so close."

"I'm dating someone she doesn't approve of," I admit, and watch as his face falls. But he catches himself and soon his smile returns.

"Dating someone, huh? Must be a great guy to catch your attention. I know, I've been trying to get it for an entire semester."

"You're sweet." I don't know what else to say.

"Who's the guy?" he asks.

I knew he would ask and I thought about how to approach this on the drive over. I could be honest and see how he reacts. That would tell me if he's deep in with his dad or if he's an innocent bystander to the family business. Or I could lie and try to trick him into thinking it's someone else, so when I bring up the club, he's more forthcoming.

Ultimately, I decided on honesty. And the element of surprise.

"You know him. Remember Will from the party?" I purposely use his real name to humanize him.

His jaw ticks and his face hardens. His reaction sends gooseflesh spreading across my skin. I was wrong to think he didn't know about everything going on. He clearly has hatred for the club.

"Not a smart idea, Tru. I thought you were bright enough to listen when I warned you about him." He shakes his head slowly.

"That's actually why I wanted to meet with you," I admit. "I don't know what business your dad is in, but I know he has something to do with the attacks on the club lately."

His expression goes from disappointment to surprise in a flash.

"You know more than I gave you credit for."

"Listen. I like you. You've been a great friend to me. That's why I'm coming to you first. Please do what you can to get your dad to back off. He nearly killed Will the other night." I blink to clear the tears that threaten to spring free every time I think about what could've happened.

"I don't think you know what you're getting yourself into."

"Probably not. To be honest, I don't know why you guys are fighting. I'm a little out of my element."

"I can tell." He leans back in his seat, studying me. "You're a sweet girl. Too sweet for the life you're involving yourself in."

His comment irks me. I know I don't fit in with the criminal lifestyle and I don't want to, but my heart doesn't care. It never has. I love Roch and I'll do anything to protect him.

"I'm not *that* sweet." It's a weak argument. I know it, and he knows it.

"I see you care about him a lot." He scrubs a hand over his beard. "I'll tell you what. Let me talk to my dad. See what I can do. I'd hate for you to get hurt in all of this."

That was much easier than I thought it would be. My chest puffs a bit, feeling pretty proud of myself. Whatever I can do to help, I know Roch would appreciate it.

"Really?"

"Yeah. I can't guarantee anything. Their beef goes way back, but maybe I can dissuade him from taking this any farther."

"That would be amazing. Thank you."

"No problem," he says. "Now, talk to me about the classes you're taking next semester."

We chat for a bit longer about our plans for the coming year. Max is getting a business degree and only has a few courses left to take before he graduates, whereas I have a few years left if I want to get my Doctor of Veterinary Medicine degree.

"This was fun. We should get together again soon," Max says as we walk outside.

"Agreed."

"I'll see you later." He gives me a hug.

"Bye, Max." I wave as I get into my car.

"Bye."

Before I leave the parking lot, I order from my favorite Chinese place so it'll be ready for pick up by the time I get there. I also shoot Roch a text telling him I'm on my way back.

He replies with a thumb's up emoji. Normally, I would consider that emoji an attack of passive aggression. But it's Roch. He doesn't have a passive aggressive bone in his body. Everything he says and does is exactly what he means. It's what I love most about him. There's no questioning his intentions.

Max is a different story. I can't help but feel like our conversation was too easy. Like he was pacifying me.

Only time will tell.

Ten minutes later, I have dinner in hand and I'm back at the clubhouse. I feel weird about walking in the front door and I feel even weirder about knocking, so I bypass the main building all together and follow the path that goes down the side of the property.

Once inside the gate, I'm swarmed by dogs whose noses go crazy with the smell of food.

"Get back, guys. This isn't for you." I push my way through to the casita where I'm met with loud bangs and the buzzing of a power tool.

I step through the front door to see sawhorses holding up sections of wood. Khan has a power saw in his hand and protective eyewear on.

What the hell happened while I was gone?

I wave to get his attention. I don't want to startle him when I walk past and have him whack off a finger. After a second or two, he notices me and turns the saw off.

"Hey, munchkin."

"Hi. Want to tell me what's going on?"

"You're getting a bathroom," he says like I've just won a prize.

"Oh yeah?"

"Yep. Your man decided shitting out in the open doesn't work when there's two of ya."

He's so crass, I can't help but like him.

"I agree."

I make my way to the back of the space where the bedroom is and find Roch with a nail gun, framing out the area around the sink and toilet.

"How long was I gone?" I ask, turning in a circle to see stacks of sheetrock and plywood.

"Hour," Roch replies, deadpan.

"And in that time, you decided to build a bathroom?"

He nods like this is the most normal thing in the world. My heart flutters in my chest though. He did this for me. He wanted to make me comfortable. This robotic man who feels exactly two emotions—angry and horny—did all of this for me.

"I love it." I hold up the food. "I brought dinner."

"I love Chinese," Khan snags the bag from me and sets it on the counter. "Where are your plates, bro?"

"Care to join us?" I ask sarcastically and reach in the bags, pulling out white containers. "Roch owns exactly one plate. But we can eat out of the containers. I made sure there were chopsticks."

We take the food outside and sit around the fire pit. Looking around, I wonder if this could be my home. I know Mom and I will eventually repair things between us, that's a given. But even after we do, would I want to stay here? I want to be wherever Roch is, and I doubt I could convince him to leave, so I guess the answer is yes.

"Do you want me to stay here with you?" I ask Roch.

"Whoa, munchkin's diving in with the big questions." Khan shoves a hunk of sweet and sour pork in his mouth.

Roch nods, eyes locked on me, completely ignoring his friend.

"Like forever? Or just until I find a place?"

"This is getting a little deep for me." Khan tosses his empty container of food in the fire pit. "It's getting late anyway. We can finish this up tomorrow. Bullet said he'd help too."

The two men slap knuckles together before Khan disappears inside the clubhouse.

"Do you? Want me here forever?" I ask again.

Roch nods while reaching over and sliding my chair closer to his. He takes my container of noodles and sets it on the ground, then tugs me into his lap. His strong arms wrap around my waist and he rests his forehead on mine.

"Love you," he says simply.

My nose stings and I rest my arms on his shoulders, my fingers weaving through the back of his hair.

"I love you too. So much."

He stands up, me still in his arms, and carries me back inside, kicking the door shut behind us.

He makes love to me that night. Not the hard and mind-blowing way he's done before. This time is intense and all-consuming.

But in the back of my mind, I can't shake the worry that something's off.

Chapter
TWENTY-THREE

Roch

I step out of the warm spray of the new shower and wrap a towel around my waist. Took two days to get the bathroom enclosed and a shower stall put in. The new walls make the place feel much smaller, but it's worth it knowing Tru is more inclined to stay here with me.

I could buy a place, maybe somewhere close by. Fuck knows I have the cash for it. But this is the first place that's ever felt like home and I don't want to give it up. Not yet anyway.

I get dressed quietly and slip out of the casita, leaving Truly asleep in bed. Got church this morning and I don't want to be late. We've got a retaliation to plan and I want to be on the frontlines. I can't wait to peel Anthony's skin from his body, slice by slice.

Miles sees me coming and has a cup of coffee waiting for me.

"Want me to take one over for Truly?" he asks eagerly.

I shake my head. When I left her, she was bare ass naked, sleeping on her stomach, the sheet barely draped across her ass. Don't need the prospect seeing what's mine.

Inside the Chapel, I take my usual seat next to Goblin.

"How's it going, bro?" he asks, cig dangling from his mouth.

"Fine."

"How're things going with your girl?"

I nod. I fucking hate small talk. It's like nails on a chalkboard to me. Don't know why everyone feels the need to fill silence with meaningless jabber.

"Gotta tell you, she's a smart one. Had a conversation about socialism yesterday. She knows her shit. I'm impressed."

I nod, surprised when a sense of pride washes over me. Truly is charming everyone in this club—including Loki— and he's hard to impress.

"Quiet down!" Loki shouts over all the talking. "Here's where we're at. That Victor asshole, Franco, and all their security are gone. I think that puts us in a better position to attack. What are our options?"

"I say we blow up his house. Take out dad and son at the same time," Khan suggests.

"I don't think we need to piss off the entire Corsetti family. They're like fucking cockroaches. We start killing them off, this is never going to end," Loki says.

I clench my jaw. I still can't fucking believe he's putting off killing the fucker. He's attacked us twice, nearly killed three of us, and Loki doesn't think we should take them all out.

"Something to say, Roch?" he asks, noticing my reaction. "I know you've got this vendetta against him—and trust me I do too—but my job is to keep us whole. Franco is letting Anthony handle us now, but if we kill two of his sons, it'll be him and the entire fucking Corsetti mafia coming after us. We don't have the manpower to fight off an attack like that."

"What about blowing up the storage unit?" Sly suggests. "They've got a shit ton of money in that thing. It'll stop him from his trafficking ring—at least temporarily—and it'll send the message that we're not going to sit by and let shit keep happening to us."

"Roch, we have the explosives to pull something like that off?" Loki asks.

I do a mental run through of what we have on hand. We've got a decent stockpile of ammonium nitrate and diesel fuel out at one of our warehouses we use for storage. It's enough to blow Anthony's entire facility up.

I nod.

"Then let's do it." Loki lights a cigarette. "Do we know what kind of surveillance they have going over there?"

"They have two guards stationed at all times. There's a construction crew there during the day, but at night, it's just the guards," Sly says.

"Okay. Roch and Khan, I want you to find out which construction company they're using and lift one of their vans. Sly and Moto, you're in charge of loading and detonating. Bullet can park the van there tomorrow night."

"Me?" Bullet's eyes widen, making most everyone laugh.

"You'll do great. Just don't crash before you get there." Khan messes the kid's hair up good-naturedly.

"Fuck off." He glowers and tries to smooth down his hair.

"We all know what to do. Let's get it done." Loki bangs the gavel.

"Gotta say, I dig your girl," Khan says from behind the wheel of the minivan. It's dark out and we're headed over to the construction company's main office where the employees store their work vehicles overnight. "Kind of makes me want to lock down an old lady of my own."

I ignore his chatter. I'm glad everyone loves Truly, but it seems like that's all anyone wants to talk about anymore.

"Don't know how you landed her. I mean, don't get me wrong, you're a pretty motherfucker, but you're not the easiest person to get along with."

I glare daggers into him. Not because he isn't right, but it seems like everyone feels the need to remind me I'm a shit human being.

"Don't get your panties in a twist. I still love you." He flips the blinker and parks on a darkened street. "Wait here, I'll go get the van. Be ready if anything goes wrong."

We both get out and I move over to the driver's seat. I watch as he does a walk by of the building to find out where the security cameras are and what direction they're pointing. My cell rings and I hit the speaker button.

"There's a corner in the back that doesn't have a camera directed at it. I'm going to hop the fence and take the van back there."

I grunt and end the call.

He disappears along the fence line. I keep my eyes on the parking lot and street, making sure there are no surprises. Five minutes later, headlights pop on, and the white van with the company's logo on the side pulls out in front of me.

I follow him down side roads until we pull up to the warehouse where we're meeting Sly and Moto. I breathe a little sigh of relief when we make it without incident.

The guns are one thing, Miguel has paid off enough people that I'm confident we would get off on charges, but this is all us, and the local law enforcement wouldn't be easy to pay off. We've been lucky to mostly avoid getting locked up and I'd like to keep it that way.

"Excellent job, guys. This is perfect." Moto opens the back up and shoves aside all of the equipment. "Plenty of room."

"You got it from here?" Khan asks.

"Yep. We'll get her loaded tonight and we can deliver the package tomorrow night." Sly pounds on the hood.

"Awesome. See you back at the house."

Khan and I jump back in our vehicle and take off for home. Truly is helping Tabitha and Sissy make a big dinner for all of us. She's trying hard to make friends with everyone. I don't get it, but it's important to her.

Tabitha and Sissy are good girls, and they get pretty territorial over us guys. Much like everyone else though, Truly has them charmed and they get along well.

We walk in the door to the smell of garlic, onion, and butter. I spot Truly setting a pot of something on the bar. I sneak up behind her and envelope her in my arms.

"You're back." She turns around and lifts onto her toes for a kiss. "Everything go okay?"

I nod. I didn't tell her what we were doing, only that it was club business. I expected kick back, but she didn't press for more. There's a lot of shit I'll never tell her, not because I want to hide things, but because I want to keep her safe. The less she knows, the better.

We get in line and load our plates with fettuccine alfredo, salad, and garlic bread. We've just sat down, when Sly and

Moto walk in the door. They give a nod to Loki, letting him know everything's set.

"Birdie!" Truly calls over, and points to the empty chairs at our table.

Loki, Khan, and Birdie join us. The two girls prattle on endlessly while they eat. I'm glad they've become friends. This isn't an easy life, and having Birdie there to confide in will only make Truly feel more settled here.

"Crazy shit, huh?" Loki says, lifting his chin at the women. "Didn't think I'd see the day either of us were locked down."

"Right? Between Loki's man whore ways and you being… well, you. I never thought I'd see the day," Khan muses.

"Oh, he's still a man whore. But now, he's only a whore for me," Birdie says.

Loki groans. "Darlin', swear to God, keep saying shit like that and you'll be in trouble."

"Promise?" She winks.

Fucking hell. This place is getting soft.

"Excuse me guys, my woman needs sorting." Loki stands up, hoists Birdie over his shoulder, and stalks down the hallway to their room.

"They're adorable," Truly says, leaning into me.

"Stupid," I reply.

"It's not stupid. It's sweet." Truly rests a hand on my thigh, kneading my muscle and inching higher and higher. My dick takes notice and thickens, causing my jeans to become uncomfortable.

"Tru."

"What? It's all your fault I'm in a constant state of arousal," she whispers.

"Done?" I ask, nodding at her nearly empty plate.

"Sure am."

Then I do something out of character. I toss her over my shoulder and carry her out the backdoor. She giggles and slaps my ass the whole time, while all the guys hoot and holler behind us.

I'll regret this later when I'm getting shit for it, but to hear Truly laugh makes it worth it. I'm surly and unemotional, detached even, but she loves me anyway. If I have to act like an idiot now and then to show her how I feel, I can make that concession.

I throw open the door and toss her on the bed. She scoots back to the headboard, her brown eyes twinkling. I yank off my shirt, kick off my boots, and let my pants fall to the ground. She gapes when she notices the bulge I'm sporting.

I climb over to her and strip her T-shirt off. She doesn't have a bra on, she rarely does, so I'm met with her perfect tits. She shimmies her pants down and throws them to the side. I palm her breast, pinching and rolling her nipple while kissing her.

I've fucked her in a lot of positions in a short amount of time, but I've never hit it from behind, and that's exactly what I want to do tonight.

I jump off the bed and grab her left ankle with my right hand and her right ankle with my left. In one fluid motion, I uncross my arms, flipping her onto her belly.

"Holy shit," she says, craning her neck to look over her shoulder.

I climb over her and take a handful of her ass, kneading her soft, smooth flesh. Fuck, she's amazing. I trace along the thin piece of black fabric nestled between her cheeks until

I reach her covered pussy. Pushing her thong to the side, I press into her with a finger. I'm immediately drenched in her arousal.

I pull out and snap her thong against her skin. "Off."

She gets up on her knees and pushes her panties down slowly. As soon as they're gone, she sinks to all fours, her ass propped in the air.

"Fuck," I murmur, unable to take my eyes off her glistening pussy and the puckered hole right above.

I lose my boxers and position myself behind her. My cock screams for me to sink into her, but I want to play first. I push two fingers inside her, and leisurely fuck her while pressing against her asshole with my thumb. She gasps in surprise, but doesn't ask me to stop.

I pull out and spread her cheeks wide, lowering my mouth to her cunt. I suck and slurp while keeping pressure against her asshole. She screams out an orgasm and I use that moment to penetrate her back entrance. She mewls and whines, pushing herself against my finger and against my face while she comes.

"Holy shit, Roch. What was that?" She falls face first into her pillow, but her ass stays up in the air.

I give my throbbing dick a few strokes before entering her. She's so warm, wet, and tight. I take a calming breath so I don't shoot my load before I can make her come again.

I fall forward, covering her body with mine, hitting her at a different angle. I play with her tits while sucking on her neck.

"Oh my God. You're going to make me come again already."

I feel her pulsate around me, so I reach even lower to her

clit. I rub small circles while she climaxes, clenching around my cock, almost painfully. Her whole body shudders, her legs shake, and she moans incoherently.

I lift up onto my knees and dig my fingertips into her hips while I bounce her back and forth on my dick. I can't take my eyes off her asshole. I want to fuck it. Not today, but someday. I want to own all her holes. Make her mine in every way possible.

Wanting to see her ass jiggle, I slap her left cheek, followed by her right. She lets out a yelp, but her pussy grips me tighter and she cries out in pleasure.

"Again," she begs.

I crack a hand against her cheeks again, a bit harder this time.

"Again. Again. Again."

I slap her ass over and over until her ass is glowing red. It's a fucking beautiful sight, and one that has my balls tightening, ready to explode.

"Fuck," I choke out before pulling out and jerking myself off until ropes of thick cum paints her ass and lower back.

I rub it into her abused flesh like a balm.

"I don't think that'll fix the damage you just did," she says, giggling.

Probably not, but I keep rubbing anyway.

"Come on, caveman. Let's shower." She crawls off the bed and walks over to the bathroom, my semen dripping off her.

Fuck, I love her.

"We should talk about birth control," she says, her hair in a sudsy pile on her head. This shower isn't big enough for two, but it doesn't stop us from squeezing in here together, at least once a day.

I nod. I fucked up again tonight, but at least I had the foresight to pull out.

"I'm not on the pill, but I made an appointment earlier. Until then, I think we should use condoms. I'm only nineteen, I don't want kids," she says, but in a way that leads me to believe there should be a "not yet" at the end of that sentence. She turns her back to the spray to rinse the shampoo.

"Not ever," I say.

She whirls back around, her wet hair smacking me in the face. "You never want kids?"

I shake my head.

"I don't know if I do or not. I guess I assumed I would." Water beads on her skin and I want to lick it off. "I don't think I'm ready to say absolutely not. Where does that leave us?"

I don't know what to say. It's not negotiable to me. Adding a child to this fucked up life I live is selfish. There's a very real possibility I could be taken from this earth too soon, and I don't want to leave an orphan out there to grow up the way I did.

"Can you promise me you'll rethink it in a few years? I mean, if we're still together. I don't want to assume."

"Forever." I kiss her long and deep.

I didn't break all my rules for a temporary relationship. I broke them for my forever.

Chapter

TWENTY-FOUR

Truly

I pull up to Mom's house feeling like a boulder has settled in my gut. Everything has been so perfect lately. Roch and I are getting into a schedule and learning more about each other every day.

A lot is learned at night when I'm naked under him… or on top of him… or pressed against a wall, but it's not only the sex. If I thought I could read his body language before, I have him down to a science now. He's an easy study when so much about him is ritualistic.

From the way he dresses, to the time he wakes up or how he eats, it's all done the same way every time. He disappears on club business now and then, but I keep myself busy. I registered for school, applied for a few jobs, and spent some time with Birdie since we're both on summer break.

But something is missing. Mom.

In a lot of ways, she and I grew up together. She was young when she had me, and alone most of the time since Dad was always on a tour of duty. We're best friends and while I'm happier than I've ever been before, it won't feel right until I settle this feud between us.

It's evening, so I'm pretty sure she's home and not in the clinic. I stand outside the door, wondering if I should knock, or go right in. I've only ever lived in this house. It's weird to not feel welcome here.

The door opens right as I lift my fist to knock.

"How long were you going to stand out here," she says, folding her arms over her chest.

"Can I come in?"

"Sure." She turns and walks into the living room, taking a seat on the couch.

"Thanks." I close the door behind me and sit next to her.

"Are you here to ask to move back in?"

"No." I trace invisible shapes nervously over the top of my jeans.

"Are you still living in that hell hole?"

"The clubhouse, and yes. But Roch has his own home out back and he installed a proper bathroom to make it more comfortable."

"All it takes are four walls and a bathroom to impress you?" She shakes her head, realizing she's being defensive. "Sorry. Why are you here then?"

"Because it doesn't matter how perfect things are, something will always be missing if I don't have my mom," I admit.

"Are you staying in a relationship with Will?"

"Yes."

"Well, kid, I don't know what to tell you. My opinion hasn't changed. He'll ruin your life and I can't watch it happen."

"Why do you think he'll *ruin my life?*" I throw air quotes around her words.

"Because he's a murderer and a criminal." Her voice rises. "And you're not. You're smart and have a future, but mark my words, he will drag you down with him. Either to an early grave, or to a jail cell. Those are the only two places those guys go."

A conversation with Birdie flashes through my mind. She told me Loki's mom and Goblin's dad were both killed by the Corsettis. It's where this rivalry began. So yeah, Mom's not wrong. But even knowing the risks, I wouldn't change it.

"I understand your concerns, but hear me out. Please."

"Fine."

"This is going to sound bad, but do you remember when Will came here that first day?"

"When you were eight. Yes, I remember."

I wince. She's not making this easy.

"I know it doesn't make sense, but the first time I saw him, something changed inside me."

"You didn't fall in love with a grown man when you were just a child," she says incredulously.

"No. It wasn't that. It was more like I thought he was mine. In my mind, Dad had sent him to me. I had it stuck in my head he would protect me and keep me safe because Dad told him to. You definitely didn't help things when you called on him every time I got into trouble."

"I see my mistakes now."

"It wasn't a mistake though. I fell in love with him over the years. It changed from something innocent to… something else. I know it's difficult for you and I know you think you don't want this life for me, but I think you're wrong." I plead with my eyes for her to hear me. "My entire life, you've told me all you want is for me to be happy. Well, I'm telling you I'm happy. Really happy."

"And you're willing to die by his side?"

"If that's what it comes to. I would rather spend a short life with him in it, than a long life without him." Tears prick my eyes. It's the truest thing I've ever said.

She studies me for a long while as tears stream down my cheeks. Eventually, she wraps me up in her arms and holds me tight.

"I'm scared for you," she admits.

"I know."

"I can't live in a world without you. You're my best friend and half my heart."

"I know."

"But you're right. Will has always put you first, even with the club. He drops everything to take care of you, and I guess I have to trust that he'll work even harder to keep you safe now that you're together."

"He will, Mom. He does."

"I want you to move back in," she says.

"I can't do that."

"Worth a try." She pulls back and wipes my tears away. "You're so young. I hope you don't regret this."

"I won't."

She sinks back into the couch, emotionally exhausted from our talk.

"So, we're okay?" I ask.

"I have two conditions."

I roll my eyes. Here we go.

"I don't think they're unreasonable."

"What are they?"

"You have to stay in school, and I want you to come back and work part-time at the clinic again."

"Done."

"Wait, one more. I want you to bring Will for dinner."

He's going to hate that, but I'm too excited to argue.

"And then we're okay?"

"Yeah. Then we're okay," she repeats my words back to me.

"I love you."

"Love you too."

It's dark when I get back to the House of Bastards, as I now refer to it because the clubhouse reminds me of a childhood play structure. Though, nothing that takes place around here is safe for a child.

Not knowing where Roch is, I decide to go through the main house instead of walking around to the back. The second I'm inside, I know something's going on. The anxious energy is palpable even though no one is around except Tabitha and Sissy, who are both watching TV.

"Hey, where is everyone?"

"Don't know. They grumbled about club business and left," Sissy says.

"Weird. Have the dogs eaten?" I ask.

"Yeah, Roch fed them before he left." Tabitha stretches along the back of the couch lazily.

"Okay. I guess I'll head out back."

"Don't go. We're watching The Bachelor." Sissy waves me over.

"Okay." I curl up on the couch. I'm not much of a reality TV person, but I'm also feeling off not knowing what Roch's up to and I welcome the distraction.

"Popcorn," Tabitha announces, jumping up. "We need popcorn. Be right back."

An hour and two bowls of popcorn later, I hear the roar of motorcycles engines. The air around me thins and I feel like I can breathe again when all the guys walk through the door, laughing and joking. Trailing behind them is my serious man, but even he doesn't have his usual constant look of disdain.

He spots me on the sofa and makes a B-line toward me. He plops down on the sofa, taking my hand in his.

"Everything okay?"

He nods and kisses the top of my hand. I know even if he wanted to, he wouldn't tell me about where's he's been, so I drop it. There's no point in getting irritated about things I can't change.

My phone rings from where it's resting on the arm of the sofa. I lift it up and see a call from Max.

"I'll be right back."

Roch scoffs at the phone like it's somehow offended him, but he releases my hand. I step outside and hit accept.

"What's up?"

"Hey, Truly. How are you?" Max asks.

"I'm great. What's going on?" I haven't heard from him since the café so I'm certain this has something to do with that.

"I asked my dad about what we talked about. He's not on board for any kind of truce."

"That's what I thought you'd say," I sigh. It was worth a shot.

"But what if we forced them to talk."

"What do you mean?"

"I mean, we find somewhere safe for all of them to meet and figure out a way to get them there."

"Without them knowing?" I ask.

"Yeah, I mean maybe if they were in the same room, at the same time, they might feel differently."

"I don't know." It feels dishonest and I don't fully trust Max. "They aren't a family trying to stay together."

"Listen, I'm not supposed to know this, but the Bastards blew up my dad's storage facility tonight."

His words echo through my head. I don't question or doubt him. They were gone tonight, they rarely leave all together. I look in the window, seeing everyone sitting around bullshitting.

"Truly?" Max calls out, snapping me back to the moment.

"I'm here."

"I'm only telling you this because they pissed my dad off, even more than he was before. He's going to do something worse and we need to stop this before we end up being the ones who get hurt."

He's right. Things will keep progressing. What's next?

"I guess you're right. But I still don't know how I'll convince them to come."

"What if you called them from wherever we decided to meet up and told them you were being held?"

I wince, knowing that would trigger some bad memories for Roch.

"I don't know."

"We're in the same boat, you and me. We can see the things the people around us are doing and know it will get them killed. I think if we did this, it could be the end of this war. Then you and I could remain friends and the people we love wouldn't have to die." He sounds sincere, like he thinks this could help.

An arm snakes around my middle and I jump two feet in the air before realizing it's Roch. He lays open mouthed kisses along my neck before sucking my earlobe into his mouth. I don't want to worry that one day he won't be here to do this.

"Okay," I say to Max. "I'm in."

"Perfect. I'll text you tomorrow to let you know where we can meet."

"Okay. Bye."

I let the phone fall onto the grass and allow Roch to do delicious things to me. We're interrupted when we hear a commotion going on inside. Roch takes my hand and walks me back into the clubhouse.

I stop dead in my tracks at the sight of eight uniformed police officers standing next to the bar. Even more shocking is that Khan is belly down on the bar with his hands behind his back, being handcuffed.

"You have the right to remain silent," a large, mean looking man starts.

"What's going on?" I ask Goblin who's looking just as dumbfounded as everyone else.

"They're arresting him for grand theft auto, arson by explosion, and arson by possession of explosive devices." Goblin scratches his chin.

"No," Roch grunts and tries to step forward, but I grip tighter onto his hand, stopping him.

"You can't do anything now. He needs a lawyer," I say.

"We have a lawyer, but she doesn't like Khan much," Goblin says. "Guess she'll have to get over it."

"Call her," Roch says, jaw clenched tightly.

Chapter

TWENTY-FIVE

Roch

"**W**hat the fuck happened? Did you see anything when you lifted the work van?" Loki asks me during church the morning after Khan was arrested. His chair sits empty, making everything feel off.

I shake my head. I spent all night going over every move we made. There was no one around. Even as we drove to the warehouse, we didn't pass anyone.

"Security camera," I suggest. It's the only variable that I didn't have control over. Khan was the one who said the camera didn't reach in that corner. I didn't check to make sure he was right.

"Have we heard from Bexley?" Moto asks.

"I talked with her last night. She was going to call the district attorney this morning and get back to me," Goblin replies, lighting a cigarette with the one he just finished.

"Is there bail set? Can we get him out?" Bullet asks.

"Not yet. Should be coming anytime now, though."

Goblin blows a plume of smoke above our heads where it settles.

"This is fucked." Loki yanks his beanie off his head. "Goblin, as soon as you hear back, let me know."

"Will do."

"This is bad timing, but we've got a run this weekend. Miguel needs a shipment taken to Vegas. Moto, Sly, Bullet, and Ford will go. I hate to lose four of you right now, but I don't see a way around it. Miguel's watching us, we need to deliver," Loki says.

"We should think about patching in Ford and Miles. Maybe taking in some new prospects. With everything going on, we need more members." Goblin lights his third smoke in a row.

"Agreed," Loki replies. "But let's get Khan home, get this shipment to Vegas, and then we can talk more about it."

He bangs the gavel and we disperse. I pour two cups of coffee and take them to the casita. Truly is curled up in bed with Karen tucked under her chin.

I set the coffees on the nightstand and sit on the edge of the bed. Truly stirs and rubs my back.

"Any news on Khan?"

I shake my head. Having the VP in jail doesn't sit right. Not when I was with him. I feel responsible. If I only got out to double check. Khan is a lot of things, but observant isn't one of them, and if they have footage of him taking that van, I don't see how he'll get out of this.

"I'm sorry, baby." She lifts to her knees and hugs me from behind.

I never thought I wanted to be comforted or have some-one to share my problems with. It seemed too messy to have to talk things out with someone. I didn't imagine there was someone out there who didn't need my words to get me.

She's the exception to everything I am.

"Are you busy today?" She massages my shoulders, pulling some of the tension out. It feels amazing.

"New bike."

"That's right. Are you excited?"

"A little." I put a rush order in on a newer version of my old bike, which is sitting in a scrap pile on the side of the clubhouse now. Moto took one look at it, shook his head, and walked away. If he had no hope for it, I knew it was a total loss. He can fix almost anything.

I'm still grieving the loss. A man and his bike have a relationship. You get to know your machine, inside and out. It becomes a part of you. Now she's gone and I have to learn someone else. Fucking sucks.

A knock on the door interrupts us. I reach onto the ground and toss Truly my T-shirt. She fell asleep with just her panties on last night and I don't want anyone else seeing her tits.

I open the door to see Goblin. In his hand is Truly's phone. I recognize it from the black, sparkly case.

"We should talk."

I motion for him to enter.

"Maybe in private."

I shake my head. This doesn't feel like club business. Not with my girl's phone in his hand. If this has to do with her, she deserves to hear it from him.

"Hey, Gobbles," Truly jokes.

"Hey, kid. I found your phone on the lawn." He hands her the phone.

"Oh, thanks. I forgot I dropped it out there after everything with Khan." She briefly glances at the screen, looking nervous as hell.

What the fuck is going on?

"Yeah, I didn't know whose it was until I looked at the screen and saw a picture of the two of you." His eyes dart from me to her. "I also saw a text message that made me a little nervous."

"What did you see?" Truly asks, defensiveness lacing her tone.

"Maybe it's a misunderstanding, but are you and Max Corsetti friends?"

All color drains from Truly's face and her jaw drops open. I grab her phone. She doesn't have a passcode set, so I get right into it. Sure as shit, there's a string of messages between her and a guy named Max. She snags the phone from my hands.

"This is my private cellphone," she bites out.

"I get it, and I swear I wasn't snooping. But when I saw who the message was from and what it said, the puzzle pieces fit." Goblin scrubs at the back of his neck, looking uncomfortable as hell. "Roch, she's planning something with Max. She was going to lure all of us to some location where Anthony would be."

"No, that's not what I was doing." Truly turns to me. "You have to listen to me. I'd never do that. It's a misunderstanding."

It suddenly clicks where I know that punk Max from. He was at the party with Truly when I ran into her. She was there with him.

"What am I misunderstanding?" Goblin asks. "Max and his family are human traffickers. They take pretty girls like you and sell them to men who do unthinkable things to them. They use them up until there's nothing left, then they're sold to the next asshole or, if they're lucky, they're killed. Does that sound like the type of person you want as a friend?"

I slam the door in his face. Whatever's going on is none of his business. Not when it has to do with Truly. I'll get to the bottom of this without him standing there judging my girl.

I take her by the hand and sit her down on the bed. I'll hear her out before I make any judgements, but I hope to God she has an explanation because the evidence is pretty damning.

"Tell me," I demand.

"I wouldn't do that to you. You know that, right?" Her eyes well with tears, but I don't want a sob story, I need answers.

"Tell me," I repeat.

"Max was my lab partner. We got to know each other and hung out occasionally. I had no idea who he was and we weren't… whatever we are. I thought it was weird he knew who you were, but a lot of people know about the Royal Bastards, so I just brushed it off.

"Then the fight with my mom happened and when I showed up here, I heard you talking about Max and saw his picture. His dad's too. I met him once. He's a slimy asshole."

My blood boils thinking she was in close contact with Anthony.

"Dangerous," I grit out.

"I know. I got that vibe off him and I never went over to Max's house again after that one time I met him. Anyway, I wanted to help because I figured out it was Max's dad behind all of the attacks on you guys. So I met with Max. I asked him to talk to his dad. Tell him to back off."

I growl, low in my throat.

"I only wanted to help. Max said his dad wanted nothing to do with a truce, so we thought we'd force you into a room together. Get you guys talking or something. I don't know."

"Tricked you."

"No, Max isn't like that, and I don't think he's involved with his dad's business. He would never do those things Goblin said. He's not like his dad. He's a nice guy. I mean, he has a little crush on me, but he knows about us. He knows I love you and I'm not interested in him."

"Truly." I deadpan.

It's not her fault. She wasn't raised in this world. Aiyana did her a favor and a disservice by teaching her the world is moral and people are to be trusted. It's one of the reasons I love her. She's my opposite in every way and I love seeing the world through her eyes.

To her, life is a vacation. Everything around her is exciting and new. But I'm a local resident in this life. I see the dark underbelly.

It's also why she needs protection. I don't want that light in her eyes to die, I want to protect it. I want to keep the bad shit away from her so she never has to see the evil in people.

Truly's face tightens and her lips pinch into a tight line. I see her replaying every conversation she's had with Max, only this time through shrewd eyes. As realization dawns, her lips part and her brows knit together.

"He was using me, wasn't he?" she asks in a quiet voice.

I envelop her in my arms. She remains limp, lost in her newfound realization.

"S'okay," I murmur into her hair.

"How is it okay?" She pulls away from me. "I almost got you killed."

"No."

"Yes, Will, I did."

I don't miss the use of my real name. When she started using my road name, it was her way of accepting this life and even me, to an extent. Hearing her say Will is like her reverting to a time where my club life was kept hidden and detached from her.

"I shouldn't be here." She runs around the room, collecting her things, and shoving them into duffle bags.

I want to stop her, to sit her down so I can find a way to convince her, but how? Pour my heart out to her? I wouldn't be able to. My thoughts are so clear, but when I open my mouth to verbalize them, they get jumbled and don't come out right.

I approach her from behind, grab onto her shoulders, and spin her around.

"Stop."

"Don't you see? I don't belong here. I'm not made for this life. I mean, look at me," she argues. "I thought our age or our life situations didn't matter, that love was enough. My naivety will not only get you killed, but your brothers too."

"Truly." I clench my jaw so tight it aches and my chest constricts painfully. I need to say something, anything to make her stop. If she would calm down, think things through, she'd see it's not a bad thing to be a decent human being.

"Yesterday my mom told me we would never work because you'd drag me down with you. She was right that we'd never work, but she was also wrong. Because it's me who's going to drag you down."

"Don't go," I say.

"I'm sorry. I can't stay. I'll get the rest of my stuff later." She throws the strap of her duffle over her shoulder and walks out, leaving me standing alone in the middle of my bedroom.

The spot in my chest that has been staying warm more and more each day turns so cold, it burns. I'm used to being left behind, but it's never felt this painful before.

I crumple to the ground, pounding on my head, trying to make my brain work right. It's all in my head. All in my stupid fucking head. Why can't I be like everyone else? Why does it have to this goddamn hard?

I hear a whimper come from behind me. When I look up, I realize I'm surrounded by dogs, all of them with their heads lowered and sad eyes. I look over my shoulder and see Karen on her back legs, her front paws paddling up and down. I reach around and scoop her up.

Sam, Tooth, and Patch lie down, resting their heads in my lap and on my legs. All of my frustration doesn't leave me, but enough does that my heart slows and I stop abusing myself.

I don't deserve them.

Chapter
TWENTY-SIX

Truly

I toss my duffle into the backseat and jump into my car. Goblin stands near his bike on the opposite end of the gravel watching me as I drive away.

I'm embarrassed. More than that. I'm humiliated. When all the guys hear what almost happened, they'll be pissed. My stomach sinks. I hope they won't be angry with Roch for letting me get so close. It's not his fault I'm a naïve idiot who doesn't know when she's being taken advantage of.

One of Dad's favorite songs comes on the radio. Garth Brooks sings about having friends in low places. I smack the power button on my stereo. Country music isn't going to help today.

I'm so angry. I can't believe Max tricked me. All this time, I considered him a friend. I trusted him. I'm so stupid. So, so stupid.

Every time he mentioned what bad guys the Bastards are, or tried to pry information out of me, I thought he was interested and cared about my well-being. Really, I was just a pawn.

I drive around aimlessly. I could go to Mom's house, but it doesn't feel like home anymore. Plus, I can only imagine the amount of gloating she would do if she saw me.

I pull into a parking lot. My hands are shaking and I shouldn't be on the road. The second the car is in park, tears spill down my face. I picture Roch's devastated face. I could see he had so much he wanted to say. Words he thought would stop me from leaving.

I hate myself for being so stupid. I was a child trying to fit into an adult world I knew nothing about. I convinced him I was ready and I could handle it. I made him love me and then ruined it.

I should've stayed in my lane. I'm a student, an animal lover, and a loner. Why did I think I could belong in a family? Have friends who genuinely care about me? That's not how my life works.

A horribly stupid idea pops into my head, but I'm so pissed, I don't care. I dig my phone out of my bag and call Max.

"Hey, Truly. Everything okay? I didn't hear from you last night."

"You're a piece of shit," I reply.

"What?"

"I know what you did. I know this was a plan to trap the Royal Bastards. You used me."

"I don't know what you think, but that's not what this was. I was being honest with you. You're a good friend and I didn't want this dumb feud to come between us."

"You're lying. We were never *that* good of friends," I spit out.

"Where is all this coming from?"

"It all makes sense now. Why you were warning me off of Roch. Why you kept asking all those questions. I thought you wanted to fix things. But that's not who you are, is it?"

"Truly, this is ridiculous."

"No, it's not. Goblin found my phone and saw your texts. He thought I was plotting against them."

"Fuck. Did they hurt you? Where are you?"

"Hurt me? They would never hurt me."

"You think they don't hurt people for less?"

"Maybe they do, but not me. Roch loves me and because of you, we broke up." My nose runs and I swipe at it with the back of my hand.

"Where are you?" he asks again.

"It doesn't matter. I don't ever want to hear from you again."

"There's an explanation for this. All of it. Please meet with me. Let's talk it out."

"So you can kidnap me? Maybe sell me into a life of slavery? That's what the family business is now, isn't it?"

"I'm not going into the family business. I'm only pretending to so my dad will pay for college. Once I graduate, I'm out. I'm done. I'd never do the things he does."

I'm so confused. I don't know who to believe.

"Truly, let me come to you. Anywhere you want. Out in public so you know you'll be safe," he pleads.

I rest my forehead on my steering wheel. I don't know what to believe, but if Max is telling the truth, maybe he'll give me information so I can report his dad to the authorities. That way he won't be killed by the Bastards, but everyone will be free from him.

"Fine. Let's meet at the café."

"Thank you for hearing me out. Give me a half hour, okay?"

It's not too late to say no. This could be me being gullible all over again. I don't trust myself, but I also have to fix this mess I made. I don't want the Bastards to hate me and I know once they hear what almost happened, they'll despise me.

"Truly," he snaps, startling me.

"Sorry. Yes. Okay. I'll be there."

I hang up and drive over to the café. This time, I don't bother getting drinks. Anything I put in my stomach right now would no doubt reenter the world in a not so dignified way.

I take a seat close to the entrance and position myself facing the door. I don't want Max's psycho family to show up without me seeing them.

I thrum my fingertips on the table, my knee bouncing uncontrollably. Sure enough, Max pulls up in his Audi right on time. He's wearing what must be his uniform these days, the same black button down and slacks.

"Hey," he greets, taking the seat across from me.

"Hi." I sit up straight, not wanting to show weakness.

It's quiet for a long moment, both of us sizing the other up. Finally, he breaks the silence.

"I'm so sorry you found out what fucked up shit my dad does, but you have to believe me, I have no intention of taking over for him. At all."

He's either telling the truth or he's an excellent liar.

"I don't know if I believe you," I admit.

"Believe me or not, I only wanted to make things better, for both of us."

"It doesn't change anything. The plan is ruined, and Roch and I broke up."

"I'm sorry to hear you're upset. I know you cared about him, but I stand by what I said about him being dangerous. It hurts now, but you'll be better off in the long run."

"How could you possibly know that?"

"Because he can't protect you. Not like I can. You know who my dad is now, surely you're smart enough to figure out having an entire crime family behind you is better than a ten-person biker gang."

I shake my head. What the hell is he talking about? Being with him was never on the table. Even if he wasn't related to the worst kind of person in the world, I don't have romantic feelings for him.

"Max, we won't ever be together."

"Not right now, you have a broken heart. But someday. I'm going to prove myself to you. After I graduate, you and I can run away together, leave Roch and my dad behind us." His voice grows louder with each word and the other customers take notice.

Chills run up my arm. He's delusional and contradicting himself left and right. Does he think he can protect me because of who his family is? Or does he want to run away and have nothing to do with them? I'm certain he wouldn't get out that easily.

"I think this conversation is over. Please don't call or text me again," I say in a hushed tone, not wanting to draw any more attention to the conversation.

I stand up and rush out the door to my car, but I'm not fast enough. Before I get it open, I'm being pressed into the hard metal painfully.

"Max, let me go," I say calmly, but firmly.

"Not gonna happen, princess." He pulls back on my arms and slams me into the door again. "Here's what is going to happen. You're going to walk over to my car and get in. I'm not done talking."

"You're hurting me. Let go." I push back on him, but he barely budges. That's when I feel it. Something sharp digs into my skin before I feel warmth trickle down my side.

"Feel that? It's a knife, and it's currently working itself into your body. Might want to rethink," he says through clenched teeth, sending spittle onto my ear and cheek.

Bile rises in my throat, but I swallow it down. I'm not going to be his victim. He digs the knife deeper when I don't respond, sending searing pain through my abdomen.

"I'll go. I'll go." I hold my hands up.

"Lower your fucking arms. I don't need to parade you across the parking lot looking like a hostage."

He removes the blade and walks me over to his car. As I slide into the passenger seat, he's ducking his head in and opening the glove box. He brandishes a zip tie.

"Hands together," he orders.

I clasp my fingers together and cringe when he feeds the plastic through the zipper and pulls tight.

"Ouch."

"Shut up."

He slams the door closed and jogs to the driver's side. Once behind the wheel, he throws the car in drive and takes off down the road.

"Where are you taking me?"

"I don't know, Truly. I didn't exactly plan this out." He slams a hand on his steering wheel. "Fuck."

"Then let me go. I won't tell anyone, I swear."

"Right," he huffs. "Don't believe that for a goddamn second."

He makes a series of turns that puts us on a street I know well. It's the one leading up to his house.

"Please don't take me to your dad. You know what he'll do to me."

"What choice do I have? Maybe he'll respect me, give me more responsibility if I deliver him a Bastard's girl."

"That's what this about? You need your daddy's approval? Has everything you said been a lie?"

His fist cracks against my cheek. The force of it has my head slamming into the window, dazing me, making me see stars and I feel my face swell instantly. I roll my forehead along the cool window and cry out in shock and pain. I've never been hit a day in my life.

"Shut. The. Fuck. Up."

I don't even recognize who he is anymore. He's not the same person that tried to get my attention with sneaky touches and compliments. The man next to me is pure evil, and I walked right into his trap.

He parks his car in the garage before getting out and opening the passenger door. He reaches inside, grabs my arm, and tosses me out of the car. I stumble and eventually fall to the cold cement floor.

"Get up."

I struggle to my feet with my hands still bound. He shoves me into the house and sits me down at the dining room table. The same table we studied at, ate meals together on.

"I'll be right back. Don't bother running, I'll catch you." His sinister smile frightens me to my core.

The second he's out of sight, I immediately start thinking of ways to escape. My eyes skim over every surface. If I can make it to the kitchen, there's a block of knives. But I don't know if I have time. I stand up and in doing so, feel my cross-body bag slap against my leg. My cell phone is in my bag.

I sit back down and maneuver it onto my lap. I unclasp it and dig inside. It's difficult to lift with my palms firmly pressed together, but I manage to get it onto my lap. Thankful I never set a passcode, I unlock the screen with a swipe of my finger.

My background image is of Roch and me. The one and only selfie he allowed me to snap of us. The smile on my face brings tears to my eyes. Things went so wrong so quickly.

I bring up my favorites in contacts. There's only one person I can call who might stand a chance of rescuing me. My finger hovers over the button. Calling him means putting his life and his brother's lives at risk... again. But not calling means my life will end in the most horrific way.

I connect the call. I can hear the faint ringing, but there's no way to bring the phone to my ear, and I don't want to hit the speaker button in case Max is somewhere close by and can hear me. The second I see the call answered, I pray it's him and not his voicemail.

"Roch," I whisper shout, bending in half to try and hear.

"Tru?" He sounds panicked already.

"I don't have much time. Max took me. I'm at his house. I don't know what he's going to do. Please help."

"Shit," I hear him say and then there's a series of crashes and bangs.

"Please, Roch. I'm so scared."

"S'okay. Coming."

I breathe a sigh of relief, but it's short lived. Leather soles clack against the marble and I know my time is up.

"I have to go now. I love you. I've always loved you," I say through a sob.

"What the fuck are you doing?" Max sprints over to me, picking up the phone and throwing it to the ground. He crushes it with the heel of his shoe.

He storms over and backhands me across the same cheek that took his fist earlier. My skin splits open and blood runs down my face, landing in a pool on my arm.

"That's enough, son," Max's dad, Anthony, says in a calm tone that strikes terror in me. "Nice to see you again, Truly. My son was just catching me up on the unfortunate events that landed you in my dining room. While this wasn't the plan—"

"What plan?" I ask.

He pulls a chair out and sits down, every movement is methodical and deliberate. He rests an ankle on his knee and leans back so casually, you'd think we were old friends sitting down for coffee.

"After your biker boys killed my brother, it put me and them on an uneven platform. They took something from me, so it was only right to take something from them. I didn't want to take over my family's business, I only wanted to reap the rewards. It allowed me a nice life where I was free to enjoy other interests." A sly grin spreads over his thin lips. "But your boys ruined that for me. Suddenly, I was in charge. I didn't want guns. It's a stupid trade and the money is laughable. Dom always did take the easy route. It was only natural for me to change our business model."

"Like buying girls, raping them, and eventually killing them?" I ask, my tone laced with disdain.

Max kicks me in the shoulder, throwing me off the chair

where I land on my side. Something snaps in my elbow when it hits the hard marble, and sharp, shooting pains run up my arm. I roll onto my back, crying out. Max grabs me by the arm and hoists me back onto the chair.

"You should learn your place. You're going to be fun to break," Anthony sneers. "As I was saying, I had my men dig into each member. The president's girlfriend was the obvious choice, but she was so well protected. None of the other losers seemed to have easy targets, until we got to William Pellman. It didn't take us trailing him for long to see he does have people in his life he cares for. You and your mother."

"Leave my mom out of this. She has no ties to the club."

"I'm not going after your mommy. Not yet anyway."

"So you planted your son in my biology class?" I ask, allowing the puzzle pieces to fall in place.

"I did. He was away at college anyway, so it was just a matter of getting him transferred. He was all too willing when I showed him your picture and told him I'd teach him how to handle pets, with you as his first."

Bile rises in my throat. Pets? Like a human pet? Roch better get here soon.

"Why go through all the trouble? Why involve Max when you could've just taken me in the first place?"

"That was my initial thought. But my son was distancing himself from the family, threatening to not come home and be part of the business." He leans his elbows on the table and steeples his fingers, his gaze shifting to Max. "He always had a soft spot for innocent girls he can ruin. I knew once he saw you, not only would he reinvest himself in my agenda, but you'd be his prize at the end."

Max unbuttons the top few buttons of his shirt and swallows

hard. This is news to him too, and he doesn't look like he enjoys being played.

"Why don't we finish this conversation in the car? I suspect your dark avengers will be here any minute." Anthony gives Max a smug look and stands.

Max lifts me to my feet and drags me back out to the garage. Instead of his Audi, he shoves me into the back seat of a black Escalade.

Max climbs in after me, while Anthony gets in the passenger seat. A large man dressed in a suit gets in on the driver's side.

"Take us to the property," he orders.

"Yes, sir," the driver replies, not caring about the bloody girl with her hands bound in the back seat.

I want to plead with him, ask him for help, but I'm certain it would be fruitless. This man works for Anthony. He's not going to go against his boss.

"As I was saying, the plan was for my son to charm you, and when you least expected it, to steal you away right from under William's nose. He would've been crushed to fail your family twice."

The mention of Dad's death feels like a knife to the heart. Roch has spent every day of the last eleven years feeling overwhelming guilt for not saving him. He's never said it out loud, but I've never needed his words to know how he feels.

"You're sick," I spit out.

We've made it out of their neighborhood and onto a main road before I hear the faint rumbling of motorcycles. They're too late. They'll never find me now. I close my eyes to ask the spirits for help, but I don't know what to ask for. That Roch will find me and potentially get himself killed? That I'll die before having humanity stripped from me by these assholes?

"No one ever said I wasn't." Anthony chuckles. "Things got derailed a bit when you decided to fall in love with your dad's best friend and not my son. I can't blame you, Max has always been a little soft."

I glance over at Max, who's glowering at his dad's rejection.

"Our second plan fell through when you caught onto the little trick my son was trying to pull. I told him it wouldn't work, but he insisted you were too sweet and innocent to know a ploy if it smacked you in the face. Guess he was wrong about that too. But he's finally redeemed himself, because here you are."

"The whole time?" I whisper to Max.

"Don't be so fucking surprised. You think any man would put so much effort into a chick who didn't put out? I didn't want to be your friend. I wanted you to suck my cock." He turns his attention out his window.

"I will never suck anything on you. I'd rather be dead."

"Don't write it off just yet. You don't know our methods. You might be on your knees begging for it by nightfall." Anthony turns around in his seat to face me. "You might even be begging for both our cocks. I'd go first naturally. To demonstrate."

"I'll bite your small dick off and spit it in your face."

"You could try, but you wouldn't be the first girl I've had to remove teeth from to stop such bad behavior."

I gasp at his words. This is so much worse than I thought. My idiotic mind wasn't even capable of imagining the potential bad things that could happen to me. I bite my lip until I taste blood. I won't cry. I won't give them the satisfaction.

If I have to live through this, I'll do it without giving them what they want the most.

To break me.

Chapter
TWENTY-SEVEN

Roch

We turn into Anthony's driveway. He's not here. I don't have to go inside to know it. After I got the call from Truly, we loaded up on weapons and headed out. We knew we'd miss him, but he doesn't have a huge head start and he didn't know he's been under constant surveillance.

Moto was tailing him all morning and then parked himself at the end of Anthony's street after he'd gone home. Paid off after he made the mistake of taking my girl.

"He's going down Veterans. Black Escalade," Sly says, his phone to his ear with Moto on the line.

"Tell him to stay on him. We'll call back after we load the package," Loki says.

Sly relays the message and we creep around to the back of the house. Everything in me screams to chase after Truly, but this has to be done first. We need insurance.

"Let me just—" Sly taps a few keys on the laptop he brought back with "—there. Alarm's disabled."

Goblin screws on a silencer and shoots the lock. It pops open and we file inside.

"Upstairs," I say. It's the only logical place for the queen's throne to be.

I walk to the far end of the hall and start kicking in doors. This place is too goddamn big for three people, and there are a lot of doors.

"Here," I call out, looking inside a darkened bedroom.

It reeks of stale air and vodka. Lying in the center of the bed is a human shaped form, covered by blankets. I approach the bed on one side and Loki takes the other. We each grab a section of blanket and I hold out three fingers. He watches as my fingers lower one by one.

We yank the covers off, exposing a passed-out woman who's so small, it's a miracle if she's alive. Bottles of liquor and empty booze surround her in the bed. A strong stench of piss hits my nostrils and I turn away.

"For fuck's sake. Ford, Bullet, get in here," Loki calls out. "Take her to the van."

The woman barely stirs when she's lifted from bed and carried to the minivan. The guys lay her down in the back.

"She doesn't look old enough to be a mom to a twenty-something year old," Ford notes.

"Especially for a pill popping drunk. Maybe she's the step monster?" Bullet asks.

"I don't give a fuck who she is, she wouldn't be here if she weren't important to Anthony." Loki slams the back of the van closed. "Let's ride."

"Moto says Anthony's heading out to the hills. We need to hurry if we're going to catch up." Sly pushes his helmet over his head and mounts his bike.

We take off, speeding out of this privileged neighborhood, toward the highway.

I can't even see straight, I'm so fucking pissed. My mind fills with all the ways I'm going to kill that asshole. I'll make it last for days. Maybe weeks. All the things that happened to me while in the middle of the Afghanistan desert will feel like child's play compared to what I'm going to do with him.

And Truly? She better believe she's never leaving my sight ever again. I don't care if she's walking to the mailbox, my grumpy ass will be by her side, making sure no one else dares touch what's mine.

I remember what Anthony's known for and pressure squeezes my throat with anxiety. Need to find her now. Right fucking now.

My phone rings in my ear and I connect my Bluetooth.

"You guys better hurry. I have a feeling we're headed toward the Minden/Tahoe airport," he says. "If he boards a plane..."

He doesn't have to finish, I know what that means. I go full throttle, picking up speed and taking the lead. Under normal circumstances, going ahead of Loki would be disrespectful, and earn me an ass whooping, but he waves me by. I know he understands what I'm going through right now.

Sweat trickles down my back. It's usually cool at dusk, but it's one of those rare nights where the summer heat sticks around. Every second feels like an hour as I speed past slower moving vehicles in a desperate attempt to not lose Truly.

Ten minutes later, my phone rings again.

"I was right. They're at the airstrip. Where are you guys at?" Moto asks, sounding stressed the fuck out.

"Two minutes," I say.

"I'm parked on the side of the road outside the gate. Meet me there."

I slow down to a crawl as we approach the airport. It's an old military training base that's now used for emergency services and corporate travel. It's not a busy area and the sound of six bikes will give us away.

I park in front of Moto and get off my bike, setting my helmet over the handlebar.

"That plane." Moto points to a small aircraft that's parked outside a garage with its lights on. Next to it, is a black SUV. "They haven't boarded yet. The pilot has been walking around doing checks. They're still in the Escalade."

"Here's how we're playing this," Loki says, after assessing the situation. "Ford, you're going to drive through that gate. We'll ride in after you. Get the bitch wife out of the car as soon as it's safe. I want him to see her before he decides to open fire on us."

"On it," Ford says confidently.

Two of the prospects were asked to help us out, leaving Duncan to keep an eye on the clubhouse. We don't normally let them get this close to the fire until we know how they'll react, but both Ford and Miles have proven themselves. Plus with Khan being locked up, we need to fast track a few members so we don't appear weak.

Ford gets back in the minivan and pulls around the bikes while we prepare to follow. He backs up a little on the road, then lays on the gas. He breaks the gate wide open. Sparks fly from the metal hitting metal. Like a biker parade, we drive through after him.

Ford skids to a halt in front of the Escalade while we fan out around it. My pistol is in my hand the second my kickstand is down. I walk around to the driver's window, staying fifteen feet away. I can't see who's driving, but I'll bet it's not Anthony. In all the time we've been following him, he's had a driver.

The pilot startles and jumps inside his plane for cover. Smart man.

My eyes snap from the SUV to the minivan and back again, watching as Ford heaves the frail woman over his shoulder and carries her around to the front. Sly and Moto cover him, despite the gun in his free hand.

Everything becomes very still. My senses go on high alert. My heart is jumping in my chest, knowing I'm this close to Truly but not being able to get to her. I swallow hard, watching and waiting.

The passenger door opens and Anthony steps out, hands raised. It's not what I was expecting, but I don't let down my guard.

"Loki, Bastards, nice to see you," he says cordially, like we're here for a fucking tea party.

"Let her go," Loki yells out.

"Or else what?"

"Or else you'll be saying goodbye to your bitch wife," he responds.

"Her? You think I care about her?" He laughs almost hysterically. "She's a whore I picked up after my wife died. Honestly, she's been a drain on me for years, but my kid had grown attached. The marriage was for appearances only, I assure you. Max is a man now, he doesn't need a motherly figure. Do whatever you want with her."

There goes our leverage. The woman lifts her head up and twists in Ford's arms until he sets her down. She howls out a pained cry, but I don't think it's physical pain that has her in tears. She falls to the ground, her knees to her chest, and her head resting on them. She rocks back and forth.

"I wouldn't keep her around long, she has an expensive habit of Xanax and Vicodin," Anthony says coolly. This is getting off track and if I don't see my girl soon, I'm going to flip my shit.

"Truly," I growl.

"The mute speaks," he says. "She's in the car with my son. He's taken quite a liking to her. I don't think you'll be able to convince him to give her up."

"Let her go and we'll let you go," Goblin tries.

"I don't think so." In one swift motion, he pulls a pistol from his side arm and opens fire on Ford and Goblin since they're closest, and standing in the way of him and the plane. They dive out of the way, leaving the pathway onto the plane clear.

Loki, who's standing at the nose of the plane, returns fire, but misses, allowing Anthony to make it inside the puddle jumper.

Probably realizing Anthony intends to leave them behind, the Escalade peels out toward Moto and Sly, who are in its direct path. To their credit, they stay in position for as long as they can, raining bullets into the windshield. I aim my gun lower, shooting out the tires.

The driver loses control, whether from being hit or because of the tires. The vehicle jerks to the right and Moto doesn't have a chance to move before being clipped. His body flies through the air, then lands with a sickening thud.

It's time to end this shit. I keep my gun aimed at the vehicle as I approach. I try to open the back door, but it's locked.

Instead, I open the driver's door and a man falls to the ground at my feet. His eyes are wide open, but there's a gaping hole dead center in his forehead. I kick him to the side and climb in.

Max has Truly on his lap, a knife to her throat. There's a trickle of blood dripping down her neck and her face is so swollen, I hardly recognize her. The look on her face is something I've never seen. Emotionless and cold. So unlike her. Ice fills my veins.

I aim at his forehead, but don't have a clear shot with Truly so close. Every muscle in my body tenses. I clench my jaw so hard, I hear my molar crack. It's the least of my worries right now.

Kill him.

Kill him.

Kill him.

"Don't do anything stupid. You're known for making rash decisions," the kid says like he knows me and the things I've done. "You don't think we looked into every single one of you? I know all about how you tried to rescue Truly's dad. You failed epically. Wouldn't it be poetic for you to fail saving his daughter too?"

"Kill you."

"No offense, but you're in no position to make threats." He shifts Truly to his side, keeping an arm around her neck and the blade against her throat. "Here's what's going to happen. Me and your girl are going to get in that plane. You're going to be a good biker and let it happen. If you do that, I promise to call when we land and tell you where to pick her up."

I don't believe a goddamn word that comes out of his

mouth, but in such cramped quarters, I can't do anything about it. I lower my gun, holding my hands up.

"You better make sure I get to that plane unharmed, or I swear to God, this knife will slice right through her jugular. I don't think her mom could fix that."

He slowly opens the back door, shoving Truly out first and then stepping behind her, using her as a shield.

"Tell your friends the plan," he orders.

I get out of the Escalade, allowing my brothers to see my hands up. They'll understand not to try anything crazy.

Max takes three steps toward the plane before the loud engine whooshes to life and taxis toward the runway. Max's eyes widen comically as he watches his dad make a run for it, leaving him behind.

He takes a few steps before shoving Truly to the ground and sprinting to our minivan. Sly is crouched over Moto's limp body, Loki and Goblin are firing at the plane, and the prospects are staring at me for direction. But the only thought in my mind is getting to Truly.

I run over to her and scoop her up in my arms. She takes one look at me and the dead expression falls away. She bursts into tears, holding me tight around the neck, and burying her face into my shoulder.

"Shh," I whisper.

The minivan's tires screech as Max makes a run for it. I point at it, letting the clueless prospects know now would be the perfect time to stop him. Gunshots echo through the air, shattering the back windows of the minivan, but it's too late. He's getting away.

Anthony isn't as lucky. The plane slows to a stop and the engine makes an ugly sound before shutting off completely.

Loki, Goblin, Bullet, and the prospects move in, surrounding the only exit. If Anthony doesn't come out before the cops get here, it'll be them to take him down and not us. There's no doubt in my mind multiple 911 calls have been made because of the gunfire.

After a few long moments, the door opens, folding down to reveal the stairs. Anthony appears, pushing a terrified pilot in front of him with a gun to his head.

"Get back," Anthony orders as he disembarks.

"That's cute you think we give a fuck about some random pilot," Loki says and rushes toward the pair.

He knocks into both of them, sending all three crashing to the asphalt. Goblin steps in and grabs Anthony by his oily hair. He slams his head into the hard ground over and over, until his body goes limp.

The pilot scampers away, holding his hands up in defense. "Don't shoot. Don't shoot."

"Where's your car?" Loki barks.

The scared man points to a four-door pick-up parked on the other side of the garage.

"Load the women and Moto up in the truck. Ford, you ride Moto's bike. Miles, you drive the cage." He turns to the pilot. "Keys?"

He reaches into his pocket and tosses them through the air. Loki catches them easily, and hands them to Miles. Loki pulls a roll of duct tape out of the saddlebag of his bike and wraps it around Anthony's hands and feet.

"Give me a hand," he says to Bullet. Lifting Anthony up by the limbs, they toss him into the bed of the truck, unfolding the bed cover over the top of him.

"Consider this a warning." Goblin aims his gun and

shoots the man in the leg. He screams out, clutching his calf as blood pours from the wound. "You have about three minutes to make up a story that doesn't include a bunch of bikers. I don't give a fuck what it is. Next time that bullet will be in your head."

The man's head bobs up and down in agreement. If it had been me, I'd kill the guy. Birdie has made Goblin soft. A witness is a witness and everyone has a price, but the call has been made and I'm not going to argue.

I carry Truly to the white pick-up and set her in the passenger seat. She clutches tighter to me.

"Don't go. Please. I need you."

She doesn't need to ask twice. I toss my keys to Miles, who's in the driver's seat. He looks at me like he's about to piss himself. He doesn't want to be the one who scratches up my new bike.

"Don't crash," I mutter, securing Truly's seatbelt.

Sirens sound in the distance. We have to get out of here right the fuck now. I jog over to the driver's side and hop in. Ford shuts the truck door after setting the woman inside. She's still curled into a ball crying. We should leave her behind. We have no use for a strung-out bitch at the clubhouse.

Sly and Goblin load Moto on the seat opposite of Anthony's wife. His face is contorted in pain and he's holding onto his right arm to keep it in place. Must be dislocated.

I take off, letting Loki lead the way. I hold my breath until we're at least five miles away with no sign of lights or sirens trailing behind us. I go the speed limit on the freeway, not wanting to attract any unwanted attention. I keep an eye on the bed of the truck as we head back to Reno. I don't think he could free himself, but I don't want to chance it.

Looking at the occupants of the truck, I don't know where to go. We can't go to a hospital. It's out of the question. I would drive straight to Aiyana's, but I swore to her I wouldn't do it again.

"It's okay. She'll understand. She'll be pissed, but she'll understand," Truly says softly, reading my mind, like always.

"Promise," I say.

"I know you promised, but it was a dumb oath to make. Until you find yourself a doctor who doesn't mind putting back together broken bikers, she's all we've got." She undoes her seatbelt and scoots across the bench seat so she can rest her battered head on my shoulder.

Aiyana is going to kill me and I'm going to let her. I promised to protect Truly but instead, I'm bringing her home broken.

Chapter

TWENTY-EIGHT

Truly

We split apart from the bikers. Loki leads the way for us and turns toward Mom's house. I'm not looking forward to seeing her again. Not like this. Not after I'd convinced her I'd be okay a few days ago. But we have no other choice.

Today was officially the worst day of my life. Between the physical abuse by Max's hand, and the emotional abuse at Anthony's, I'm tired and in pain. Not to mention the ache that still resides in my heart from all the trouble I've caused the club. If I was embarrassed before, that's nothing compared to how I'm feeling now.

We turn down the gravel driveway. It's dark out now, but the light in the clinic is still on.

"She's up there." I point.

He travels up to the building with a giant paw print on the sign that reads, 'Harvest Hills Animal Clinic'. Once he's parked, he jumps out, coming over to my side of the truck first. He lifts me out and takes my hand. Loki helps Moto out and follows us. We leave both Corsettis in the truck for the time being. Anthony's tied up, and his wife passed out the minute we started driving and hasn't moved since. I should have more sympathy for her, but it's hard when I know who she's aligned herself with.

We enter through the back. Not wanting to startle Mom, I call out, "Mom, where are you at?"

"Truly?" Her head pops out of an examination room. Her smile falls when she gets a glimpse of me. "Oh my God. What happened?'

"There was an accident," I say, keeping my feelings hidden.

"There are no accidents when it comes to the Royal Bastards." If looks could kill, Roch would be dead on the ground right now. "Only innocent people getting hurt. Truly, Room Two. Loki, take Moto to Room Three. Is there anyone else?"

"No, ma'am," Loki replies. He must not want to bring up the drugged woman in the back of the truck. I don't say anything. Mom can't help her anyway. She needs detox and priorities.

Mom follows Loki and Moto, deciding he's worse off than I am. Roch sits on a padded bench in the room and pulls me across his lap. He gently cups my face, studying my injuries. I don't know how I look, but I can see the swollen flesh of my cheek and eyelid in my periphery, so I know it must be bad.

He tilts my head to the side, inspecting the shallow cut on my neck. His lips purse in a tight line and his brows knit together.

My serious man.

"I love you and I'm sorry." I brush my cracked lips over his in a chaste kiss.

"S'okay." He traces my jaw with the tip of his finger, then trails featherlight kisses across my cheeks and forehead, not caring about the dried-up blood.

"It's not okay. After I left you, I had to do something. I met Max at a coffee shop. I thought I'd be safe meeting in a public place. But he took me anyway. It was so stupid."

He nods in agreement, features hard and unyielding. He's scolding me with only a look that makes me feel shittier than I did before. It's the same look he's given me countless times before when I get myself in trouble.

"Trust me," he murmurs.

"I do. There's no one I trust more." I hug him around his neck. My heart overflows when he squeezes me right back. "Does this mean we're good?"

He nods.

Mom walks in, pausing in the doorway at our position. Roch shoves me off his lap and onto the bench next to him. I watch a badass biker turn into a Boy Scout in the blink of an eye.

"Let me look at you." Mom flashes a light in my eyes, feels around my neck, takes my blood pressure, and checks my heart rate. "I think you have a mild concussion, but I'm used to examining dogs, so who knows. You want to tell me what happened? Because the cowards in the other room are pleading the fifth."

"You remember Max?" I ask, and peek a look at Roch. He's nervous I'm going to say too much. "Well, turns out he's an asshole who doesn't take no for an answer. I called Roch and he brought the cavalry."

Roch growls, and I clear my throat to try to disguise his alpha gesture.

"What? Oh my God. You need a rape kit. Has he been arrested?"

"Calm down. He beat me up, but didn't rape me. No need for tests. And no, he hasn't been arrested. He got away." I leave out the fact that his dad is currently in the bed of the stolen truck parked out front. That feels more like a *need-to-know* piece of information.

"Are there any other injuries besides your... entire face?"

"I have this." I lift my shirt, exposing the cut on my side.

"Fuck," Roch spits out.

He didn't know about this and looking down, it's worse than I thought. There's a three-inch gash with exposed tissue.

"You need stitches. I'll be right back."

Roch jumps to his feet and gets a closer look. His semi-calm from earlier is gone. His icy eyes darken to navy, and the long vein going down his neck pulses. He's pissed.

"It's okay. It doesn't hurt much." I let my shirt fall to hide the evidence of Max's handiwork.

"I'll inject a little lidocaine so it won't sting so much," Mom says, returning with a tray of supplies.

I lie down on the exam table and let her do her magic. Roch stands over me, holding my hand.

"I guess I owe you an apology," Mom says to Roch, ripping off her latex gloves. I sit up, feeling a bit woozy and tired.

He shakes his head adamantly, with a look one could only describe as guilt. He's an idiot.

"No, I do. This kid"—she cringes at her use of the word—"Truly has given you a lot of trouble. You've always been there for her. And me too. I won't stand in your way. I couldn't ask for a better man for my daughter."

Roch's head lowers, the same posture his dogs take when they chew something up.

Pathetic.

"But if your illegal activities touch her, I'm coming for you. Ask those little puppies in the room next to us, I'm scary."

Roch opens his arms wide and Mom steps in them. My jaw drops. He doesn't do hugs. Not with anyone but me. Not only that, he's so emotionally detached, he wouldn't know the appropriate moment to give a hug if there was a neon sign telling him.

My eyes well with tears. He thinks he's defective, that something's wrong with him. What he doesn't understand is he's perfect in his own way. He's perfect for me.

"So we understand each other?" Mom asks, and Roch nods. "Okay, now take Moto home. He had a dislocated shoulder and a pretty nasty bruise on his hip. I gave him some pain meds, but he needs rest and to keep his arm in a sling."

"Okay, I'll make sure he stays down." I hug Mom.

"I still want that dinner," she whispers into my hair.

"Deal."

The drive home is quiet. Moto's doped up on pills and snoring. The woman is still lying on her side, curled into a ball. I rest my hand on Roch's thigh and he covers it with his own. Things are pretty fucked right now, but we're solid.

When we pull up to the House of Bastards, the Bastards themselves descend. A couple of them help Moto inside, while some of the others lug Anthony away. I can't think about what's going to happen to him. Rationally, I know he deserves whatever is coming. But my moral compass tells me what they're doing is wrong and he should be turned over to the authorities.

I need to forget he ever existed.

Tabitha and Sissy help the black-haired waif of a woman in the back get out of the truck. The four of us head to Sissy and Tabitha's suite. We sit her down on one of the beds while we decide what to do with her.

"She's shaking uncontrollably, her teeth are chattering, and she's sweating by the gallon. Bitch is drug sick," Tabitha says, folding her arms under her huge tits, propping them up even more than they accomplish on their own.

"I don't know how to help her," I say.

"You help her by tossing her into rehab."

"I'll talk to Roch. See if it's a possibility." I steal a glance at her. She looks so frail in her white cotton nightie. "But she knows stuff."

"I figured that's why you guys didn't leave her where you found her," Sissy says under her breath.

"Well, let's get her cleaned up. I'll have one of the guys bring a cot in here so we can keep an eye on her." Tabitha picks up her phone to type out a text.

"I'm not doing it." Sissy says, propping a fist on her hip.

"I'll do it," I say. "Find me a change of clothes for her."

I take the woman by the hand and lead her into the bathroom.

"I'm going to help you get cleaned up, okay?"

She doesn't respond, but she willingly raises her arms so I can lift her nightgown off. I suck in a sharp breath at her protruding ribs and prominent hip bones. My guess is most of her meals are replaced by pills and booze. But what shocks me the most, is seeing a brand on her hip. The skin has long since healed, but it's obviously a burn.

A tear leaks down her cheek at my perusal.

"Sorry, this must be uncomfortable. Here, step in." I open the shower stall door and set her under the spray. "It'll be like a spa date. I'll wash your hair. Give you a nice scalp massage."

She turns her back to me and I squirt shampoo onto my palm before rubbing it in. She stands under the water to rinse, then I repeat the process with conditioner. Her hair is thick and long like mine, but black as night where mine is more a brownish black.

"I'll give you some privacy so you can finish up." I hope she'll wash herself. She smells like body odor and urine.

I wait patiently until I hear the water turn off. I open the door, holding up a towel. She steps into it and wraps it around her body.

"There are some clothes right there for you. Not sure how well they'll fit, but they'll do for now." I pat the leggings and T-shirt the girls brought in. "I'll leave you to it."

"Thank you," she whispers softly.

"What's your name?" I ask.

"Petra."

"Nice to meet you. My name is Truly." I step out and close the door behind me. I don't know what her story is, but it must be a painful one.

"Is she okay?" Tabitha asks, spreading a blanket over the cot someone brought in while I was gone.

"Yeah, I think so. Her name is Petra. If you need anything, text me," I say, and leave the room.

I shower and change into one of Roch's T-shirts back at the casita, before sinking into our comfortable mattress. Roch beat me here. He's on his back, one arm behind his head, the other resting on his chest, and his eyes fixed on the ceiling.

It's been a long ass day and I read the weariness on his face. I know he's worried about me, about us, about how we're going to make a life together.

I've turned over a new leaf, though. No more thinking I'm part of the Royal Bastards. I'm not. I'm a college student training to be a veterinarian. I'll support my man in whatever he needs and I trust him to stay as safe he can, but other than that, I don't want to know what they do.

I'm adopting Birdie's mentality. What I don't know won't hurt me.

I reach under the covers and drape an arm around Roch's abdomen, loving the way his muscles flex under my touch. He snakes his arm under my head and tucks me into his side.

"Love you," he mutters, kissing my crown.

"I love you too."

Chapter

TWENTY-NINE

Roch

I wait until Truly's sleeping to sneak out of bed. I have things to do tonight. Things I didn't have time to do earlier without her asking questions.

I saw the way she watched Loki and Goblin drag away Anthony's body. I could tell she was confused about how to feel. It must be so hard to see things like that when you still have a moral compass.

I put on a pair of jeans and a T-shirt before slipping out the door. A couple of the dogs lift their heads, but they stay in their beds. They're used to me leaving at all hours. Hazard of the job.

I walk inside the back door of the clubhouse. Everything's quiet and no one's around. It was a long ass day, so I'd imagine they're all passed the fuck out. I make a stop at Moto's room. Cracking the door to check on him, I find Sly sleeping on a chair in the corner. I'm not surprised.

I pad down the stairs and step inside the kill room. It's

cold in here and the air smells strongly of chemicals from the last time it was cleaned.

Hanging from the ceiling by his arms, is Anthony. He studies me, but there's a faraway look in his eyes, like he's only halfway conscious.

His bastard kid got away, but we'll find him. And when we do, Anthony's death will look like a vacation. He dared lay a hand on my girl, securing his place in Hades with all the rest of us assholes. The difference is, when I'm burning in the fiery depths of hell, I'll know all my actions had good intentions. Same can't be said for the Corsettis.

I undo the chains holding him up, and let him fall to the ground. He cries out like the fucking pussy he is.

"Don't do this. I'll do whatever you want. Give you whatever you want," he says scrambling away from me. "You want women? I can get you an obedient one, not like that Truly bitch. I'll bet she won't even suck your cock, she's such a prude. My girls, they're trained to handle a man like—"

He doesn't get to finish his train of thought before I rear back my fist and land a punch that knocks him out cold. His eye splits open with the force and sprays blood all over me.

After dragging him back to the middle of the floor, I use the wench to lower the chains to the ground. Then, circle them around each of his ankles and raise him up until he's suspended in the air, his legs wide open. I fill a bucket of cold water up and toss it over him, jolting him awake.

He flops around, sputtering nonsensically. Over on the stainless-steel table, I pick up a handsaw. I press my finger against one of the teeth to test for sharpness. My skin splits and a drop of blood surfaces. I suck the blood off and return to my prisoner.

"You got away with killing Dom, but do you think Franco will allow you to kill both of his heirs without retaliation? Your whole club is going to burn for this."

If Franco cares we killed his shit stains for sons, we'll take care of him too. We can't lie back and let them walk all over us or it'll never end.

I tap the saw against the V of his legs and relish in his screams as he realizes what I'm about to do. Holding him by the calf, I saw through his pants and into his limp dick and saggy balls, in one fluid forward motion. His cries are other-worldly when I drag the saw back toward me.

I'm suddenly back in the desert, picturing the masked faces of the rebels who bent me over and slammed their dicks into my dry asshole, ripping me open. I picture the bearded man with golden eyes who pissed on me every night before his shift ended. But mostly I picture the guards who took a machete to Ricky's neck, decapitating him.

Kill him.

Kill him.

Kill him.

The demons in my head take over as I temporarily lose my humanity. With a crazed vigor, I saw Anthony down the middle. Every push of the saw brings blood pooling and spilling onto the ground. Every pull, fills my ears with the tinny sound of bone grinding against metal.

Because he's hanging by his ankles, his blood rushes to his head, and keeps him alive and awake for his own execution. He claws and scratches at my legs as I work my way through his body, pleading with incoherent words. Long, strings of mucus hang from his mouth to his hairline.

Disgusting piece of shit.

Eventually, his body sags lifelessly. I release his leg and he sways from side to side, a grotesque wound extending beyond his naval. I toss the saw in the corner and sink to my haunches. I tuck my head between my arms, and a primal roar rips from my lungs.

My heart slows and sweet relief washes over me like a warm blanket. The demons slip away, tucking themselves into the dark corners of my mind. I've appeased them for now.

"You're one sick fuck," someone says behind me. I whirl around, seeing Goblin. "That's saying a lot coming from me."

I shrug.

"Can't let this sit all night. Let me go get the prospects."

Minutes later, he's back with a bleary-eyed Ford and Miles. They both turn white as a ghost at what they see. A man, nearly cut in half, with his organs dripping from his body. It's remarkable the things a person can grow accustomed to. If they patch in, it won't be long before they don't bat an eyelash at shit like this.

It takes three hours to get the kill room cleaned, and Anthony's body tossed into the back of our only remaining minivan. Miles and Ford will be in charge of disposing of him tomorrow.

I quickly shower in the main house, bagging another pair of sweatpants and a T-shirt to be burned. It reminds me I need to order new clothing. Been going through a lot of it lately.

Clean and relaxed, I slide back into bed. It's nearly morning and the sun is starting to climb over the horizon, but I'm beat. I tug Truly's body against mine, and run a hand up the outside of her thigh. Her skin is silky smooth and she smells so fucking delicious.

Her body reacts to my touch and she unconsciously arches her back, pushing her ass into my crotch. I bite down on my lip, trying not to get hard. She's hurt. Her face is so swollen, I hardly recognized her. Then there's the gash in her side.

I've never been more enraged than when I saw Max holding her in front of him like a goddamn pussy. Real men don't hide behind women. Blood whooshes in my ears thinking about him getting away. I press my nose into Truly's hair and breathe in deeply, feeling the instant calm she gives me. I'm addicted.

I'll deal with the kid later.

One sick fuck down, one to go.

"I'm sorry. They've denied bail, claiming he's a flight risk because of his connections. Any number of your associates could get him into Mexico." Bexley crosses her long legs. Normally, we don't allow outsiders in here, but a meeting with Bexley is the exception.

Our hoity-toity attorney is dressed in a black pantsuit with a lacy corset top underneath. Her make up is perfectly done and her long brown hair is styled into loose curls. She drives the guys crazy, but I prefer Truly's natural beauty. Take all that shit off Bexley's face and who knows what you'd end up with.

"And you can't change their minds?" Loki asks, glaring at her. Any other woman would cower under that look, but Bexley is nonplussed.

"No. The decision has been made. He's inside until the

hearing. We can file another request for bail at that time. I'm sorry."

"When is the hearing?" Goblin lifts his glasses to the top of his head and rubs at his eyes.

"Three months."

"Jesus Christ." Loki turns his attention to us. "Who do we know on the inside?"

"Nathan and a few guys from his crew. They were pulled over with a shit ton of blow," Moto says. The guy almost looks himself today. He spent seventy-two hours in bed after being hit by the van, milking his injuries while Tabs, Sissy, and even Sly doted on him.

"Get in touch with him. I want Khan protected. No matter the cost," Loki orders.

"On it." Moto steps out of the Chapel.

"What kind of evidence do they have? Is this something you can get him out of?" Loki asks.

"They have surveillance footage of him stealing the van. The same van that blew up an entire storage unit the next day. Thankfully, no one was hurt, but it's enough to keep him locked up for a long time."

"Not if the footage disappears," he says.

"Stop right there." She holds up a hand. "I don't want to know anything about that. But to answer your question, without the footage, they have nothing."

Loki nods, lost in thought.

"But this judge, he's a hard ass. You won't be able to pay him off or threaten him into submission. Matter of fact, I wouldn't even try. You don't want to make an enemy out of him." Bexley stands and organizes her file folders before stuffing them into her briefcase. "I'll be in touch soon."

"Thanks, Bex," Loki says.

"No problem. Do you have anything you want me to tell Khan? Unfortunately, I have to meet with him this week to discuss everything." She rolls her eyes. Khan drives her insane by hitting on her relentlessly.

"I'll let you know before you see him."

"Okay." Bexley waves and struts out of the room.

"Now that she's gone, where are we at with Max Corsetti?" Loki lights up a cig.

"Our van was found on the border of Arizona and New Mexico. From there, the trail goes cold," Sly says, chewing on the end of a pen.

"Were there any missing vehicles reported around that area and time?" Goblin asks.

"Let me check." Sly taps on the keys of his laptop for three minutes before he hacks his way into the local police department. "No. There's literally nothing but a rest stop there."

"Where could he be going in that direction? Would he drive all the way to Franco in New York?" Loki leans back in his chair.

"What about Memphis?" Sly tap tap taps on the keys.

"What the fuck is in Memphis?" Loki chuckles.

"That Victor Knight guy. Anthony's contact into the trafficking ring." Sly spins around his laptop screen, showing surveillance images of the ugly bastard. "When he left here, I had him tailed. I figured if we knew what he was up to, it would help us keep a better eye on Anthony. He's been holing up in Memphis."

"You think Max would go to him?"

"Why not? Franco won't want to lose the contact or slow down. Dom and Anthony are toast, so that leaves the kid.

Without him, his blood lines are gone. You know how that whack job family feels about blood relatives. I mean, he put Anthony in charge and that asshole didn't even make it six months before getting himself killed. Fucking moron." Sly brings the computer back in front of him.

"Let's try and get eyes on Max. I'm calling Koyn to see if they mind intercepting our package." Loki digs his phone out of his pocket.

"Who's Koyn?" Bullet asks, looking sheepish.

"Prez of the Tulsa chapter," Loki responds.

"Are you asking them to deliver Max back here?"

"Nah, I don't want to deal with the logistics. Although Max probably would rather get stuck with us. Koyn is fucking brutal," Loki says.

"You say that like you didn't sever the eyeballs out of that strip club owner, and shove them into his mouth." Goblin chuckles.

"That asshole deserved it," Loki defends and then slams the gavel down. The loud crack echoes in the empty room. "Meeting adjourned."

Loki stays in his seat, and so do I. I'm not done with this conversation. Max hurt my girl, so he's mine.

"Want him," I growl after everyone is gone.

"You want him dead, or do you want to find a way to bring him back here and run the risk of him getting free?"

I pinch the bridge of my nose. Logically, I know the sooner he's in a grave, the better. But the demons inside scream to be set free and take care of the problem.

"I know it's personal. Trust me, I fucking know." He stamps out his lit cig. "I'm going to tell you something no one else knows."

I nod.

"When we brought Dom back here, everyone thought I was the one to take him out—"

"Trucker," I say, putting the pieces together.

"Yeah. It was fucking hard to let someone else do the job, but in the end, all that mattered was handing him over to Hades."

I scrub a hand over my face.

"I'll tell Koyn to get creative. He'll get a *proper* death."

I nod. It's for the best. Plus, we don't even know if Tulsa will be able to find him. My chance at revenge isn't gone.

"So, does this mean you're making Truly your old lady?" Loki smirks. "Out of everyone else, I'm glad it's you, brother. You deserve some happiness."

My lips twitch and Loki cracks up laughing.

"Come on. You drink now that the icicle up your ass is melting?" He punches me in the arm and stands up.

"Asshole," I mutter.

"Fuck you."

Chapter
THIRTY

Truly

I wrap my arms tighter around Roch's middle and crush my body against his back. Between my legs, the Harley engine vibrates, causing my clit to engorge, and my nipples to pebble.

I move my hand lower to the waistband of his worn jeans. His body tenses and his abs flex hard. As I rest my cheek on his warm leather cut, breathing in the rich scent of leather, I hold my position, not wanting him to stop me before he's had a chance to warm up to the idea.

After everything going on lately, we decided to take a ride up to Tahoe for the weekend. Loki and Birdie are letting us camp out on their property. I know Roch would rent a cabin or hotel if I wanted, but the idea of sleeping in a tent and cooking over a fire sounds more romantic. Plus, Roch will need the open air and space after I tell him what's on my mind.

I pop the button on his jeans. We're on the backroads and no one's around. Zero harm in getting our weekend started now. I rub over the crotch of his jeans. He's hard and thick. It's all the encouragement I need. I slowly lower his zipper and reach inside his underwear. His elbows snap to his sides, trapping my arms and stopping me from proceeding.

I don't let it deter me. I tease the head of his dick, smearing pre-cum over his tip, and proving he's not going to stop me. His arms loosen up and I pat his tummy in approval. I wrap my hand around his cock and free him. Using one hand, I keep him steady from the slapping wind. With the other, I jerk him off using teasingly slow strokes.

The veins that run along his length swell and he twitches under my palm. I'm so turned on, I know I could orgasm right here. I tilt my hips forward and back, rubbing my sex on the seat. It feels delicious.

Suddenly, Roch turns off the road and drives us around down a dirt path, parking behind a large Jeffrey Pine. He throws the kickstand down and gets off the bike. With his hands on my hips, he lifts me off. In one swift movement, he yanks my leggings down my legs and bends me over the seat of the bike.

He reaches between my legs and cups my pussy. His hand is warm. Energy passes between us, a tingling awareness I've never felt before. One toughened finger traces my outer lips. Everything in me wants to rock back on his finger, force him to do more. The anticipation is driving me crazy.

As if he can hear my thoughts, he cracks his palm against my ass cheek. It feels like a warning, so I rest my forehead against the seat of the bike and take deep breaths to calm myself.

He kneels down and spreads me wide open. It feels dirty having him that close to my center in the broad daylight, out in the open. It's a delicious experience that has another wave of arousal dripping from my body. He must notice because next thing I know, his mouth is covering me, sucking, licking, and nibbling on every inch of my pussy.

It takes an embarrassing twenty seconds for me to lose my mind in an earth-shattering orgasm. My legs go weak, but Roch's right there, holding me up until I finish quaking.

"Wow," I say on an exhale.

He stands and smacks my ass again. I look over my shoulder in time to see him grab himself by the base, and guide his cock into my wet opening. The sound is obscene and seems to echo in the trees around us. My core throbs, ready for round two.

"Fucking beautiful," he grunts. His entire focus is the place we're joined, and from behind, I'm sure he can see *everything*.

My instincts are proven correct when he drags my arousal up to my asshole and presses in. My legs straighten and I clench down on him. It's such a foreign feeling, but not altogether unpleasant.

He fists my hair, gives it a sharp tug, and leans over my body. He tilts my head to the side and flicks my earlobe with his tongue, then trails kisses down my neck.

Releasing my hair, he skims his hand down my spine as he stands to his full height once again. With a punishing grip on my hips, he pounds into me. The bike shifts back and forth so much, I worry it will tip, but it doesn't.

A soundtrack of our bodies slapping together, our heavy pants, birds chirping, and the wind blowing plays on repeat.

He slows down to guide my hand between my legs. I rub circles on my clit and Roch resumes his pace. I climb higher and higher, loving his rough and hard fucking. Tingling goosebumps take over my body as I spasm around him.

He squeezes the flesh of my ass, slowing his pace, but thrusting deeper and holding himself inside me for long seconds each time. He grunts low and guttural, then pulls out and spills his semen onto the ground next to us. It's not necessary, but I don't tell him that.

Not yet.

I collapse over the bike, feeling boneless and sleepy. The sound of Roch pulling up his zipper has me lifting my head and peering over my shoulder.

"I don't know how you expect me to move after that," I mumble.

One corner of his mouth tips up. It's been happening more and more often since he took care of Anthony. I'm holding out hope I'll hear him laugh someday. I'll never stop trying to make this serious man happy.

He crouches down and pulls my pants and panties back up my legs. I'm a mess down there and I cringe when my panties cover my wetness. Loki said there's a river, it better be deep enough to rinse myself off.

Roch tugs me into his arms. He cups my face and kisses me deeply. It's the kind of kiss that means something. The kind of kiss someone gives you when they *love you*.

"Love you," he murmurs against my lips, once again reading my mind.

He said it once before, but I didn't believe him. It's easy to say I love you when emotions are high and you're fighting for something. It's harder in the quiet moments when you have time to think about your feelings, and you're not worried they'll be the last thing you say to a person.

"I love you so much." I squeeze him tight around the middle.

"Go," he says as he swats my ass.

He throws a leg over his bike and holds his hand out to help me on. We don't have far to go, but he takes his time getting there. Going slow and pointing to things he sees, like a patch of wildflowers.

Off in the distance, I spot Loki and Bridgette's cabin. It's practically hidden in the trees, but the copper tin roof shines in the sun. Roch turns down a dirt path. It's a tight fit, so I crouch behind him, letting his arms scrape along the low-lying branches.

We drive a half mile into the forest before Roch brakes and shuts off the engine. Instantly, I can hear the trickle of water. He helps me off the bike and I turn in a slow circle, taking in my surroundings. It's beautiful out here. The ground is covered by a bed of pine needles and the trees are so tall, I can hardly see the tops.

We're mostly in the shade, but there's a meadow to our left with bright, warm sun shining down on it. I follow my ears to the river. It's slow moving and appears to be waist deep. I shift my weight, once again feeling pretty gross.

"Think I can wash off in there?" I ask.

Roch nods and opens up one of the saddlebags to unpack. He hands me my small backpack of clothes and toiletries. We're here two nights, so I didn't need to bring much.

I remove a clean pair of shorts and panties from my bag, and a travel size bottle of body wash. Birdie said I could shower at their place, but I don't want to be pulled from this experience. They're close by, but you'd never know it. We feel alone out here and I want to keep it that way.

I strip down, but leave my bra on, and step into the water. It's so cold, it burns. I screech loudly and Roch rushes over.

"It's freezing," I whine.

"Runoff," he says.

"I know it's snow runoff. I grew up here, remember?" I sass. "Doesn't make it easier."

I inch my way in, whining the whole time. My bare foot slips on a moss-covered rock and I fall in. The ice-cold water sucks the air from my lungs. I try to stand up, but my feet keep slipping. I splash and flail until my foot hits a patch of sand. I come out of the water gasping for air and my wet hair covering my face.

I brush it away to find Roch, standing on dry land, with the biggest smile I've ever seen on him. His lips are still together, so it's not a broad smile or anything, but it's blinding none the less.

I grin back at him and slosh my way to the water's edge. Roch holds open a towel and I step into it. Screw soap. I'm certain my dunk into the frigid water did a decent enough job.

"You think that's funny, huh?" I smirk. He pats my head and leaves me to dry off and dress.

By the time I've sorted myself, he has our tent fully erected, and the sleeping bags spread. I throw a braid into my long hair, knowing it's going to be a tangled mess after the river.

"What do people do when they go camping?" I ask. I've never been, and now that our camp is all set up, I don't know what I'm supposed to do now.

Roch shrugs, but he takes my hand and leads me deeper into the woods. We walk in silence and I know I need to tell him the secret I've been keeping. My stomach aches thinking about it. Maybe I should wait until we're leaving so I don't ruin our weekend.

No, I need to tell him now. At least out here, he won't be

able to run away without leaving me stranded. Eventually, the trees clear and Roch leans against a boulder and backs me up between his legs. His head rests on my shoulder and his arms wind around my middle.

I collect my thoughts in the quiet moment we're having. Last week, I realized I'd missed a period. He's mostly worn a condom every time we've had sex, but a few times he's pulled out, and then there was a first time where we didn't use any method of birth control, flimsy or otherwise.

I texted Birdie and made her go to the store with me. In the bathroom of a CVS, I peed on a stick, and was met with two pink lines. I kind of like the idea of our first time being the one that knocked me up, though I'll never know for sure.

I'm equally happy and scared to find out about a baby on the way. I'm young and still have a lot of schooling to finish. A baby might slow me down, but it won't deter me. I will be a veterinarian someday.

It's Roch's reaction that terrifies me. We've never spoken properly about kids, I mean, it was mentioned briefly in the shower right before he fucked me into oblivion, but I don't think he wants them. I don't know much about his own childhood, but I know it wasn't healthy. I asked him where his parents were one time and he told me he didn't have any.

"I'm pregnant," I blurt out, unable to hold it in any longer.

The moment freezes in time. Neither of us move a muscle, except for Roch's heart that's pounding against my back. His arms fall to the side and I flip around to see his expression.

His head is lulling back and his eyes are closed. His Adam's apple bobs dramatically and sweat beads along his hairline.

This can't be good.

This can't be good at all.

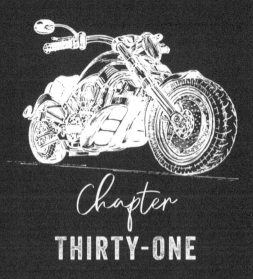

Chapter

THIRTY-ONE

Roch

Pregnant. She's pregnant.

My mind fills with a million different things all at once. It's so loud, I can't think. I can't wrap my head around it.

I slide around Truly and walk away from her. I need a goddamn minute. Hell, I need a few goddamn years before I can even think about the possibility of a kid.

I never wanted kids. Not ever. This world is a dark and dangerous place, and I contribute to all the darkness and danger. It's no life for a baby. It's no life for Truly either. I battle that every day of my life.

"Roch, don't walk away. Let's talk about it," she calls after me.

Talk about it. Yeah, right. I don't fucking talk. I grumble and growl one-word sentences. What kind of example would I be to a kid?

My feet move quickly through the woods. With each

step, I know I'm breaking Truly's heart. She's probably excited about the news. She was meant to be a mother. She's patient, kind, and has a curiosity about the world that a child would love. Probably because she's more kid than adult.

What the fuck was I thinking? Why couldn't I be happy fucking club sluts and riding my bike like my brothers? They're back at the clubhouse right now, having the time of their lives, without a care in the world.

I had to go and fall in love with a woman who hasn't had a chance to live yet. I'm a selfish bastard and I don't deserve any of the happiness she brings me.

Aiyana's going to kill me. She'll cut off my balls and have them made into sausage for the dogs.

That thought right there proves I'm not the type of man who should be a dad. What kind of father thinks about making testicle sausage?

An image of a pregnant Truly flashes through my mind and I pause, my feet slowing. She'll be so fucking beautiful round with my baby.

Footsteps thud behind me and I whirl around to see Truly jogging toward me. Are pregnant women supposed to run? Seems like the fetus would get jostled.

"Stop," she shouts, sterner than she's ever been with me. "Stop right there. I'm not letting you do this. I refuse to let you storm away and think you aren't good enough to be a dad."

She puts a voice to my number one concern.

"And I know the club life isn't a place for kids, but you know what? We did this together and we need to figure it out together." Her face is pinched in anger. I want to kiss it away and bring her smile back. "I know everything you're thinking and I agree, there are things we need to work out, but we need to work it out as a team."

Usually when someone says they know what you're thinking, it's condescending and manipulative because it's impossible to know those things about someone, but not with Truly. She knows me better than I know myself.

"I can't," I say somberly.

"You can. You love me and protect me. I know you'll do the same for our baby." Her hands rest on her lower belly in an unconscious move.

I want to believe her, but it's far too optimistic for me. It's going to be hard and she might regret having this baby with me. She'd be better off moving in with her mom and leaving me in her memories.

That thought hits me in the gut and has my breath hitching. I can't imagine her and my baby out in the world without me there every day, making sure they're okay and taken care of.

"You're scared. Of course you are. I am too. I have so much to accomplish still, but I want to do it with you and this baby at my side." She reaches for my hand. I reluctantly let her place my palm over her stomach. "There's a baby in there. Don't you want to see if it has your pale blue eyes or my brown ones? Or if it'll be a grumpy giant like you or a dork that exudes crackhead energy like me?"

I do want to know all of those things and more.

"Y'okay?" A wave of guilt rushes over me. She shouldn't be stressed out or upset in her condition.

"That depends. Are you going to force me to become a single mom at nineteen?"

I flinch with the blatant reminder of her age.

"If it's any consolation, I'll be twenty by the time I have the baby." She gives me a small smile.

"Love you," I say, drawing her into my arms. "And baby."

She audibly exhales and relaxes against me.

I'm going to be a dad.

"Where is my pink sundress?" Truly tears through the two drawers she's taken over. Every day she grumbles about space and not having anywhere to hang her clothes. It's a constant reminder I need to find us a bigger place.

We're deciding on the desert hills near Aiyana or the wooded acreage near Loki and Birdie. We need to make a decision soon though, because both properties require us to build.

The casita is big enough for a newborn, but not a toddler.

I push my feet into my boots and sit down on the edge of the bed. I know she isn't looking for an answer to her question, but she does want an audience to complain to. I'm nothing if not a good listener.

"Would it have killed whoever built this place to put in a closet?" She holds out a flowy pink dress. "Found it."

She disappears in the bathroom. While I wait, I scoop Karen up and tuck her into my hood. I wonder how she's going to do with the new addition. She's used to being the baby around here.

Truly emerges, looking like a goddess. The fuchsia dress stands out against her golden-brown skin. Two long braided pigtails hang over each shoulder, stopping at the swell of her breasts that have grown bigger in the past few weeks. She isn't showing, not yet, but there is the beginning of a pooch on her lower abdomen you can't see unless she's naked.

I stand up and crowd her space. I twirl her pigtails around my fingers. They make her look her age and make me feel like a dirty old man. But later, when this dress is gone and she's underneath me while I fuck her, I'll be reminded she's all woman.

I kiss her long and deep, thrusting my tongue in her mouth to taste her, while grabbing a handful of her ass. Her palms flatten on my chest and she shoves me away.

"Oh, no you don't. We're going out there, we're eating Khan's smoked meats." She pushes me toward the door. "And we're telling your biker buddies they're going to be uncles."

I hoped I could distract her. Give her enough orgasms to forget about a stupid cook out and telling everyone she's knocked up. She saw through my plan.

Outside, Tabitha and Sissy set out bowls of salads and condiments. Birdie tails them with an arm load of buns. The back yard is full of people, but only with my brothers and whatever *date* they chose to bring. No outsiders are welcome tonight.

Khan's standing in front of the smoker and it's a good fucking sight. He was released on bail yesterday, which is why we're having this barbecue in the first place. Truly decided now's the perfect time to tell everyone about the baby. She thinks it'll be the happy news everyone needs right now.

I'm not so sure. These guys don't want a baby running around. Loki has settled down, but he's as anti-kid as I am. Or was. Maybe even still am, a little. It's been three months since I found out and I'm still not certain I've made the right choice to be present in my kid's life.

Aiyana walks out the back door, cautiously. My girl's been

keeping the baby secret, and for some reason, along with everyone else, she thought it would be a good time to tell her too.

If I walk away from tonight with a heartbeat, I'll be lucky.

"Mom!" Truly rushes over and hugs Aiyana. "I'm so glad you came."

Aiyana gives her a weary smile. She's accepted her daughter's future with a biker, but that'll probably change within the hour.

"Food's done," Khan announces, carrying a tray of hamburgers, hotdogs, brisket, and pulled pork. He sets it down on a table and smiles big. "Dig in."

Everyone dishes up plates of food and settles at a picnic table. Loki and I arranged them in a circle earlier, as per Truly and Birdie's directions. Before there were permanent women around here, we wouldn't have bothered with such formalities.

Things are changing.

Loki stands up and pounds a fist on the picnic table, gaining everyone's attention.

"It's been a shit year. We lost a brother," he says, referring to Jake. "We went to war twice, but we're stronger for it."

The crowd hoots and hollers, pounding their fists on the tables.

Loki swipes a hand through the air, silencing us. "And we're growing."

Birdie stands up next to him, smiling huge, and tears in her eyes.

"You're knocked up?" Khan asks.

Birdie's face falls. "No, asshole. Loki asked me to marry him, and I said yes." She plucks a ring from her pocket and slides it on her finger. "We're getting married."

Truly jumps up and rushes over to her friend. They both visibly swoon over the ring.

I clear my throat and stand up. My palms sweat, and if I had any food in my stomach, it would be threatening to come up. Everyone's eyes turn to me, as Truly makes her way back to my side.

"Pregnant," I say dumbly. I planned to say more than that. I ran it through my head all day, but the second I opened my mouth, it left me.

Eyes widen in all directions, everyone freezing in place. I don't know what it means. Are they happy or pissed?

I don't dare look at Aiyana. I'd go against some of the seediest people in this world, but I cower from that woman like a pissant.

"You're pregnant?" Birdie calls out in a high-pitched tone. Truly nods, tears welling in her eyes now.

Suddenly, I'm surrounded by my brothers. They pound me on the back and shake my hand. The nerves fall away, until I see Aiyana making her escape, wiping at her cheeks. Truly pulls away from me, but I stop her. It should be me. I'm the one she's mad at.

"Be back," I whisper in her ear.

I catch Aiyana getting into her car.

"I don't want to talk to you right now," she says.

"Stop, please," I stutter.

"How could you?" She charges toward me and smacks me across the face. I deserve it and a lot more. "A child, Will? Really? Do you have any idea what a bad idea this is?"

I nod. If she was expecting an argument, she won't get it from me.

"This was irresponsible of you."

I nod again.

"She's still a kid herself."

I might as well be a fucking bobble head with all the nodding I'm doing.

"You have no argument? You're not going to tell me how this is going to be okay?"

I shake my head.

"Then why are we having this conversation?" She opens her car door.

"Need you," I admit.

"You need me? Why?"

"Baby," I say.

She sighs, closes the door, and rests against the hood. "I think it was Ricky's fourth deployment he mentioned you for the first time. He said there was a new guy, young, and despite his hard shell, he could tell he was scared. He said he made it his personal mission to make you feel needed, because he didn't think you'd ever had that before. He said, you can't value your own life if no one else values it."

A pang shoots through my chest remembering all the stupid shit Ricky did that I had to save him from. Was he doing those things for my sake?

"Did you read the letter he had you give me?" she asks.

I shake my head. It wasn't my business.

"Of course he said all the things you'd expect. That he loves me and Truly, he's sorry we'll have to find a way to be without him, but he also said he's never been prouder of someone than he was of you. He told me you took punishments and purposely drew the attention to yourself to spare him. He said to make sure Truly finds a man just like you. Someone who puts others before themselves, no matter the consequences." Her voice pitches high on those last words.

"Sorry," I say. I've apologized for the way things turned out over and over, but I'll never stop. It should be him still on this earth and not me.

"I know you are." She pushes off the car and rests a hand over my folded arms. "It was those final words that had me not fighting Truly's decision to be with you, but a baby?"

"I know it's not ideal," Truly says, joining us.

"Not ideal." She rolls her eyes. "Understatement of the year."

"But," she says calmly. "No matter our unique situation, the same reason you accepted us is the same reason you should accept this baby. Do you know anyone who would protect our family like Roch will?"

"That's just it, though. He will have to protect you. Most men don't ever have to go so far as to protect their families. It's a far-off idea they never have to make good on."

"I know. And you're right, it's scary. I'm not so naïve I don't know that. But I also know me and this little peanut are safer in his world with him by our side, than in your world, alone."

I extend my arm around Truly. Not only did her mom need to hear her reasoning, but I did too. She's right. She's always right.

"I can see you believe that. I'm not there yet. Give me some time, okay?"

"As much as you need, but this baby will need their grandma, so try not to take too long."

"Grandma," Aiyana huffs, getting into her car.

We watch her pull away. I expect Truly to crumple under the weight of her mom's rejection, but she doesn't. Instead, she lifts onto her toes and hugs me around my neck.

"She'll come around. Don't worry."

I nod and peck her on the lips.

"Now let's go. Biker baby is craving a brisket sandwich."

I tuck her into my side and we walk back to the party. I don't know how a callous asshole like myself got so fucking lucky.

Truly pats my chest over the place where her pendant is sewn in. "Fate brought me to you, and it's fate we need to trust in order to stay together."

Once again, she answers my unspoken question, reading my mind. And while I still don't believe in fate, I believe in her.

I believe in us.

THE END

EPILOGUE

Khan

The guard leads me down a long hallway, my foam sandals clacking against my foot with each step. The cuffs around my wrists and ankles squeeze my joints painfully, but I'd never ask for them to be loosened. Weaknesses like that are exploited when you're locked up.

We stand in front of a closed door until a buzzer sounds, unlocking the door to a private room. Inside, sitting at a shiny stainless-steel table, is motherfucking Bexley March, the defense attorney the club keeps on retainer.

The sexy as hell brunette is wearing a fire-red dress suit, with a deep V that shows off her long neck and her ample cleavage. I want to bury my face in those tits. Hell, I want to suffocate in them.

I usually prefer tiny women I can toss around while I fuck them, but there's something about Bexley's exaggerated curves that make my mouth water.

I want to watch her ass jiggle while I fuck her from

behind, feel her thick thighs squeeze my head while I eat her out, and grip onto her padded hips while I sink into her pussy.

Jesus fuck. I need to get out of this place. My dick can't handle the celibacy.

"Wes," she bites out like my name's a curse word, but I ignore it, and focus on her pouty red lips.

What I wouldn't do for her to leave lipstick stains on my dick from sucking me dry.

My cock chubs in my cotton prison uniform, leaving nothing to the imagination, if the wide-eyed expression Bex has is any indication.

She clears her throat. "Have a seat."

The guard gives my shoulder a hard shove, making sure I remember who's in charge. On the streets, I'd break his neck for doing something like that. But in this place, I have to play by the rules and not make waves. At least that's what Bex says.

I plop down in the plastic chair, feeling the legs bow under my weight. I wait for them to snap in half, but it must be my lucky day, because they stay strong.

The guard lifts my cuffed hands from my lap and drops them on the table. He locks them in place before moving to my feet and securing them to the bolt in the cement floor.

"That's not necessary," Bex says.

"My job is to keep you safe, Mrs…"

"*Miss* March," she corrects.

"Oh, so I stand a chance," he flirts.

I roll my eyes. He's wasting his time.

Bex notices my reaction and since she loves to irritate the fuck out of me, she leans over the table, tracing a black painted nail over the swells of her breasts. "Are you asking me for a date?"

I growl, low and menacing. Some wannabe douche on a power trip can't keep her satisfied. Bex is powerful and strong, the key to winning her over is convincing her she's in charge. Not making her feel like the weaker sex because he has a pair of handcuffs and a badge.

This game she's playing is a personal attack on me, not genuine interest in him.

"That's enough." The guard pulls out his baton and takes a threatening stance. I shake my head. "We can talk about this date when you're finished with him. You sure you're okay? I'll be right outside the door."

"We'll be fine. Wes will be a good boy, won't you?"

"A regular Boy Scout," I reply, keeping my gaze on her.

The guard nods and leaves us alone. Bex pulls a few files out of her briefcase and stacks them neatly on the table. If my hands were free, I'd toss them on the floor to watch her head spin. I fucking love messing up all her perfection.

"Whatever you're thinking, don't do it," she says, without lifting her eyes.

"Wasn't thinking about anything other than how beautiful you look today, darlin'."

"Ha," she laughs humorously. "What is it? You want to knock my papers on the floor, don't you?"

"Don't know what you're talking about," I lie.

"Are you trying to tell me you don't get off on annoying me? Let's count all the reasons that's a lie." She lifts a finger for each of my recent crimes against her. "You gave Roch's dogs my brand-new pair of Manolo Blahniks to use as chew toys—still trying to figure out how you got them out of my car since you were with me the whole time. There was that time you intentionally spilled motor oil on my Mercedes, even though you claim it was an accident, I know the truth. Or, how about the time you tripped me and I sprained my ankle?"

"It's not my fault you didn't see my foot." I smirk.

"Whatever. I didn't come here to argue about your schoolboy crush. I'm here to talk about the pre-trial next week."

"Is there a problem?"

"You were caught, on camera, stealing a van that was later used to blow up a building. Yeah, I'd say there's a problem." She scowls at me, causing two lines to form between her eyes. I bite my lip to stop myself from telling her. She'd run out of the room and to the nearest plastic surgeon for another round of Botox if she knew.

"So, how do we get out of it?" I ask. I need to keep my head on straight. I'm facing steep charges.

"You can't. The best I can do is try for a plea deal, and even that's a long shot because of your extensive record."

"Would the plea deal get me out on parole?"

"Wes, you're not hearing me. You're facing a minimum five-year sentence, and fines in the hundreds of thousands." Her lips that were so plump when she arrived, are now a flat line.

Her words hit me like a ton of bricks. Five years behind bars? I'd lose my mind.

Memories of all the times I've been locked up on drug charges flood my mind. Detoxing in a cement cell is a special kind of torture. The cold sweats, constant shivering, and body aches from withdrawal were only intensified by the frigid temperature they kept the facility at.

Each time I was released sober, I swore I'd never go back,

but it was a lie I told myself. Within a week, I'd be back to shooting myself up with heroine, if I could afford it, or meth, when I couldn't.

It was a vicious cycle, I only freed myself from because of Goblin's old man. He was serving time for gun charges and took a liking to me. He explained what the Royal Bastards were about and said they were always looking for new members, especially big motherfuckers who knew how to shoot a gun, like me. He said if I stayed clean for a month after I was released, to stop by the club.

It was a tough month, but I was determined.

The club is the best thing to ever happen to me. Loki and I quickly became closer than brothers, and now I'm the vice president. Of course, I won't be for much longer if I can't get these charges dropped.

"What about bail?" I ask, my mind figuring all the ways I can make the footage of me stealing that van disappear.

"I'm going to ask for house arrest. I'll claim you need to work in order to pay for my representation." She taps her lip with the end of her pen. "You guys still have the construction business, right?"

I nod. We started a phony company years ago to clean our money. I keep a small crew employed, taking on bullshit jobs for appearances.

"Okay then. It's settled. I'll work on getting you out on bail. You'll be released for at least six months, and we'll put together your defense during that time."

"Thanks," I say, meaning it. I like to razz the girl, but she's saved my ass more than once, and I appreciate it.

"Are you doing okay?" she asks, concern lacing her tone. "Anyone bothering you?"

I smirk, the seriousness of the moment leaving me. "You worried about my safety?"

"You *are* in jail."

"Darlin', have you seen me?" I twist my arm to the side and flex. Since my hands are chained to the table, I'm only able to show off my triceps, but they're impressive.

"You're not indestructible."

"The only weakness I have, is you," I say.

"God. You can't be serious for longer than two minutes, can you?" She huffs and gathers her things, tucking them away in her bag that probably costs more than everything I own put together, including my bike.

"Did Loki ask you to give me any messages?"

"He said to tell you the footlong Italian sub is on ice, but the six-inch was left out in the open. Not to worry though, because Tulsa is hungry, and will finish it before it spoils." She cocks her head to the side. "Whatever that means."

It means Anthony's dead and Max got away, but Koyn's crew will be taking him out soon. Good. I fucking hate I wasn't there to help take them out. Maybe if I had been, Max's body would be out in the middle of the desert alongside his dad.

"An Italian sub sounds so fucking good. That'll be my first meal when you get me out of here," I groan. The food here sucks.

"It's lunchtime, and that does sound yummy. I think I'll go get one right now. With onions and peppers. Maybe a drizzle of oil and vinegar. My tummy is growling just thinking about it." She holds my gaze while she licks her upper lip suggestively.

Fucking hell.

"You're a cruel bitch, you know that?"

"Yep, I know. See you next week. Don't drop the soap." She struts over to the door, swinging her curvy hips the whole way. My eyes catch on her juicy ass and I'm unable to look away.

She pounds on the door and the guard holds it open for her.

"How about next Friday night for that date?" he asks.

"What's your number? I'll text you."

"Do you have a piece of paper?"

"Just tell me. I'll remember."

I chuckle, knowing she has no intention of ever calling the poor sap.

"555-2703."

"Got it. Talk soon." She pats his chest, and I listen as her high heels clack down the hallway.

"Goddamn, she's sexy as hell," the guard says, confidently strutting into the room to unlock my cuffs.

"Don't know what you're talking about, Boss."

"Yeah, you do. I saw the way you looked at her. You want her." He crouches and unlocks my feet. "A woman like her doesn't want a con, though. She wants someone with a decent job who knows how to deal with criminal assholes like you."

I rise to my full height, looking down on him. I'm six-foot-eight, and two hundred and fifty pounds of solid muscle. I could sit on this twig and break him.

"Don't worry, I'll take real good care of her." He grips me by the arm. "You think she likes her ass fucked? A chubby girl like her probably has a loose pussy."

Without considering the consequences, I ball my hands together, creating one large fist, and swing to the side, connecting with his jaw. The force of it knocks him on his ass. I stalk over to him and crouch next to him. He cowers, holding his hands up in defense.

Like that could stop me from ending him.

"You listen to me. You touch a hair on her body, and swear to God, I'll send you straight to Hades. And your bitch mom who's letting you live in her basement? It'll be her ass that gets fucked by every one of my brothers."

His face turns an ugly shade of red. I was guessing about him living in his mom's basement, but judging by his reaction, I was spot on.

"Back the fuck up, inmate," he growls, but it's all for show. His hands are shaking, and the wet spot in the front of his pants tells me he pissed himself.

"Not until we have an understanding." I kneel on his neck, cutting off his air supply.

He chokes and sputters comically, but nods in agreement.

"I'd like to go to my cell now, please," I say.

Officer Dumbass gasps for air as he struggles to stand up. As soon as he's upright, he takes me by the arm again.

Only this time, we both know who's in control.

And it's not his pathetic ass.

A soft man like him couldn't handle Bex. She needs a challenge, someone to verbally spar with who doesn't back down. She can't win without a fight, and Deputy Dipshit would buckle at the slightest raise of her voice.

But I have no problem pissing her the hell off, and I'm damn good at it too. When I say something that makes her eyes narrow and her lips purse tight, I can practically smell her sweetness dripping between her thighs.

All because of what *I* do to her.

Not this loser.

Bex doesn't know it yet, but she's mine. The second I get these charges against me dropped, I'm coming for her. And there'll be nowhere for her to run.

Need more Khan and Bexley? You can preorder *Bexley's Biker*, coming October 12, 2021, on Amazon.

Dying to know what happened to Max Corsetti? Find out in *Dragon*, by K Webster, coming this fall. If you haven't started her Tulsa, OK chapter of the Royal Bastards, you can purchase the first book in that series, here.
www.amazon.com/gp/product/B08CBGJ93H

ABOUT THE AUTHOR

Misty Walker writes everything from dark and delicious, to sweet and spicy. Most of her books are forbidden in some way and many are age-gap, because that's her jam.

She's lived quite the nomadic life, never staying in the same place for long until she met her husband. They've recently settled in Reno, NV with their two daughters, two dogs, and two hamsters, because everything's better in pairs.

Misty is fueled by coffee and the voices in her head screaming for their stories to be told. Which is why the coffee is necessary, because there are only so many hours in a day and who needs sleep anyway?

If you'd like to keep up to date on all her future releases, please sign up for her newsletter on her website. You can also order a signed paperback of this book, or any of her releases, there.

Connect with Misty:

www.authormistywalker.com
authormistywalker@gmail.com
Instagram: www.instagram.com/authormistywalker
Facebook: www.facebook.com/authormistywalker
Twitter: @mistywalkerbook

Turn the page for a list of all of Misty Walker's books.

ALSO BY MISTY WALKER

ACKNOWLEDGMENTS

Kristi, you are my sanity, my voice of reason, and my motivation. You're the hardest working person I've ever known, and while I think you're absolutely bat shit crazy, you inspire me to push harder and do better. I love your face.

Ty-bot, thank you for helping to make my dreams come true. You're my real-life book boyfriend.

Sultan, my hype girl! It's been the shittiest of years, for you especially. Remember you're a tough bitch and I'll always have your back.

Genevieve, thanks for having my back in all things!

Sara, Sarah, Ariadna, & Elizabeth, y'all be the best beta bitches ever. You each bring something to the table that make my books better. Don't ever leave me.

Sarah Goodman, thank you for making my words sparkle and shine. You might be regretting answering my pleas for help, but you're mine now. I'm not letting go.

Molly Whitman, your insane attention to detail boggles my mind. Thank you so much for being my book's figurative spit shine.

Stacey Blake, thank you for making the pages of this book as badass as the bikers themselves.

Mom, your friendship means more to me than you'll ever know. It's a pretty darn good feeling knowing you're out there believing in me more than I believe in myself. I love you!

To my readers & my reader group, Misty Walker's Thirsty Readers, thank you the most! You guys rock my world and motivate me to keep writing. I love nothing more than to get your messages and read your reviews. It's a great big book world, but you choose to read my books, and that means everything.

Lorelai and Mabel, quarantining with you dorks has been the highlight of this disastrous year. I'm going to miss you when you go back to school and this is all over. Not enough to homeschool you anymore, but I'll still miss you. Love you both.

Lightning Source UK Ltd.
Milton Keynes UK
UKHW020837190123
415611UK00009B/615